The LIE

WASHINGTON WOLVES

KARLA SORENSEN

© 2021—Karla Sorensen
All Rights Reserved
Cover Designer-Najla Qamber Design www.najlaqamberdesigns.com
Cover Photography: Regina Wamba
Interior Design—Champagne Book Design
Editor—Jenny Sims, Editing4Indies
Proofreading—Julia Griffis, The Romance Bibliophile

No part of this book may be reproduced or transmitted in any form or by any means, electronic or mechanical, including photocopying, recording, or by any information storage and retrieval system without written permission of the author, except for the use of brief quotations in a book review.

This is a work of fiction. Names, characters, businesses, places, events, and incidents are either the products of the author's imagination or used in a fictitious manner. The author acknowledges the trademark status and trademark owners of various products referenced in this work of fiction, which have been used without permission. The publication/use of these trademarks is not authorized, associated with, or sponsored by the trademark owners.

The LIE

Chapter ONE

Dominic

It took two things to ruin my first day with the Washington Wolves—an asshole journalist determined to pick a fight and a bottle of tequila I should've said no to.

The first managed to take a perfectly good press conference and turn it to shit. The second didn't come until later.

And more than anything, when I woke up happy on a day I normally hated, when I signed my contract with genuine optimism at the change in my career, I should have known something would blow it the hell up.

His name was Kevin Carter, from a two-bit sports network, and he overcompensated for a pencil dick by being a bully in press conferences. Most of the time, I avoided his questions, but he yelled over everyone else that day.

The moment he stood and gave me an oily smile, I knew he was going to piss me the hell off. (Never, ever a good thing for me.)

"Dominic, what do you say to the *many* critics who think your aggressive style of play and tendency for drawing flags won't fit in here at Washington?"

If you thought the first day at a new school was bad, try transferring football teams when no one thinks you can hack it with the "good guys."

I leaned back in my seat and gave Kevin Carter a tight smile. "Are people saying that?" I asked casually.

His answer was sly. "You know they are. You weren't exactly known for your ability to keep your cool in Vegas. Didn't you set the record for most unnecessary roughness flags in a single season?"

Around him, the journalists filling the rows of my first press conference in Washington shuffled uncomfortably. In every fricken one of these things, one asshole made it his job to piss off the football player, and it was almost always Kevin. If I snapped, tossed a mic at his face, and stormed off because he was wrecking my mood, he'd probably get a bonus.

So with a grit of my teeth and a deep breath, I managed a smile, even as a cold ball of dread filled my stomach. "That was my first year in the league, Kevin. I've matured over the past three years."

The dipshit snorted loudly with disbelief.

"*Watch out, Washington,*" he read from the screen of his phone, "*Walker the Wild is your problem now.*" He lifted an eyebrow. "That's my headline for tomorrow, if you were interested."

The woman sitting next to him, with the ESPN badge around her neck, rolled her eyes.

What I wanted to do was call him a prick and walk away from all the eyes waiting impatiently for me to react. I wanted to tell him that Walker the Wild was a byproduct of an aggressive team with an aggressive coach who knew exactly how to amp up his players.

"Nice alliteration," I told him. "I bet it took you all day to think of it."

His smile flattened at my dig and the small ripple of laughter that moved through the room.

"I read an article claiming knowledge from inside sources at

Washington that they're not all that excited about your *type* of energy in the locker room," he continued. "Any comment?"

I shook my head. A calm reaction. One I was really fucking proud of, considering I wanted to throw a chair at his head.

The reporter next to him—I think her name was Julie—raised her hand, and I nodded. But before she could ask her question, a slickly dressed PR guy interrupted. "That's all for Mr. Walker today. We've got another player who'd love to answer some questions." He spoke quietly into my ear. "Just go. We'll handle Kevin's headline. Don't say a word to anyone," he warned.

His voice didn't even have a sharp edge, but that warning was still there.

They all expected me to explode, even the guy who was paid to make me look good. Not like I could really even blame him for that. My reputation of Walker the Wild had preceded me. From my days playing in college at Texas, where I was still chippy as hell and didn't know exactly how to prove my worth as a walk-on player without going overboard. My days being built into that player on a professional scale in Vegas, as an undrafted player who'd heard the critics say over and over that I wasn't good enough.

My hand curled into a fist under the table, but I nodded at the PR guy. He didn't see the fist. No one did. It was the only outward hint that something dangerous was building under the surface of my skin.

Don't be so cranky, Dominic, I heard my sister's voice in my head. My fist uncurled, and I stood from the table before I did something awful, like burst into tears or some shit.

A few cameras followed my exit from the Washington press room, and I kept my gaze straight ahead when a few journalists made a move to follow me.

No one waited for me outside of the room because the circus portion of the transfer was over. I glanced down a long corridor, and without thinking too hard about where I was going, my legs took me in the direction of the field.

The Wolves facility was impressive. It had been as long as I could remember. Even though I grew up with the shape of the stadium on the skyline, we'd never been able to afford tickets. Even before Ivy was born, on the eve of my tenth birthday, and even before she got sick, we'd never had the kind of money to see a professional game. Back then, even if I kept saying it would happen, no one actually thought I'd end up doing what I was doing. Maybe my parents would've pinched pennies even further to take me.

My senior year of college, Texas played a bowl game at Wolves stadium, and it was when I knew eventually I'd play the game I loved wearing the black and red jerseys. I knew I'd make my way back to that stadium. With that team.

I remembered going back to the hotel room and wishing I could call my sister—call Ivy—and tell her about it. Then I drank half a bottle of Jack and passed out because it was the only way—back then—to keep myself from doing something really stupid.

With a careful glance over my shoulder, I walked down the tunnel toward the dark field. The roof was open, and again, I heard my sister's voice in my head.

Wouldn't it be fun to sleep in the middle of a field someday?
Sounds uncomfortable, Ivy Lee, I'd told her.
Just once. If you can do it someday, you better do it for me.

Rubbing the back of my neck, I took a deep breath. I could still hear my sister's voice so clearly even though five years had passed since I'd heard it. Five years to the day, in fact.

Instead of hopping the last of the barriers to go out on the dark field, I leaned up against the wall of the tunnel and stared at the logo until my eyes started to burn.

The day hadn't gone the way I thought it would. Instead of the excitement I'd felt that morning, the tremor of anticipation I'd felt while scrawling my name across the white paper that was bringing me back home, now I simply heard that fucking reporter's voice in my head too.

They're not all that excited about your *type* of energy in the locker room.

I took a deep breath and tried to shove it out of my head.

"Walker?" a voice called behind me.

I turned and saw the rookie who'd taken my place with the press. He looked a little dumbstruck at the sight of me, and I could hardly remember a time when seeing veteran players gave me the same feeling. Probably because it didn't take long in Vegas to realize no one gave a shit if you were excited to meet them. The entire locker room was a study in guys with anger management issues.

"Rookie," I said. I knew his name, but I was just feeling a little chippy after the press conference.

He stood shoulder to shoulder with me, staring out at the field. "Fucking awesome," he breathed. "I wanted to see it empty."

Something about him tugged at me. I didn't know much about him, but like me, he hadn't been some flashy draft pick. He was undrafted, someone with raw talent and a love for the game. My hands curled into fists again because unlike me, he still had stars in his eyes, a visible excitement he didn't worry about hiding.

It wasn't that easy for everyone.

"You played for Florida, right?"

"Go Gators," he said with a grin.

I stared back at the field. Something about his enthusiasm grated, but not because he annoyed me. Because I was annoying myself. My mood had changed so abruptly, and since leaving that room, it only got worse.

The rookie slipped a backpack off his shoulders and gave me a sly look that probably should've made me bolt back down the tunnel. Then he produced a bottle of really fucking expensive tequila.

"Bad idea, rookie," I said.

He waved the bottle at the sprawling field. "No one's out here.

Besides, I promised my little brother I'd take a shot on the fifty-yard line if they signed me."

I eyed him. "That's a weird fucking thing to promise your brother."

Rookie shrugged. "He's eighteen, so it sounds like his idea of a good time."

His words had me imagining Ivy if she'd lived to turn eighteen. Before she got sick, she'd shown the kind of youthful hints of a girl who'd grow to be naturally beautiful. But instead of knowing what she'd look like, I'd only ever remember her as she was. Not even ten when she died.

Something dangerous shook inside me, and I held out my hand for the bottle.

He handed it to me with a grin. "We doing this?"

For one second, I wondered exactly how stupid this was. If I should stop and message Turbo to ask her if this was a really fucking dumb way to honor the fifth year without my sister. But my online friend had no idea what I did for a living or that I was back in Washington. And trying to explain any of it sounded like too much noise to add into my already loud head.

"Why the hell not?" I mumbled. Without checking to see if he was following, I gripped the tequila in one hand and strode to the middle of the field.

Hours later, I realized that stopping to message her might have been a smart idea. But then again … I wasn't exactly known for my restraint.

"We won't get kicked off the team for this, will we?"

I stared up at the sky, felt the slight spinning warmth of the alcohol in my veins as my fingers ran over the cropped grass of the field underneath me. "Nah."

I felt like shit. Not because I'd gotten drunk, but like I'd anticipated, falling asleep on the turf was really, really uncomfortable. Another thing I couldn't tell Ivy.

But would it get us kicked out? No. To get kicked off a team usually meant you'd committed a crime, and the last time I checked, getting drunk wasn't against the law. Especially since neither of us had driven under the influence. But still … the Wolves organization might not appreciate our attempt at a first experience on the roster.

The rookie glanced over at me. "You sounded a lot more excited about this idea before."

"Didn't know you were so fucking chatty when I said yes."

In his drunken state, he thought it was the funniest thing he'd ever heard.

After his laughter faded, he held up the bottle of tequila and took another swig. "Taking shots with Dominic Walker," he mused. "Epic."

Normally, I would've smiled or made a joke. But I kept my eyes on the stars and felt an uncomfortable pinch in my chest when I realized that with the slowly rising sun, the stars were no longer visible.

"Want another one?" he asked. Thankfully, his drunk ass was oblivious to my lack of reaction.

I shook my head. "I'm good."

He stared at the half-empty bottle. "Didn't you only have like … two shots?"

"Three, I think."

"Shit," he groaned. "No wonder I feel like this."

He flopped onto his back with a groan, the bottle forgotten between us. My eyes remained open as I stared up at the sky unblinking. When I blinked, it felt like there was a layer of sand coating them.

For a moment, I let my eyelids fall closed, but it was a mistake because as soon as I did, I saw her face when she talked about sleeping on the field.

She couldn't have been more than eight at the time, already sick and hooked up for her treatments at the hospital, where we used to discuss all the different things we could do after she was done and feeling better.

I rubbed at my chest, hoping it would send the aching feeling away, but it didn't.

And instead of sadness, I just felt a slow crescendo of anger, like a snowball rolling down the side of a mountain. This always happened to me—it eclipsed everything. Whatever I kept buried inside me, it didn't explode like people expected. It wasn't an immediate reaction, like a bomb going off or a grenade exploding.

It was slower than that. Eventually, it came out in a way that other people could see. It was what got me in trouble. But to me, it was never a surprise. If you'd ever watched someone heat glass, it was a lot like that.

For a while, you couldn't see anything changing, but if you watched long enough, the color turned bright molten orange, and the shape of it became something fragile. One wrong move, one twist in the wrong direction, and the entire thing broke in a way that couldn't be repaired.

If you were still tracking my little analogy, my temper was the broken glass. More than one "unnecessary roughness" flag came from that part of my personality.

As I lay on the grass with the sky turning light, thinking about Ivy after the press conference as the doubts clawed past my excitement of being in Washington, I felt the heat rise and the color of my mood change.

Tequila wouldn't help it. Very few things did. My parents never wanted to talk about it. My only friend who would was someone I'd never even met face-to-face, but she was still the only person I could vent all this bullshit to. I picked up my phone, swiped until I found the right messaging app, and for the first time all damn day, I didn't question what I was about to say, or if I was phrasing it the right way.

NicktheBrickLayer: I don't want to do anything this year, Turbo. No gestures, no commemoration, no stupid little purchases that don't mean anything. Because no matter what I do, she's still gone, and it pisses me off, and nothing I ever do feels like enough anyway.

NicktheBrickLayer: And that's fine, I don't feel bad for feeling that way. Ivy doesn't need me to do those things, she never has. But I'm me, so it's never that simple.

NicktheBrickLayer: Instead, I did something stupid on my first day at a new job, and I'll probably never live it down.

NicktheBrickLayer: When will I fucking learn? I'm too old for this. Yet here I am.

Just as I hit send, someone flipped some master switch and all the floodlights in the stadium came on in a painful, bright burst. I held my hand up to block it, and the rookie groaned miserably. For some reason, those lights triggered the worst possible reaction for a guy who'd just drunk half a bottle of tequila. He rolled to the side and threw up.

"Oh, this was a stupid idea," he moaned. "Who do you think it is?"

"Wipe your mouth off," I hissed.

As I stood, I thought about helping him up, but I wasn't sure he could actually stand.

"I hate tequila."

"A little late to realize that now, asshole," I whispered. Finally, they came into view. The looming silhouette of a security guard ambled in our direction with someone shorter and petite next to him.

Rookie sat up and rubbed his eyes. "Oh, we're fucked."

If I thought my doubts were loud before, they were screaming in my face now. This was exactly what I should have thought about before grabbing that stupid bottle of tequila and walking out on the field. Walker the Wild would never live this down if the press got wind of it.

The security guard stopped, hands on his hips, and spoke to the person next to him, who was still hard to see because of where they stood with the lights behind them. "What do you want to do with them, boss?"

She sighed. "Do you two need to sober up before we talk about this?"

My eyes fell shut as soon as I heard her voice. Of course, it was the owner of the team. Allie Sutton-Pierson had been the owner of the Washington Wolves for the past two decades and was not someone I necessarily wanted to face for the first time when I was like this.

That anger, the slow climb of my internal temperature, skyrocketed. And the only person I was pissed at was myself.

"I'm fine," I muttered. "Nothing for the last few hours for me."

The rookie stared down at the bottle, then the puke on the ground, and hiccuped.

He opened his mouth to say something about it, but a stupid impulse had me laying a hand on his shoulder. I shook my head when he glanced up at me.

I turned and met the guard's eyes. "That was mine from … earlier."

The rookie hiccupped again. The guard's eyes narrowed, like he knew I was lying.

But come on, this kid—even if he was dumber than shit for carrying a bottle of tequila in his backpack—would never get a fair shot at a place like Washington if this was how he started.

Everyone would expect it from me. They'd shake their head and move about their day, that the hothead from Vegas would do something as stupid as throw up on the fifty-yard line.

The guard's craggy face bent in a frown, and Miss Sutton-Pierson rubbed her forehead. "Walker, let's go to my office." She pointed at the rookie. "A driver will take you home, but you better be back in my office at eight a.m. tomorrow."

He gave her a salute. Sort of. "Yes, ma'am."

When she shook her head, she moved to the side, and I could finally see her face clearly. She wasn't happy, but when her eyes landed on my face, it wasn't anger I saw. It was disappointment, and somehow, that was worse.

To the security guard, she said, "Can you get him up and call a driver to get him home?"

"Sure thing, boss." He swooped down and helped the rookie to his feet. "You two gonna learn the hard way, aren't you?"

I swiped blades of grass off the front of my shirt and fought the way my hackles rose along my back. This guy couldn't have known it, but I learned everything the hard way. Every battle I'd won had come from actual blood, sweat, and tears. My success was in spite of my background, not because of it.

"Thank you, Keith," my brand new boss told the guard while he started off the field with the rookie.

He paused and assessed me with shrewd eyes. "You sure you got this one?"

She gave me a look. "Oh yeah."

I swiped a hand over my mouth and decided not to snap back with something at the guard's back. He was a big dude, probably could've played linebacker if he hadn't already.

Out of the corner of my eye, I studied her for a moment. From what I knew of her, she was in her mid-forties, but with her blond hair pulled off her face and the white shirt she was wearing with dark jeans, she looked about a decade younger.

Allie Sutton-Pierson assessed me equally, and I could tell by her facial expression that she wasn't intimidated by me in the slightest even though I towered over her at six-four.

Owning a team for two decades while being married to a former elite quarterback would do that.

She gave me a smile and gestured toward the tunnel that had let me out onto the field. "Shall we?"

The words were said so pleasantly, and for some reason, her impeccable manners and her kind smile wrapped in implacable resolve set my temper on edge again. The flames roared dangerously inside me, even as I kept my face blank. "Do I actually have a choice?"

She faced me. "Not if you want to have the role on this team that you're capable of. I suppose in that regard, yes, you have a choice, Dominic. You can choose not to speak to me about this, and I'll sit down with you later, along with Coach and our GM. I don't think that conversation will be as pleasant."

Crossing my arms over my chest, I took a second to roll through those scenarios. *Check your temper at the door, Walker,* my beleaguered agent had told me when he finalized this trade. Washington wasn't the place to showboat. It wasn't the place to break single-player records if it came at the cost of a win. My last team had been that way. Many players did all sorts of amazing things individually, but as a cohesive unit, we were terrible.

"Lead the way," I told her after a loaded beat of silence. Our steps made no sound as we left the field, and I took a second to take in a deep breath and hope that my hours on the field were enough of a tribute to mark the passing of this day. Last year, I'd gotten a tattoo. The year before, I donated a huge chunk of my signing bonus to the children's hospital where she'd stayed for so many months.

"Is this going to be a regular occurrence, Mr. Walker?" she asked as we cleared the tunnel. "Because I was promised by your agent that it wouldn't be."

I winced, but considering she was staring straight ahead as she maneuvered us through the empty passageways of the building toward some of the offices, she didn't see.

"No, ma'am." Was ma'am the correct thing to call her? Miss? Boss? I wasn't even sure.

She sent me an amused grin. "Most people call me Allie. Except

Keith, who's called me boss for the past twenty years. I can't break him of it now."

She led me through an intricate maze of tunnels and hallways. This was a building she knew intimately. We reached a wall of glass doors that slid open when Allie waved a security badge in front of a small panel to the left. There were lights on, but given how early it still was, only a couple of people were at work yet.

"You have your office at the stadium?" I asked.

She waved at someone sitting in a cubicle, greeting them by name.

"I have one at the team facilities as well, but I split my time because I get to know the stadium staff better when I spend some of my days here."

A man pushing a custodial cart greeted her with a wide smile as he came down the hallway. His blue eyes were a little cloudy with age. "Morning, Allie. You're in early today."

She tilted her head in my direction. "Had to initiate the new guy. Max, meet Dominic Walker. He's our new tight end." She gave me a look that I roughly translated as *if you don't treat this man like you're meeting a dignitary, I'll castrate you.* "Dominic, Max has worked for the Wolves longer than anyone else in the organization. We couldn't do a single thing well without him."

He held out a hand that looked bent with arthritis. I shook it. "Pleasure to meet you, Max."

Those blue eyes held a twinkle as he did his own assessment. "You're a troublemaker, aren't you?"

Allie smothered a laugh with a polite cough.

"I've been told that a time or two," I answered honestly.

"If you see Faith, let her know I'm in my office, okay, Max?" Allie said with a smile.

He nodded. "Sure thing. You know she always brings me those muffins I like, even if I tell her not to."

Allie laughed. "Sounds like her. Dominic, we're right in here."

She pointed at a dark office with large windows overlooking downtown Seattle. From the room, large and perfectly decorated with comfortable seats and framed black and white photos of moments in Wolves history, I caught sight of a shot of Allie, her husband Luke Pierson, and two girls. Allie saw me looking. "Our daughters, Faith and Lydia."

Faith. It was the name she mentioned out in the hallway. But I didn't ask. I just wanted to get out of this meeting and figure out a way not to end the day pissed off and self-destructive because the way I was starting it certainly wasn't good.

Allie took a seat on a long black couch and gestured for me to sit across from her. I held my body stiffly, aware that she had the power to make or break my career at Washington with this one meeting. It kindled that anger all over again.

It was just like I'd messaged Turbo—when would I fucking learn?

"Do you feel like telling me why you were drinking on the fifty-yard line?" she asked.

I met her gaze unflinchingly. "Not particularly."

Allie nodded. "I've been here for twenty years, Dominic. Not once have we ever had players try to wreck their livers midfield before the season has even started." She crossed her legs and reclined on the couch. "Makes me a little curious about you."

"And not the drunk rookie?" I asked dryly.

"Oh, he and I will have this conversation as well. But you weren't drunk, and I don't actually think you were the one who puked on my precious wolf logo. That makes it even more interesting."

I didn't like that she was being kind about this, that she was reacting with curiosity and not an iron fist. This approach of hers made me uncomfortable.

Because I found myself opening my mouth and handing her one small snippet of truth.

"This is my least favorite day of the entire year. Something shitty happened a few years ago, and I don't like talking about it."

She hummed. "I don't know much about you other than your years in Vegas. If it's something you'd like to explain to me, I'm always here to listen."

"No thanks," I said evenly. "Can I go now?"

This time, her smile held an edge. "Nope. Whatever happened on this day in your life, you don't get to bring it here in the form of empty bottles of alcohol in my building. Every inch of this place is important to me and every person who works in it, on or off the field."

She had no fucking clue about my life or what I went through. No clue how important this was to me too. Because in her mind, I'd bet, she looked at me the exact same way that all my teammates in Texas had. They walked in with scholarships and an excuse to dick off in their classes so they could spend all their time on football. I worked my ass off to afford that schooling, moving across the country because my dad had an old buddy who gave me a job and a place to live.

To them, my attitude somehow meant I didn't care. And that couldn't be further from the truth.

She sat in her glass enclosure, overseeing her billion-dollar enterprise with a smile on her face. I'd smile too if I was as rich as her, had the kind of problems she probably had. I crossed my arms and let out a hard breath through my nose.

"You have an opportunity, Dominic, and by signing that contract yesterday, you promised a certain level of professionalism. I expect it from everyone who receives a paycheck with my signature on it, no matter how many zeros that check has. If you showed up tomorrow and told me you wanted to scoop popcorn on Sundays, I'd expect that same professionalism. You are an excellent player, but I won't tolerate you acting recklessly and disrespecting the home we've built here."

I held her gaze unflinchingly, and she had no clue what was happening under the surface of my skin, how hot my blood was as it rushed through my body, pumped furiously through my heart.

"I won't consider that strike one because I've never believed in consequences without a warning first. Now you know what I expect from every person on our roster, and I'm going to have to trust that you won't let this happen again. But you will do something to earn my trust and learn some humility."

"What's that?" I asked.

She looked at her watch. "My daughter Faith will be here any minute. You're going to spend some time doing volunteer work for me and my husband's foundation, Team Sutton."

I slicked my tongue over my teeth. As punishments went, it wasn't nearly as bad as I thought it might be. "What does your daughter have to do with it?"

I saw her look over my shoulder into the hallway. "Faith, at the moment, is the director of the foundation. And I think she'll have no problem keeping you in line."

I snorted because I couldn't even manage to keep myself in line. Some rich girl, handed a job by her rich parents, didn't stand a chance.

Chapter TWO

Faith

NicktheBrickLayer: I don't want to do anything this year, Turbo. No gestures, no commemoration, no stupid little purchases that don't mean anything. Because no matter what I do, she's still gone, and it pisses me off, and nothing I ever do feels like enough anyway.

I couldn't get that first message out of my head. I wanted to answer him, but because of my terrible tendency to hit snooze one too many times, I didn't have enough time to properly answer my friend before I drove downtown to the stadium to meet with Allie. But because of what day it was, how hard I knew it was for him, I couldn't make him wait a couple more hours without saying something.

Before turning the corner where the big glass door would lead me to the offices, I tucked myself against the wall and pulled out my phone. Tapping my thumb onto the screen, I opened the messaging app but deflated a little when I saw no unread notification and no new messages waiting from him.

Every year on this day, I received a message first thing in the morning from my one and only online friend. I'd never seen his face nor spoken to him on the phone. Sometimes, we'd go weeks without messaging at all, but because this day—three years earlier—is how we "met" in the first place, it had yet to pass without him reaching out to me.

> **TurboGirl:** I'm sorry I'm just answering. I woke up late for work.

> **TurboGirl:** I'm sure whatever you did wasn't stupid. And even if it was, it's been five years since Ivy died. Be nice to my friend, okay?

I bit my lip and watched the time click past the start time of my meeting with Allie. She'd forgive me a couple of minutes, especially because she'd been married to my dad since I was like … seven … so my always-a-couple-minutes-late arrival would be no surprise to her.

> **TurboGirl:** Tell me something about her. What was her favorite restaurant? Or her favorite movie? I love hearing you talk about your sister. It's the best way you can honor her life, N. <3

Hitting send, I glimpsed at the clock on my phone again. "Oh, fracksticks," I whispered.

Swiping my badge in front of the glass doors, they slid open soundlessly as I hustled through, almost colliding with Max. He steadied me with a laugh. "Easy there, kiddo. You running late?"

"Always," I said. Tucking my phone into my pocket was a feat with the bakery bag shoved under my arm. Max saw the bag and started shaking his head. "Don't even argue," I told him. "You haven't tried this flavor yet, and it's divine."

With a gesture of his gnarled hands, I gave him the bag. When he opened it and took a deep inhale, his eyes fell closed, and he released a sigh that had me laughing out loud.

"That smells illegal, Miss Faith."

The LIE

"Raspberry cream. Let me know how you like it after my meeting, okay?"

He nodded his head toward Allie's office. "She's got someone in there—one of the new players—but she said you could head on in."

"Huh. Okay." My interaction with players was fairly limited to foundation events, despite the fact that my stepmom owned the team and my dad was practically an unofficial member of the front offices.

I preferred it that way, though. Football players had this terrible tendency to fall into one of two camps.

Camp One: Can I find a way to sleep with the owner's daughter?

Camp Two: I shall treat the owner's daughter like she's my long-lost sibling.

It was why my most important addition to the Pierson Family Rule List was *No Dating Football Players*. I knew from my own regrettable experience in college what the Camp One players were like. Hence the rule.

"How're you liking that fancy new job?" he asked.

"It's a lot to learn. We just expanded to taking grant applications from the Midwest," I told him. "But Ruth was an amazing director, and she's helped me a lot since she retired."

He smiled. "You've got a big heart, just like your momma does."

Everyone at Washington knew Allie wasn't my biological mom—my birth mom died in a car accident when I was little—but in all the ways that mattered, she was the only person to ever fill that role for me. I patted him on the arm. "Hopefully, that big heart of hers forgives me for being a bit late."

His blue eyes had a twinkle to them when he answered. "I reckon she's not all that surprised, Miss Faith."

I sighed. "You're probably right." I waved. "See you around, Mr. Max."

He winked, pushing his cart past me.

Allie's door was cracked open, and when I approached, I heard the rumble of a low voice. He came into view before Allie did, and if someone had written a caption for the image of him that I saw, it would've been *pissed-off bad boy bucks authority*. His arms, big and tattooed, were crossed over his chest, and he stared at Allie like she'd done him personal harm.

His jaw was a sharp line coated in dark stubble, and there wasn't a hint of emotion on that chiseled face. For a moment, I stared at him. Something about his demeanor made me feel very much like I was approaching a wild animal, and that danger made the air vibrate at a different frequency.

"There you are, Faith," Allie said as she appeared into view. With a warm smile, she opened the door for me. "Come on in."

"Thank you for waiting," I told her, tucking some of my brown hair behind my ear. "I know I'm a little late."

She rubbed my arm. "Dominic and I were just getting to know each other before you got here."

He snorted, and my brows bent in on my forehead at the derisive sound. Allie's eyes met mine, and I saw a gleam of humor in them, which made me relax a little. Then she gestured toward me. "Dominic, this is my daughter Faith. She runs the foundation I was telling you about."

I gave him a friendly smile and held out my hand. But instead of standing to take it, he gave me a head-to-toe study without rush, then nodded curtly.

Ahh, okay, so he was one of *those* football players. That was Camp Three. The ego-the-size-of-Everest, I'm-too-talented-for-basic-manners football players who made me want to shove bamboo splints up my fingernails rather than spend time with them.

Those players made it very, very easy not to break my no dating the players rule. Kinda like when you went camping and they told you not to feed the bears because they might eat you alive.

Allie cleared her throat sharply, and Dominic sighed, reaching forward to shake my hand. His skin was rough and warm to the touch, and I fought a shiver when his palm scraped against mine.

"Do you need to finish up with him?" I asked Allie. "I can come back at a better time."

She shook her head. "No, this is perfect. Dominic is actually going to be spending some time at Team Sutton, and I'd love it if you could find one or two of our grant recipients that would benefit from his presence."

My eyebrows shot up. Benefit from Oscar the Grouch's presence? When Dominic's glower intensified, I realized just how transparent my reaction had been and tried to smooth my face. Another thing I needed to work on now that I was in charge of the foundation. "Umm, sure thing. We can find ... something."

Allie's beautiful face split into an amused grin because she knew me all too well and just how horrible I was at hiding my feelings. "Perfect. I was thinking maybe a couple of hours a week for the next month?" She turned her gaze to Dominic, and oh my, I saw the way she was not even remotely asking for permission from him. "Sound good?"

"Like I have a choice," he muttered.

I blew out a slow breath, eyes wide.

"We all have choices in life, Dominic," Allie said, unfazed by the attitude. "Spending time with the kids who benefit from Team Sutton might not be something you get to choose, but I promise you, I expect glowing reviews from Faith once your time is done."

If I thought my eyes were wide before, they must've been taking up half my friggin' face when she finished that little speech. Now I was his babysitter?

Allie's assistant knocked on the door. "Allie, do you have five minutes to check out this piece before we send it down to PR?"

"I'll be right there, Connie." She looked back and forth between Dominic and me, then nodded. "These two need to talk anyway."

After a gentle touch to my shoulder, she left the office, and the resulting silence was sonic-blast-level awkward. I stood there studying him. My mind rolled through the snippets of conversations I'd heard recently. He was no rookie and had transferred from Vegas, where he'd garnered a reputation as an explosive player, on and off the field.

He started to unfold his great big body off the couch, and I held up my hand. His eyebrows, just as dark as the stubble on his chin, rose in disbelief. "You're going to stop me from leaving?"

At his rudeness, my jaw fell open. "I... well, we need to set something up for you at Team Sutton. At least give me your email address so I can get in touch with you."

"Don't email." He held my eyes, a blatant challenge that had alllll the stubborn feelings coursing through my five-foot-seven body.

I let out a slow breath. "I think maybe we got off on the wrong foot, Dominic." I gestured to the couch. "May I sit?"

"Do you often ask permission to sit on Mommy's fancy couch?"

"I'm sorry," I said crisply, "Did I piss in your Cheerios this morning and not know about it? You don't even know me, hotshot."

He leaned forward, bracing his muscular forearms on his knees, pinning me in place with those dark eyes. "I've known people like you my whole life, little miss sunshine," he said, and I fought the urge to tug on the hem of my bright yellow shirt that was emblazoned with exactly that. "Let me guess, after your parents paid every single red penny for your fancy degree, they ushered you straight into your fancy job with a corner view? I might be forced to spend time with you because my boss just told me I had to." He leaned forward more, and again, I battled the impulse to move back from the sheer force of him. But I'd be damned if I gave this jack-hole a single inch in concession. I hated players in Camp Three. "But no one told me I had to make friends."

A defense of my parents—the way they'd raised me, the privileges that I'd been afforded because of their jobs were never, ever lost on me—sprang to the tip of my tongue, but I swallowed it down.

I tilted my head to the side. "And what did *you* do to deserve the honor of spending time with me at my fancy job that I didn't earn?"

My sarcasm wasn't lost on him, and he rolled his eyes. "The rookie and I decided to test some tequila last night. Never made it off midfield before he passed out, and I didn't feel much like moving either. I guess that type of activity is frowned upon here with the perfect people."

"Oh my gosh, what a poor football player you are," I whispered with a shake of my head. "Paid millions of dollars and you can't get drunk on private property? *For shame.*"

When he leaned in, closer this time, his eyes flashed dangerously, and I wondered vaguely if I'd pushed him too far. "You don't know shit about me, sunshine."

I leaned in right back. "Right back at you, hotshot. And you better hope that I'm in a good mood when you show up at my office Tuesday at ten a.m." My voice sharpened, the same dangerous edge that he held in his eyes, and he actually sat back when he heard it. "Because if you cop a single shred of this attitude when you're around the kids, I don't care who you are or how much money they paid you, I'll have no trouble telling Allie everything. You hate my upbringing, hotshot? I couldn't care less. But I will be damned if you take any of that out on our kids." I thrust a finger at him, stopping just shy of his broad chest. "Do we understand each other?"

He stood off the couch, face smooth, eyes hard. "Perfectly."

I pulled out my phone. "What's your number?"

He clucked his tongue. "Aww, can't manage to get a date on your own, sunshine?"

I gave him a long look, and his lips almost curved into a smile.

Then his eyes tracked over my body again. "No, I bet you don't have any problem with that. Nice boys, too, I'm sure. They wear khakis and button-downs. They play golf, like expensive whiskey, and got straight A's at their fancy schools."

"Better than a drunk football player who couldn't pluck basic manners from their asshole if their life depended on it." My smile was soft, beatific, and it made his face turn even stormier. "I don't date football players, and guys like you are exactly why it's so easy to remember why."

Dominic simply stared me down, every word somehow making him look grumpier. It was awful just how attractive he was. Why couldn't he have a weak chin or pube hair or worm lips?

No, men like him somehow always managed to be the most attractive specimens I'd laid eyes on. That's what made Camp Three players so dangerous. Because with faces like his, they could make you go stupid in two seconds flat if you weren't careful.

I tucked my phone away and crossed my arms over my chest, much like he had when I first arrived. "Tell you what, I'll get your number from HR if you don't do email. I'll send you a text tomorrow with the address for my office."

He gave me a sharp salute. "I'll do my very best to show up sober."

With a long-legged stride, he left the office, the width of his shoulders filling the doorframe ominously because he was the kind of big you just couldn't not notice.

A minute later, Allie walked in, stopping short when she caught me glaring at the door. "Dominic left already?"

I pointed at the hallway. "You cannot be serious, Mom."

Her face softened because I only called her Mom on rare occasions. Not because I didn't love her or because she *wasn't* my mother, but I'd called her Allie for years, so when she and my dad got married, it stuck.

"He's a trainwreck," I told her.

Carefully, she nodded. "It would seem that way. But I think he's got a lot of potential."

"To be a cautionary tale?" I asked.

She laughed. "Faith, you have the biggest heart of anyone I know. If anyone can handle him, it's you."

I covered my face with both hands. "I called him a drunk asshole who couldn't find his manners from his asshole if his life depended on it."

Allie sat next to me on the couch, laughter clear in her voice. "That's an impulse we should probably work on, but trust me, if anyone understands how provoking a cocky, tattooed football player can be, it's me," she said gently. That had me lowering my hands because no way was she equating that interaction to how she met my dad. She gave me a steady look, something she was so, so good at. "What?" she asked.

"You trust him around the kids?"

Immediately, she nodded. "I do. Yes, he's got a temper on the field, but you know we don't only look at their game-day stats. Dominic has fire in him, and when channeled positively, people like that can change the world." She cupped my chin. "You have fire in you too, my dear. It's why you'll do great leading Team Sutton."

Oh sure. With my face that couldn't hide anything and my inability to show up to meetings on time, I was going to be the best boss ever. I sighed. "Thank you."

How could I explain that to Allie, who'd led the Wolves with grace and vulnerability and a core of steel for twenty years?

I couldn't. That was the answer.

"How are you so good at this?" I asked her. "It comes so easily to you."

Allie leaned back on the couch. "It didn't always. Being a good leader is about so much more than wielding your power and clubbing people over the head with it, Faith." Allie glanced out the window of her office and smiled at the Seattle skyline. "Someone like Dominic can push back against that kind of display without thinking. It's a natural reaction due to his personality and the culture of the team he played with for the past three years. You can handle him," she told me. "But the key is figuring out what motivates him. Not what elicits the greatest reaction. Those two seldom overlap."

Glumly, I stared at where he exited the office like I expected him to pop his stupidly handsome face back in and snarl at me some more. "He reminds me of this grouchy bear at the zoo. I tried to give him a treat the other day when I was helping Tori, and he about took my hand off."

"See? You're perfect for this."

Great. Just what I wanted to hear.

Faith Pierson, the perfect asshole-football-player babysitter.

Chapter THREE

Dominic

By the time I pulled my truck into my parents' driveway, I was just as pissed off as I'd been hours earlier when I left the stadium. Nothing worked to settle the raised hackles I carried out of that fucking office, the image of Faith Pierson's shocked face as I said admittedly dick-ish things to her.

Moments like that, it was like someone else took over my body and took a sledgehammer to the filter between my brain and my mouth.

I wasn't sure what I expected out of the owner's daughter, but it wasn't her. Allie was a stunner. There was no other way to say it. Even into her mid forties, she could hold her own against some of the most beautiful women I'd ever seen. And when Faith Pierson walked into the office, wearing that Little Miss Sunshine shirt, I just … got even angrier.

Because under normal circumstances, she was exactly the kind of woman I'd go for. I had a type, and Faith Pierson was fucking it. She'd hate it if she knew. Because in her mind, I was a problem to be solved. And in my mind, that was a role I'd never be able to break free of if I didn't figure out a way to stop pulling such stupid shit.

Seeing her, realizing all of that, was what destroyed that leash I held on my tongue.

I didn't want her to be young and beautiful. Fresh-faced with a wide smile and big eyes. This was no polished glamazon. She had Chucks on her feet and a Wolves badge around her neck like she was born wearing one. Probably because she had been.

Jamming the truck into park, I laid my head back on the rest and took a few deep breaths. The home in front of me was the same place they'd lived my entire life. Last year, they'd painted the exterior a bright white, but the front door had stayed a vibrant red. No matter how much money I'd sent them to buy a new place.

My dad's idea of a splurge was that he'd hired out the exterior paint job. My mom's had been a new couch and recliner for their family room. No matter that I'd sent them a check with a shit ton of zeros on it when I got my signing bonus, they constantly reminded me that how much I got paid was not nearly as important to them as if I was a hard worker. Not just that, but a good person, too.

When I walked through that red door, on this day especially, I wasn't sure I could tell them that I'd been either of those things. Coming home to play for Washington, my home state, was a dream. As I punched the steering wheel, it was easy to turn that slow simmer of anger at myself.

For everything I'd done, because it was the kind of bullshit that could ruin my chance before it had even started.

With a loaded exhale, I stood from the truck, waving at Miss Rose across the street as she wheeled her garbage container to the curb.

"Saw you on the news yesterday," she called. "You look real handsome, Dominic."

I smiled. "Thank you, Miss Rose."

The LIE

She peered over the edge of her glasses. "Except for all those tattoos. Marking up the Lord's temple like that."

The smile broadened because she commented on them every time I saw her. "I'm adding your beautiful face next time." I tapped my chest. "Right here over my heart."

Her wrinkled face, the color of burnished mahogany, softened into a smile like I knew it would. "Oh, get on with you. Tell your parents I said hi. Been praying for 'em today. Missing that little girl like you must be."

Now my smile felt brittle, but I kept it firmly in place. "Thank you, Miss Rose. I'll do that."

Miss Rose had known my parents long enough that saying those things to me was the only time she could say them. My parents, given the gift of Ivy about ten years after they'd had me, didn't handle it well when they lost her. Who would?

They'd done their best with me, but they'd both worked so much just to be able to live that I'd practically raised myself. With Ivy, they'd been different. My mom didn't want to lose time with another child, so she cut back to part-time. My dad was always home for dinner. The years before she got sick were the best we'd ever had as a family.

And now, they just ... tried to forget them because it was too hard to remember.

Miss Rose gave me a last wave, then shuffled back up her driveway. Once she was back in her house, I took a second to steady myself before I jogged up the front steps and opened the door. "I'm home," I called out.

So much of this day was predictable to me. My anger no longer took me by surprise. I'd learned a few years back to embrace it. The fact that I'd walk into their house and smell Ivy's favorite meal—chicken cordon bleu—was also expected. I hated eating it, but my little sister had loved it, the way the chicken was stuffed with ham and cheese. And I also knew that this was one of the only ways my parents showed their grief. We'd eat the chicken, eat the tater tots on the side, and ignore the elephant in the room. Five years later, and there was still a hole punched through our family that we'd never quite been able to heal.

My dad was in his recliner, glasses perched on the end of his nose, work boots on his feet, and a line from his hard hat forming a crease in his dark hair. "How was your day, Dom?"

I tipped the edge of the paper back to see what he was reading. Sports, of course. He flicked his eyes up to mine with a smile.

"Just fine," I told him. "Met the owner today. She already hates me."

He sighed, flipping the page on the newspaper. "Not funny, kid."

"Not joking, Dad."

When I entered the small kitchen, my mom was still wearing her scrubs from work. She was pulling a pan of the chicken from the oven, and when she smiled over her shoulder, I hated how tired she looked. "Hey, honey. I made up your bed in case you want to stay here tonight."

The life of a professional football player, ladies and gentlemen. My mom made the sheets on my full-size bed down the hall, in a room across from theirs in the small ranch where I'd grown up. Where my dad taught me how to build a house—a skill I used to work through college as the only way I could afford it. Where my mom showed me how to fold a fitted sheet because *you better not end up as one of those asshole husbands who thinks his wife is gonna do that stuff for him.*

I laid my hands on her shoulders and kissed the top of her red hair. "Thanks, Ma."

As she laid the pan of chicken on the stovetop, I noticed she couldn't meet my eyes. We did this dance every year. I always wanted to talk about Ivy, but they never did.

And because I knew the role I was supposed to play in this macabre little memorial dinner, I kept my mouth shut.

"She doesn't really hate you, does she?" Mom asked.

"I don't know." I snagged a tater tot and popped it in my mouth. "There was one reporter at the press conference that really pissed me the fuck off."

She eyed me. "Mercy, Dominic, watch your mouth."

The way she said it, the look on her face, I couldn't help myself. "You sound like Ivy," I said around a small smile.

And just like that, my mom's features flattened out, and her cheeks lost all their color. "Dinner will be ready in five."

She busied herself filling the same water glasses we'd used for the past twenty years, and that reaction—even if I understood where it came from—made me want to chuck one of those light blue glasses against the wall, just to see if I could break the tension.

I was ready for the day to be over.

With the smell of our dinner surrounding me, the kitchen started to feel like it was closing in on me. There was this strange chasm between the two worlds I lived in. Downtown Seattle, I owned an apartment with glass and tile and chrome, fancy views and a fancy address, but half the time, I crashed here because it was home.

Somehow, I didn't seem to fit in either place. It had been my problem in Vegas too. The lifestyle of that city wasn't good for me, and my agent fighting for this trade was probably the only thing that would keep me playing because half the teams he talked to weren't interested in having me. Not with my temper.

The longer I went feeling out of place in the city where I lived and worked, the more I felt the need to explode out of my skin, which came out in destructive ways on the field. Add to that, my coach had been kind of a dick who liked it when we got rough with the opposing team, no matter how many penalty flags we drew.

As I walked down the hallway, I didn't stop to look at the framed pictures of Ivy and me. I turned into my bedroom, the walls covered in dark gray paint and posters of football players I'd idolized my entire life.

Including Faith Pierson's father.

He won the championship in his last year in the league, one of the quietly strong leaders who never had to roar too loud to be heard. But every once in a while, I remembered him getting into trouble. At the time and the age I'd been, it had made him more likeable to me. He wasn't perfect, but he had grit. He came from a normal family, and it wasn't easy to remember that when I saw his wife and daughter and their empire that was worth billions by now.

I flopped on my bed and laid an arm over my eyes. An angry buzzing came from my pocket and I sighed. I'd ignored my phone the entire day.

When I pulled it out, it was a text from my agent making sure I hadn't gotten fired yet. I rolled my eyes but didn't respond.

Scrolling to the messaging app, I curled my mouth up in a tiny smile when I saw her messages waiting for me, asking about Ivy. It was another thing about this day that wasn't surprising—her reaction, this online friend of mine, was exactly what I needed.

Without overthinking, I started typing a response.

NicktheBrickLayer: Don't judge her for this, but Ivy's favorite restaurant was Bob Evan's. She loved the little kids' menus, loved all the crap they sell up by the register and the breakfast food. If my parents had let her, she would've eaten a pound of their hash browns.

NicktheBrickLayer: Her favorite movie was *A League of Their Own*. She probably watched it two hundred times. To this day, I can't hear the music without wanting to cry.

My eyes burned as I typed that out because it made me think about the last time she was in the hospital for treatment, and we'd turned it on in her room. Even hooked up to all the machines, all those fucking cords, she told me she was going to be an athlete someday. Even though that movie was her favorite, she was going to play women's soccer for team USA. My parents could hardly afford the meals at Bob Evan's at the time, let alone the thought of entering her into sports, even if she was healthy enough.

If she'd beaten the cancer, if she'd gotten her strength back, I would've worked ten jobs if it meant fulfilling that dream for her.

"You wait and see, Dom," she told me. "I'm going to break all the records, and someday, they'll put me in a museum, and it doesn't matter if the boys make fun of me, I'll do it."

"I believe it, Ivy Lee," I'd told her back.

I liked that I could tell Turbo these two new things. Because over the years, she'd learned a lot about Ivy, considering Ivy was the reason we started talking in the first place.

At the time, my paychecks at the construction company hardly covered my books and tuition, but I'd set enough aside to do something that year to commemorate Ivy's life. The Seattle Zoo, Ivy's favorite place, had this thing where you could digitally adopt an animal. Watch it on a camera, see it grow, and the zoo sent you a dinky little stuffed animal as a thank you.

She was the one who responded to my comment online when I asked if there was a koala available because it was my sister's favorite animal. A week and countless messages later, she mailed me a special stuffed animal that she'd found. A larger koala holding a smaller one—me and Ivy, she told me.

Even though she didn't seem to be online, I clicked on her profile and stared at the picture again, the tiny gold charm on her necklace … a delicate snail against smooth tan skin. TurboGirl was her username, and mine was NicktheBrickLayer. Mind-numbingly clever, I know. But for a walk-on college football player who wasn't there on a scholarship and built houses for a living, it seemed appropriate. At the time, I figured I'd be laying bricks and nailing two-by-fours for the rest of my life.

The green circle appeared on her profile, and my heart sped up when I saw her typing.

TurboGirl: I LOVE THAT MOVIE. Ivy and I would've gotten along very well.

NicktheBrickLayer: No comment on Bob Evan's, I see. You're judging, aren't you?

TurboGirl: I'd never. I'm just hiding my face in shame as I've never eaten at one before.

I grinned, thumbs flying across the screen.

NicktheBrickLayer: It's a life-changing experience. You should go sometime.

TurboGirl: How are you? What happened at work?

NicktheBrickLayer: It's been a shitty day, T. No other way to put it. And I wish I could come here and talk to my parents about her. But I think it just hurts them too bad. I don't want it to piss me off so bad, but God, it does. They're the ones I SHOULD be able to talk to.

NicktheBrickLayer: It's like we had this small window of years when our family was so fucking strong. We did everything together, and now I can't even tell my mom that she sounded like Ivy without ruining her mood.

TurboGirl: I can't even imagine losing a child like that.

NicktheBrickLayer: You lost your mom, though, right?

TurboGirl: Yeah, but I was a baby. I don't remember her. I didn't even know Ivy, and I think of her every time I see something with tie-dye on it.

Breathing out a laugh, I didn't fight the single tear that slid down my temple this time.

"Tie-dye can't be your favorite color, Ivy Lee," I told her. The nurse asked her what her favorite color was, and they'd try to find her a hospital gown.

"Yes, it can," she announced. "It's all the colors, and that makes it even better. Nothing is prettier than tie-dye."

The koala that T sent me had been fitted with a small tie-dye ribbon that she'd tied around its neck. It sat on the top of my dresser, and if anyone gave me shit about that fucking stuffed animal, I'd rip their ballsack off.

NicktheBrickLayer: What are you up to tonight?

TurboGirl: Hanging out with my roommate. Nothing too exciting. Maybe I'll tell her we should watch *A League of Their Own*.

My fingers paused before responding because for the millionth time since I moved back, I thought about telling her that I lived in Seattle again. When we "met," I'd been at school in Texas. There was no option for us to meet up for lunch. For drinks. For a walk. And now that I was here, in a place where she still lived, I found myself hesitating.

T didn't know who I was or what I did for a living. And she was the only relationship in my entire life where I could be myself. Be Nick, the guy who built houses in order to afford college. Nick, who lost his sister and still knew how to help his dad frame a house, and who ordered breakfast for dinner at Bob Evan's because his sister loved it.

There was no one else in the world where I could be those things as easily. And I knew I risked ruining it if I met her.

My mom called from the kitchen. "Dinner's ready, guys."

NicktheBrickLayer: Gotta go eat the shitty cordon bleu. Talk tomorrow?

TurboGirl: Busy day at work, but I'll check in after.

NicktheBrickLayer: Thanks for messaging, T.

TurboGirl: Anytime. I wish I could've met her, N.

NicktheBrickLayer: Me too.

I set my phone down and sighed. Thank God I had her.

Chapter FOUR

Faith

"**D**on't you have your own office?"

The baby kangaroo in my arms jammed his feet against my body, pulling harder on the bottle I was feeding him, and I laughed. My best friend Tori shook her head, adjusting the joey in her own embrace.

"Yeah, but my office doesn't have them," I pointed out.

"You should've changed your major freshman year when we met because if you'd done it then like you wanted to, you'd get to feed these greedy little jerks every single day like I do."

One of the greedy little jerks looked up at her with massive brown eyes, and she smiled down at it like it was her own child.

She wasn't wrong, though.

Non-profit administration didn't sound nearly as cool as feeding baby animals for a living, but it was the path that unfolded in front of me with ease when my dad married Allie. My afternoons and weekends, through middle school, high school, and college, were spent helping out at the Team Sutton events, then at the office as the organization grew.

It was also when my grooming had started. Not in a creepy way. But anyone with eyeballs could tell I was meant for that type of work.

I had a knack for it, as we'd discovered. The kids liked me, the school administrators liked me, and as evidenced by the mountain of scholarship applications currently leasing space on the corner of my very big desk in my very big office, the scholarship applicants liked me too.

And really, I loved all of them. As I'd grown older, it was obvious that I had a heart for volunteering. It was never work and never punishment. I loved helping out at Team Sutton, or the local animal shelter, or—in my college years when I needed some official volunteering hours *not* at Team Sutton—the zoo.

It's where I met Tori, the jerk who lived with me and got to feed baby kangaroos all day long.

"Ouch," I muttered when I got kicked in the boob again. I gave the joey a stern look.

"I told you to put him back in his bag," she said, then tossed me the canvas tote that mimicked a mama's pouch. She wasn't getting kicked in the boob, so I listened to the smart zookeeper.

I scratched the side of his face while I maneuvered the rest of his body back into the bag and settled him on my lap. "You be careful, buddy. That's the most action I've gotten in a while."

Tori snorted. "There really is a shocking lack of men knocking down our door right now."

"Right?" I shifted the bottle, my treacherous mind pulling up an image of Dominic Walker and the words he'd flung at me like darts. Every single one of them had landed with unerring precision. "All we get is handsy kangaroos and jackass football players."

Tori gave me a sympathetic smile because I'd verbal vomited the entire story the night before.

"I bet once he gets to know you, he won't think you're a stuck-up rich girl who's never worked a day in your life," she said, oh-so helpfully.

I gave her a look. "It wouldn't matter if he did. Rule number one."

"I know, I know, I remember the douchebag. But honestly, it's a tragic rule to adopt, considering the bevy of available men at your disposal. Honestly, each and every year, there's a whole list of them drafted just for your perusal."

I laughed. "Is that why they're drafted?"

"They should be." She shifted on her seat. "You watch. He'll be following you around with heart eyes in no time."

"I highly doubt that. You didn't see him. This guy doesn't just have a chip on his shoulder. He's carrying around an entire freaking mountain."

My roommate was undeterred. "Listen, it's part of the Faith Pierson charm. We all go through this cycle when we come into your life. Like the stages of grief."

"Oh my word, Tori," I muttered.

"First is denial," she continued. "I mean, look at you. You are smoking hot in that *girl next door that could break the internet if she posted a nudie* kind of way."

"Which is totally my style."

"You know what I mean. If you did. And it's just a sad fact in this society, Miss Pierson ... looking the way you look, with all those bajillions of dollars your parents have, the knee-jerk reaction of people whose parents don't have a bajillion dollars is to deny the possibility that you are a kind person with a big heart and a recovered foul mouth who works really hard at whatever you do."

I pointed a bottle at her. "I am around kids a lot at work, or I used to be, and I cannot be the one who's teaching them creative ways to curse, okay? I like my swearing alternatives."

Tori ignored me. "Then we all inevitably move to anger," she said with a meaningful raise of her eyebrows.

"Why is your face doing that?"

"Mr. Walker is a perfect example of stage two in the Faith Pierson discovery cycle."

I groaned. "Stop. I beg you."

"He took one look at you, dipped his toe into denial, and went straight to anger." She kissed the joey's head and took the empty bottle away, hooking her tote bag around her neck so she could carry him around. "Which makes sense, if you know his background. He's a scrapper, walk-on player in college, undrafted into the pros because no one thought he would do much—"

"I don't want to know his story," I interrupted. "Because I know exactly what kind of guy he is. I have no choice but to put his grumpy-tattooed-*look at me I'm a bad boy* ass into a situation where he's trying to inspire and encourage the youth of Seattle." I held her gaze. "Does that feel like a fun time to you?"

She sighed. "No."

"No." The bottle in my hand was empty too, so I set it on the floor and settled the joey—safely in his pouch—into a comfy chair next to me. "It was just … the way he looked at me, Tori. I've met a *lot* of football players in my twenty-six years, and I'm never surprised by the giant egos that can hardly fit through the door, the players, or the partiers. That comes with the territory. But the ones who come to help out at Team Sutton are good guys who work hard and love to give back."

"And they're usually very respectful of you because of who you are," she pointed out gently.

"It's not even that," I hedged. "I mean, you're not wrong. Sure, I've been judged for who my parents are. I've even been used for it," I said lightly. "But I don't think I've ever met someone who so quickly *hated* me for who I was."

"Heavy is the burden of greatness," Tori said lightly. We'd been friends long enough that she didn't tiptoe around me, which I appreciated. Tori's childhood was normal, and mine just *wasn't*. My dad and Allie worked very hard to keep my sister and me grounded, but you could only instill so much normalcy when he was a championship-winning quarterback and my stepmom owned a professional football team. "Your life has been pretty sheltered, cupcake, and if his wasn't, I can kind of understand why he acted like that." She gave me a gentle smile. "Kind of."

Suddenly, I wished I had the fuzzy little kangaroo shield in my arms again because her assessment made me feel kinda naked. "He looked at me like I was…" I paused, shaking my head. "Something to be pitied."

Tori's eyes took on a fierce gleam. "Then he has no idea how wrong he is, but you will show him tomorrow."

"What stage of grief will he be in then?" I asked dryly. "I don't think I want to know what Dominic Walker acts like when he's trying to bargain with me over anything."

"I'm teasing."

"I know."

She shifted the joey pouch. "You going to the office soon?"

With a groan, I stood from the floor of her office and wiped off the front of my jeans. "Yeah. I need to plan my day with the giant man-baby who can't regulate his emotions."

Tori laughed. "Good luck with that. I have a school tour in a little bit anyway." She gave me a sly look. "You gonna go visit your boy's koala?"

My face went hot, just like it always did when she teased me about Nick. "He's not my boy, and for your information, no, I wasn't planning on it."

Her eye roll was proof of just how badly I'd lied. I always stopped and visited Ivy's koala when I was at the zoo. For three years, he'd paid the digital adoption fee, and for some reason, it struck me as sad that he'd never been able to visit. So I always did it for him even though he'd never asked me to.

"Someone should," I continued primly.

"Mm-hmm."

"He lives in Texas, okay? It's not like he's going to hop on a plane to come see it."

"He *used* to live in Texas," she pointed out. "You're too chickenshit to ask him if he moved after college, and don't you even deny it, Faith Pierson."

I pulled my purse strap over my head. "You know what I like about my friendship with Nick?"

She pursed her lips. "The complete and total anonymity it affords you because it feels like he's one of the only people who knows the true essence of who you are without all the weirdness of your day-to-day life?"

My face froze in a pained smile. "Yes?"

"And in other language … chickenshit. Because if you met him, you guys would probably fall in love and get married and have babies and save the world with all your do-gooding tendencies."

The conversation I had with Nick the night before, a balm to my shitty, shitty day which started at the Wolves' offices, was proof positive of what my friend was saying. Even without admitting it to her, I knew she knew she was right. And she knew that I knew it. One of those annoying unspoken true friend things.

In my head, I'd built him up to be tall and handsome, a good, decent man with a big heart and strong hands. In my head, he had a wide smile and sparkling eyes, and he spent his days creating homes for people to start their lives in. It felt impossibly wonderful that the reality of him matched the version I'd created. His profile picture was nothing more than the brim of a hat, white with the edge of an orange T-shirt showing, and a glimpse of his cheekbone, dark hair, and golden tan skin.

He talked about things that no guys my age usually talked about. How could he possibly measure up in every way?

Maybe it made me a chickenshit, like Tori said, but I would never sacrifice my friendship with him simply to see if the face-to-face version of us caused sparkage. Or flames. Or anything heat-inducing.

If I tried to explain who I was to Nick, explain my parents, our life, any of it ... he'd get weird. And the last thing I wanted was to kick-start the Faith Pierson stages of grief, or whatever BS I'd never be able to get out of my head now that she said it.

"And there's something wrong with wanting to keep that friendship the way it is?" I asked. When I imagined Nick reacting like stupid-asshole Walker—the anger, the pity, the disdain—my chest started aching, tightening the space around my heart.

Her face softened. "No. But gawd, Faith, what if he looks like a Hemsworth or something? You could be tapping that right now if you'd just ask to meet him."

I laughed. "There's no way I'd get that lucky."

"Why not? He probably thinks the same thing about you, and you're a fricken ten, Pierson."

"Lydia is a ten," I corrected because the hotness of my sister was something no one could argue with. With a rueful glance down at my My Little Pony T-shirt and dark jeans, I shrugged. "I'm an eight who can fake it with some good makeup."

"Get outta here." She laughed, then glanced at the clock on her desk. "Ooh, you actually need to get outta here. I have to go meet the school group."

I blew her a kiss. "See you at home."

"Plan something really good for the asshole," she called behind me.

As I walked down the hall and out the doors into the zoo, taking the path toward the koalas, I had the tiniest of evil smiles on my face because I was going to do exactly that.

WASHINGTON WOLVES

Chapter
FIVE

Faith

"**T**HIS WAS A GREAT IDEA," THE SCHOOL DIRECTOR GUSHED. The parking lot was configured for easy traffic flow with buckets and brushes and stacks of towels set up next to orange cones on the asphalt.

"I think it'll go over well."

Shielding my eyes, I watched two soccer players from the Seattle team chat with a couple of baseball players. Next to them was the quarterback for the Wolves and one of his linebackers. Dominic Walker hadn't arrived yet.

Behind them, up against the brick walls of the school, were hoses, dog shampoo, and even more towels than the cars might need. I got this idea while helping Tori out at the zoo, washing down some of her babies. She made a joke that we needed a service to wash the animals and her car at the same time, and how much she'd pay for someone else to do it.

So that was what we did.

The joint fundraiser was for one of the Team Sutton elementary schools and an animal shelter right around the corner—people could bring their cars and their dogs for a scrub down by professional athletes.

For a donation, of course.

The Team Sutton staff had tables set up with team swag for purchase, all the sports teams represented from each of the athletes who'd shown up to help. Beyond the few I could see were players from the professional women's team and a retired WNBA player, all chatting with the head coach from the men's basketball team at UDub. It was one of our best athlete turnouts all year.

I blew out a slow breath because these were the moments when I loved my job so much, it was stupid. When shifting stacks of paperwork and attending endless days of meetings all paid off in one epically awesome event that should raise a frack ton of money.

When I heard the rumble of a truck pulling into the far side of the parking lot, I knew he'd finally arrived. The two Wolves players approached me as I watched Dominic Walker unfold his big body out of his truck.

"Why's he here?" Brody asked. He was a fifth-year linebacker, and I had to tip my head up to meet his confused gaze.

"Serving some Allie-mandated time," I told him.

James, the QB and one of my favorite players on the roster, laughed under his breath. "Yeah, I heard about what he did."

"And you're laughing?" Brody said to James. "He puked on the field, man. I don't want that shit in our locker room."

Hearing it left a sour taste in my mouth, and I was glad I'd invited him here first. A test run where there was a lot less possible damage he could inflict if he couldn't pull his shit together.

James gave a chiding look to his teammate. "I'm not laughing at that, and you know it. But I don't think we should rush to judgment either."

Brody huffed out a humorless laugh. "Well, he said he's the one who did it. I left that partying bullshit behind in college, and I'm not okay with someone taking up a starting spot who can't respect the opportunity we have."

As Walker approached us, Brody gave me a deferential nod.

"Thanks for inviting me, Faith. Let me know if there's anything else I can do."

I smiled. "Just wash a lot of cars."

"You got it, boss."

James tucked his hands into his pockets as we watched Dominic come to a stop a few feet away from us.

"Good to see you, Walker," James said.

Dominic nodded. Just once.

"I thought I had to work with kids or something," he said to me. Under the brim of his black hat, his eyes were in shadows. It lent him a dangerous edge, one that worked for his entire demeanor. But even in those shadows, I saw his gaze skirt down to my vintage Wolves shirt with the faded logo from the 80s. Allie ran a limited edition printing a few years back, and the entire campaign had sold out in a day.

"I don't trust you yet," I told him.

James coughed, covering his mouth to smother what I suspected was a laugh.

Dominic tilted his head to the side. "I'm hurt."

"I don't think you are." I motioned to a five-gallon bucket filled with two sponges, some towels, and a chamois cloth for drying off the windshield. "Today is when you prove to me that I can, though."

His jaw clenched.

Brody approached behind us. "Faith, how do you want us to split up washing cars or the dogs?"

Dominic must've seen something on Brody's face because his entire frame tensed.

"Walker," Brody said. "Can you keep your food down today? There'll be cameras here."

James pinned the linebacker with a look, and Brody lifted his hands up.

"Just sayin.'"

I rubbed my temples. "You guys are worse than children."

"I didn't say shit," Dominic protested.

My head came back. "Should I recap our first meeting for them?"

"Can't stop thinking about it either?" He flashed a crooked grin that had my stomach go weightless for just one stupid second. "I'm flattered, sunshine."

My eyes closed for a moment, and I held up a hand to Brody, who opened his mouth like he was going to say something. "If you're comfortable washing dogs, I'd prefer you there, Brody. We have a couple of athletes who don't want to deal with it, but you will have a grooming tech with you from the shelter to help."

"Whatever you need, Faith."

I smiled. "Thank you."

"Suck-up," Dominic mumbled as Brody walked away.

James shook his head. "Walker, I don't think this is how you want to start here."

"Are you my boss that I don't know about?" The look in his eye was so combative that I actually felt the hair lift on the back of my neck. What was Allie thinking? This guy was walking around looking for people to piss him off.

But James wasn't intimidated. He smiled widely. "Today? Nope. That's her," he said, tilting his head at me. "By the end of the day, you'll wish it was me. Faith doesn't mess around with her events."

"Dogs or cars?" I asked James.

"I'll stick with the one that can't bite my throwing hand."

I handed him a bucket. "Good call. Thanks, James."

As he walked away, I was left with the big brooding baby, and I had to remind myself that while it wasn't my job to get his ego in check, it was my responsibility for these events to go off seamlessly.

As I picked up the next bucket, he eyed it cautiously.

"It's just a bucket," I told him. "You afraid of a little hard work?"

He exhaled a laugh. "Sunshine, you have no idea how little I'm afraid of."

"Ahh, the fragile male ego on display. A rare specimen indeed." I handed him the bucket.

"Just didn't want you clocking me in the balls with it."

I smiled. "Could I find them if I tried?"

Dominic narrowed his eyes.

"You can wash cars," I told him.

"What if I want to wash dogs instead?"

I met his gaze. "Tell you what, you can wash the dogs if you want."

His eyebrows lifted. "Why do I feel like that was too easy?"

I took the bucket back from Dominic. "Because it's a good test. When I said I don't trust you, I wasn't kidding. There's no way I'm letting you work with kids until I know you're not going to blow it. The kids who benefit from Team Sutton's grants have been through enough, and a guy like you with an attitude problem is the very last thing they need."

His mouth flattened, but he didn't argue.

"So if you can manage this without one of those friendly little pooches biting your face off, we'll call it good."

He eyed the lineup of dogs ready for their baths. "How much are these people paying for me to wash dog shit off their animals?"

"A lot," I answered cheerfully. "Now run along, hotshot. I'll be taking notes from my position of power."

Dominic gave me a look that might've withered a lesser woman, but instead, my smile widened. I waved my fingers in a happy wave, and his glare deepened.

But about ten minutes later when I looked in his direction, he was on his knees, hat turned backward, carefully scrubbing a tiny, used-to-be-fluffy white dog while it licked his face. Whatever he'd done to start that tiny dog's bath had ended with a metric ton of water where it shouldn't have been because Dominic's shirt was plastered to the hard, muscular planes of his chest. And he had a lot of hard, muscular planes.

And he was laughing.

Dominic's gaze lifted, and he locked his eyes with mine. *Now* the hair on the back of my neck lifted, not because of his temper or anything he'd said, but because something foundational seemed to shift with the way he looked at me.

I didn't know exactly what it was, but I tore my gaze from his and let out a deep breath.

"It was nothing," I whispered. "Just a little harmless eye contact."

But still, when I glanced at him underneath my lashes, he was still looking in my direction with his brow bent in confusion. He blinked, then carefully rinsed off the dog, chatting amiably with the owner as the tiny little animal shook off the water.

I had a feeling, the kind of gut reaction that rarely steered me wrong, that Dominic's reactions to people like Brody or me were far more bark than bite.

It wasn't much to go on, but it was something.

Chapter SIX

Dominic

THE FIRST SHOULDER-CHECK IN THE WEIGHT ROOM COULD'VE been chalked up to coincidence.

The second clued me in because the offensive tackle in question actually knocked me back a few inches. Rock music blared in my earbuds, and I glimpsed over my shoulder at his retreating back. A couple of guys quietly going about their workouts watched the exchange with veiled interest.

What a warm welcome I was getting here in Washington. So much for any of the prodigal son feelings I'd had before.

In their mind, I had crossed some invisible line by doing what I'd done—they thought I'd puked all over the Wolves logo.

By the time the third attempt came my way, I managed to side-step actual contact because he was the outside linebacker, big and mean-looking and talented as hell. Yeah, I was no shrimp, but even though I could meet him eye to eye, he'd be able to snap my body in half without breaking a sweat. And he'd been playing in Washington his entire lauded career.

Beneath my frustration that my time in Washington was starting like this was a small kindling of something unfamiliar. It took me a few reps at a couple of different machines before I recognized it.

Embarrassment.

They didn't know what my problem was. They didn't know why I did it. They just saw me as an interloper. Someone who didn't respect the system they'd all worked so hard to build. It was a marked difference from Allie's approach.

If she'd met me with this same closed-off energy, it would've been so much easier to write her off. Write off this entire place as an experiment gone wrong. And maybe it still was. Maybe I belonged somewhere like Vegas, where they cheered and applauded when I acted out. Where my coach used to grab me by the helmet and scream at me to go knock people out on the field.

Literally. He told me to actually knock people out once.

Even as self-destructive as I could be sometimes, I knew it wasn't a good environment if I wanted to do this job for at least a decade.

But I wasn't in Vegas, even if these guys thought I belonged there.

My focus narrowed in on the equipment I was using, the ability to take whatever I was feeling and channel it onto the weights until my muscles were warm and my chest was loose. It was the kind of energy I needed gone before I left the facilities freshly showered and ready to meet with Little Miss Sunshine again.

As I curled my arms, hefting my weight through some pull-ups, I couldn't banish the image of Faith Pierson from my head.

Her dark hair and her big smiles and her absolute refusal to take any of my shit. I'd never met anyone like her, and it showed, considering I'd struggled to keep my mind off her even after I'd left the first event.

Making me wash dogs to see if I could be trusted.

Gritting my teeth, I did one more pull-up before dropping down onto the rubberized floor of the weight room.

Coach walked in, followed by his longtime defensive

coordinator, Logan Ward, the clear shoo-in for the Wolves' next head coach once the position was open. They had the same steely-eyed look about them, even if Coach was a decade or two older than Ward, who didn't show his age much except for some silver at his temples.

Hands on my hips while I tried to catch my breath after the pull-ups wasn't how I wanted to meet him for the first time, but I nodded as they approached. Coach looked me up and down, nothing in his expression that made me think he was about to rip me a new asshole for what I'd done. Ward, however, had a look in his eye that made my balls shrivel up.

I straightened in the way I know my mom would expect of me when meeting my superiors. "Coach Marks, Coach Ward."

Coach shook my hand. "Coach Torres is running a little late, but I expect he'll try to find you before you leave," he said, referring to my offensive coordinator.

With a quick glance at the wall of the weight room, I nodded. "I'll be around for a bit longer."

"Got somewhere important to be?" Ward asked, his arms crossed over his chest.

Judging by the expression on his face, he knew exactly where I needed to be. I wanted to match his stance, cross my arms over my chest and spread my legs wide, tighten my jaw. But I kept my arms loose, attempted a smile. "Mrs. Sutton-Pierson was kind enough to…" I paused, searching for the right word. "*Volunteer* me for some time spent at her foundation."

Coach's lips twitched, but he kept the smile from spreading. "She's good at that. Team Sutton is a world-class organization, so if she wants you to help out, it'll do you good." He glanced at Ward, nudging Logan with his elbow when he didn't move a muscle. "You know he's not yours to intimidate, Ward."

"Shame," he uttered in response. "You got off easy, Walker."

Coach Ward couldn't have known how I was feeling all morning, that there was a slow simmer to my anger just under the surface. And unfortunately for him, it was his tone that unclipped the leash on my reaction. "Did I? I haven't done shit to anyone in this room, but every single person in here is acting like I slashed your tires or something. I thought Washington was supposed to be the good guys," I said smoothly. "Maybe you're all just a bunch of hypocrites."

He stepped closer, hands dropping to his side. The entire weight room watched us as the temperature went from chilly to downright fucking arctic.

I'd heard so many stories about him as a coach, stacked on top of his reputation from when he played. Well-respected didn't even come close to touching what people thought of him. If you listened to the pundits, to the guys who he used to coach, he damn near walked on water, and he was looking at me like I was less than dirt.

Logan's chest was only a couple of inches from mine. "You don't disrespect this house, this family, Walker. When you make the choice to treat it like a frat house"—he leaned in, and I felt my hands curl up into fists—"I have a problem. From the top down, we operate under the belief that everyone here demands respect, and when you act like you're too good to give it, don't expect me—or anyone in this locker room—to kiss your ass because you're good at this job."

I tilted my head and studied his face. He meant it. If I moved wrong, I had a feeling that this guy—twenty-plus years my senior—would kick the shit out of me.

From the corner of the room, the rookie edged away from a machine and opened his mouth to say something. I silenced him with a mighty glare and a short shake of my head. Then I looked back at Ward.

At my silence, which was born out of whatever shred of self-preservation still held on by a single, sad thread, he pointed at the locker room, to the rapt audience watching us. "They're all good at this job. The whole league is filled with guys who can play this game. And outside of it, there's no end of untapped potential just waiting for you to waste this chance." He lifted his chin. "If you fail here, there's only one person to blame, and you look at him in the mirror every single morning. You made a choice when you started here." His voice carried through the whole room, and my face burned hot as I realized the full spectacle we were putting on. "Make a better one, Walker. Because you could be key to this team's success, but only if you actually shut your punk-ass mouth, work harder than you've ever worked in your entire life, and learn some respect for this place. You got it?"

If I closed my eyes, I could visualize the devil on one shoulder and the angel on the other. The devil, red-horned and hissing, whispered in my ear that I should shoulder-check someone on my own, starting with the guy in front of me. But louder, calm and steady, was the angel.

Don't blow this, you idiot.

I swallowed, stepping back, and gave Logan a slow nod.

He relaxed, his eyes softening only a fraction. Coach watched us with interest, the good cop to Logan's bad cop. He wasn't even all that bad, if I had to be honest. Just pissed off. And if there was any reaction I could understand, even if it was aimed at me, was being pissed at someone for a perceived disrespect.

Even if I knew all that, I desperately wished I could just hold my hands up and explain why my first day played out the way it did. Explain how thrilled I was to be playing for Washington, amongst some of the most talented players in the league. Explain how awful it felt that I might never live down the persona that I'd cultivated in Vegas.

But judging by the look in their eyes, no one wanted that from me. Not yet.

Activity resumed in the weight room, some of the defensive players grinning broadly at their leader giving me the dress-down.

The coaches walked away, and I let out a slow breath. The heat left my face, but I braced for another interaction when our

QB approached. He was cool under pressure on the field, unflappable in the pocket, and he held out his hand instead of offering me a cold shoulder.

We'd played against each other over the years, but other than our small interaction at the event the day before, we'd never spoken. Warily, I shook his hand.

His smile was wide at my expression, teeth white against the dark burnished color of his skin. "Peace offering," he said warmly. "Besides, I think you got the point from him." He jerked his chin at Logan.

I nodded. "Thanks."

"No problem," he offered.

"He usually chew out players he doesn't coach?" I asked.

James laughed. "Only when they really deserve it."

"Touché." I glanced at the clock. "I need to hit the showers."

"I'll walk with you." It wasn't a question. This was the on-field leader of the team telling them that he was taking some time with me. A hothead I might be, but I wasn't an idiot. Getting along with my quarterback was about the most important thing I could manage to do.

We left the weight room, quiet for a few moments while I followed his long-legged stride. He was tall for a QB, and with his style of play, we'd be able to create magic.

"There's no perfect team," he started. "Like you, I didn't start at Washington. I transferred here four years ago, and it's always an adjustment when you switch."

"You could say that." I rubbed the back of my neck.

"But this place..." James paused, looking at the logo on the wall. "It's something special. Guys will fight sometimes. Coaches will get on our asses if we mess up, which we do. We don't always get along, but I've never played anywhere like here." He clapped me on the shoulder. "You've got a good future here, Walker, if you can see it for what it is and not for what it's not."

"So far, it seems like a place where no one in that room wants me here," I admitted.

His eyes were steady. "Can you blame them?"

I let out a slow exhale, my body still edgy from the interaction with Ward. "No."

"Give them some time, and don't prove their first impression of you right. We all make mistakes, but once we start repeating them, they're not mistakes. They're choices." He tilted his head at the logo. "This place is a good choice. But the rest of it is up to you."

With his parting words, I felt a little bit better. And I tried desperately to maintain that calm as I showered and changed, then made my way to my car and pulled up the address that had been texted to my phone while I was working out.

Sunshine: Meet me here at 10. Don't dress up. - Faith

I glanced down at my jeans and plain black T-shirt. Not a problem. The interactions I'd experienced in my first few days at Washington cycled through my head as I drove down the 405. My hands tightened on the steering wheel because this block of time doing ... whatever the hell little miss sunshine had planned for me, was my next test.

Maybe I could just toss a ball in the schoolyard with some school-age kids, tell them not to do drugs and work hard, and be done with it.

But when I took the exit, and the buildings got a little shabbier, a bit more run-down, I knew I wasn't meeting her at the Team Sutton offices for some "volunteer orientation." The GPS had me turn, and I pulled into a parking lot with only a few cars and a two-story brick building. A bright white sign with purple, red, and blue painted letters proclaimed it as a community center.

The schoolyard had clean basketball hoops and a court painted with crisp white lines. The property was kept up nicely with potted flowers on either side of the double doors. As I parked my truck, the double doors swung open, and Faith Pierson walked out, shielding her eyes from the sun.

There was no printed T-shirt today, but her long legs were covered in dark denim fitted to her curves and a simple white tank top that probably cost as much as my truck payment. The ponytail from the other day was gone, her dark brown hair in a straight, shining sweep around her shoulders, which was covered in an expensive-looking blazer buttoned in the middle.

Her face didn't change when I climbed out of my truck, and I could see her hand tapping the side of her thigh in a nervous gesture that she couldn't quite hide.

"Morning, sunshine," I said as I drew closer.

Her lips only hinted at a smile at the edges. "Good morning, Mr. Walker."

My eyebrows lifted slowly. "So formal today."

She tapped at a sleek and professional-looking name badge clipped onto the pocket of her jeans. "I'm on the clock."

"You were on the clock yesterday," I pointed out.

Faith's dark eyebrows bent in. "That was different. We were at a big event."

"So now you're nicer to me because there are no other football players to help you antagonize the new guy?"

"Th-that's not what I was doing."

"Wasn't it?" I murmured. "I think all you've done since the moment we met was give me shit."

"Because you…" She stopped short and let out a slow breath. "You're right. Even if I can't control your reaction to me, I can control my own."

"I usually am right, sunshine."

Color flushed her cheeks at my lightly teasing tone, but today, there was no witty comeback. Yeah, Faith Pierson was exactly my usual type, and it made me want to tug on the proverbial pigtails just a little bit more to see what happened.

Determined to unnerve her, I reached forward and hooked the edge of the badge with my finger and pulled, once I saw it was on one of those retractable cords. In the thumbnail picture of her, she was smiling widely at the camera without a care in the world.

"Fancy," I murmured.

Careful not to brush her skin against my fingers, Faith plucked the laminated card out of my grasp.

"Ready to go in?"

I stared at the building. "What am I supposed to be doing?"

"This community center has been a longtime grant recipient for the foundation. I used to volunteer here before I started working for Team Sutton, and I love their reading program for kids who struggle with literacy." She smiled at the shrieks of laughter that echoed down the halls. "There's a strong tie between secondary education drop-out rates and reading issues. All you're going to do today is visit with one of the groups and read a couple of books." She glanced at her watch, a sleek black and gold number that encircled her slim, fine-boned wrist. "I think today is the girls' group. They're all eight or nine, I think."

My skin went ice cold. "No fucking way."

Her eyes went wide.

Panic had me stumbling over my words. But there was no way I could sit in a room of girls Ivy's age. Not this week. "I just … why would they want me to read to a bunch of little girls? Can't I like … throw a football to some boys or something?"

Faith Pierson studied me for a moment, and I held my breath, waiting for another verbal attack for the day. Someone telling me I was disrespectful, a punk. Then she smiled. It was soft, and it made me so uncomfortable that I desperately fought the urge to sprint back to my truck.

"Follow me," she said.

Without another word, she walked into the building. And even though my heart was thrashing in my chest, I did as she asked.

Chapter SEVEN

Faith

Walking through the hallways, it very much felt like I had a growling animal behind me. One with no manners and zero training and the temperament of a rabid raccoon. When I woke earlier in the day, I'd made a decision of how to approach Dominic Walker, once I'd seen tiny glimpses of softness at the car wash. I was adding it to the rule list.

Don't Engage with the Tantrum.

No matter how he baited me, what names he called me, I would ease us through the day exactly as if he was one of the dogs I walked at the shelter around the corner from my apartment.

Once they acclimated to your presence, and you kept your calm, kept steady, they'd relax. And one could only hope that it would work with a six-four tight end with attitude problems.

And like I thought he would, the pushback from Dominic started quickly. That wasn't the surprise. It was his reaction when I told him he'd be working with the eight-year-old group with their reading.

I hated how curious it made me, that a man like him would

panic so visibly at spending time with a bunch of girls. It didn't fit neatly into any of the categories that I could've defined for him. In all my years of doing this, no players had reacted that way.

And now, more than anything, I wanted to know why.

The man piquing my curiosity walked a bit slower than I was, maybe to unnerve me by staying just out of my view.

"This particular community center has been one of the Team Sutton recipients for almost fifteen years," I explained. "We have a few programs that we've funded the entire time, providing necessary staff and training that they may not be able to afford otherwise, along with some new classes and groups for kids who live in the area."

Dominic was as quiet as the grave, and I blew out a slow breath. Okay, he wasn't going to make this easy.

These were the moments when I felt woefully unprepared for leadership, but I thought about what Allie had said. It wasn't about eliciting the greatest reaction. It was about figuring out motivation.

"The literacy program is one of those programs. We've seen an uptick in grant requests for things like this." There was a stack as tall as a toddler in my office to prove it, but he didn't need to know that. "We can't help all of them, of course, but we do what we can."

"That make you lose sleep at night, sunshine?"

The silky hairs along my forearm lifted slowly at the gravelly sound of his voice.

I kept my voice casual. "What?"

"That you can't hand out all your billions with one magnanimous sweep of your arm."

Slowing my steps, I glanced over my shoulder at him. "In a manner of speaking, yes. There's a lot of red tape involved in granting people money. It's not the fastest process in the world, a lot of steps to make sure they're going to use it in the way they say they will. That's one piece of my job."

"A hardship, to be sure." Disdain dripped from every syllable, every sound that his mouth formed.

It was harder than I thought not to snap back at him in the same way I had during our first couple of meetings. But something in my gut told me it would only make it worse. He didn't need attitude thrown back at him. Not this time.

Hands clasped innocently in front of me, I stopped, tilting my head as I studied him. His jaw clenched, coated in even more dark stubble than the last time I'd seen him. Everything about this man looked hard-edged and dangerous. But for some reason, Allie thought this was the best course of action, that it would help him, maybe just as much as it would help some of these kids.

Even knowing that, even knowing what I'd decided about how to handle him, I could only keep my tongue on so tight of a leash.

"And how many zeros did your signing bonus have when you signed with Vegas?"

Dominic's eyes, dark and piercing, never wavered. But his mouth stayed shut in a firm line.

"What about your contract with Washington?" I raised my eyebrows at his continued silence. "You act like you're better than me, like you can judge me because I come from a wealthy family, but I don't think you'll be suffering economic hardship anytime soon, hotshot. What are *you* doing to help people who don't make millions of dollars catching a ball?"

Surprise lit those eyes, pleasant surprise too, which made me instantly wary. "Now, what would Daddy think listening to you make fun of my job?"

I blew out a slow breath and pivoted away from him. "That's not exactly what I was doing."

Dominic clucked his tongue. "Sure sounded that way to me."

Stick to the plan. Stick to the plan. Do not engage, I reminded myself. Digging into whatever mental reserves I had at my disposal, I schooled my face just as a loud burst of young girlish laughter came from a classroom at the end of the hall.

At his side, I saw Dominic's hands curl into fists, then his fingers stretched back out. An unconscious gesture, I was pretty sure. We'd worked with so many different players over the years, all sorts of personalities, but no one who was flat-out unwilling to help.

I didn't like that Dominic Walker was hard to define. One moment he was rude and judgy. Then he was laughing while fluffy little dogs licked his face. Everything in my life could usually fit neatly into a category, and I got uncomfortable when it didn't.

Still, watching him, I wasn't entirely sure he could actually do this.

"A couple of the girls in there do better reading when someone sits next to them to listen. One day a week, they bring in a therapy dog program and the kids read to the dogs." I gave him a wry smile. "So if you can match the enthusiasm of a golden retriever who doesn't understand what they're saying, you'll be just fine."

But my quip didn't make him laugh. He looked pale, his body tight with tension. My brow furrowed as I realized this wasn't just plain old hesitation. This was actual panic at the thought of going in that room. Before I could say something, though, the door to the classroom opened.

One of the program directors came into the hallway, her eyes lighting up when she saw us. "Faith, I was wondering where you were. The girls are excited to have a guest today." She held her hand out to Dominic. "I'm Keisha. Nice to meet you."

He nodded. "Dominic Walker."

Okay, so he was capable of basic manners as long as the person wasn't me.

I laid a hand on Keisha's arm, yet again, going with my gut. "Do you mind if we switch things up a little?"

"What are you thinking?"

Without checking with Dominic, I tilted my head toward the exit that led to the playground. "Can we keep it a bit more relaxed today? Maybe have him toss a ball with some of the kids outside? He could just get to know them a little bit for now."

Keisha must have seen a look in my eye that begged her not to say no because she nodded slowly, then gave Dominic an encouraging smile. "Absolutely. There's a handful of kids out there right now." Another burst of sound came from the room, and she breathed out a tired-sounding laugh. "Let me go check on them. I'll be out on the playground in a little bit."

"Thank you, Keisha."

Dominic exhaled quietly, but I noticed that his frame had relaxed. My brow furrowed as I led him toward the playground. Maybe he wasn't a good reader.

"It's killing you not to ask, isn't it?" he said.

I looked over at him in surprise. I hadn't even realized he could see my facial expressions.

"You do a shit job of hiding what you're thinking." His gaze touched on various points of my face, and my cheeks warmed at his careful perusal. "You plan on prying, sunshine?"

"Everyone is entitled to a degree of privacy," I answered carefully. "Especially with the life you lead."

We reached the door that led to the playground, and he lifted his chin toward the banged-up metal door with a small window that allowed a block of bright sunlight into the hallway.

"What am I supposed to do out there?" he asked.

At his disgruntled tone, I couldn't stop my smile.

"What?" His voice got grumpier and grumpier the bigger that smile got.

I laughed quietly. "Just ... be yourself. Maybe a little nicer to them than you are to me," I corrected. "Play catch. Give them some tips. Tell them about how hard you worked to get here."

"That's it?"

"These kids don't have a ton to look forward to once they go back home. In the summers or on their days off from school, they hang out here because either their parents work themselves to the bone to provide for their families or they don't do much of anything.

It's a safe place, yes, but they also want to breed opportunities for the kids. Show them how to utilize those opportunities for growth and give them the confidence to try."

He sighed. "Let's get this over with."

I pushed open the door and walked into the yard with him behind me. As his big frame filled the doorway, I heard a little girl shout, "Heads-up!"

The football hurtled in our direction, and I ducked down, but with the sun directly into his eyes, Dominic never saw it coming until it hit him square in the balls.

Chapter EIGHT

Dominic

"I THINK I KILLED HIM," A TINY VOICE WHISPERED ABOVE where I'd sunk to my knees on the concrete.

My hands still cupped my throbbing balls, and holy hell, it was all I could do to breathe, so there was no chance I could correct her even if I wanted to.

Faith exhaled a laugh. "I don't think he's dead. You just ... hit him pretty hard in a not-so-fun spot."

I pried my eyes open and caught a glimpse of Faith's wide smile. She had the tiniest gap between her two front teeth, and I'd never noticed it before.

A bunch of kids gathered around us, and I heard one of them whisper, "Holy shit, that's Dominic Walker."

"Maggie, you knocked off *Dominic Walker's* balls," another said.

A sound came from my mouth, possibly a whimper, a little bit of a curse word, and Faith cleared her throat loudly to cover my swearing. "Okay, guys, give him some room to breathe." She laid a hand on my shoulder, nothing more than a light touch, but her fingers were cool and soft against the skin of my neck where they brushed the edge of my shirt. "Are you okay?"

I blew out a hard breath through puffed cheeks, managing a nod. "I think so."

She grinned. "Can you stand?"

I gave her a look. Her hand left my shoulder, and she placed it on the little girl hovering at her side. As I braced a booted foot on the ground to stand, I finally realized just how small she was ... the one who about castrated me.

There was no way she was much older than six or seven, but her wild, messy crown of auburn hair and big terrified brown eyes knocked the air from my lungs for a completely different reason.

She didn't look like Ivy in her coloring or her stature. But something about those eyes had me frozen.

"I'm really sorry," she said, turning her petite frame into Faith's legs. "Are you mad at me?"

"No," I managed, pushing myself up to my full height. I mean, sure, all my blood was currently throbbing between my legs in painful pulses, but I wasn't mad. "You've got quite the arm."

The little girl smiled. "I'm better than my brother."

"You are not!" a taller kid with the same coloring yelled.

"Am too!" she yelled back. "You couldn't hit the side of a semitruck, Blake."

He started to argue, and I held out my hand. "Your name is Blake?" I asked.

Eyes filled with awe, he came over—skinny chest puffed out—and shook my hand. "Uh-huh. And she's not better than me. I taught her how to throw."

Faith laughed quietly, casting her attention to all the kids starting to circle around us. "I think we should start a little game, don't you?"

They all cheered.

Maggie, the girl who'd thrown the ball, still stared up at me like

The LIE

I was going to lash out or lose my temper on her simply because I walked out of the door at the wrong time.

"You gonna be my QB?" I asked.

"Me?" she squeaked. The boys all groaned.

I nodded. "Quarterback has to have a strong arm, good aim, and a cool head. Can you manage that with all these guys trying to keep me from catching the ball?"

"Totally," she breathed.

Her brother opened his mouth, but I gave him a stern look. "She gets first up, no arguments."

"She's a girl," Blake said.

"No shit, Sherlock."

Faith cleared her throat again.

"Sorry," I murmured in her direction.

"It's okay," she answered.

The kids spread out, following my direction, and to my surprise, in her silk tank and expensive shoes, Faith lined up opposite my four-person offensive line.

"You think you can defend me, sunshine?"

She didn't answer, just gave me a sly grin that had me questioning whether I wanted to play this game at all.

But within a few minutes, any apprehension I'd had walking through the door was gone.

We attracted a crowd of other kids, older and taller, who wanted to join in once they realized it was me out here with the young ones.

"Next game is yours," I told them, wiping a sheen of sweat off my brow.

Maggie took the ball from my hands, and our team huddled up. "Pass to you again?" she asked.

A skinny kid next to her, with thin braids along his scalp, raised his hand. "Can I try to catch this time?"

"You bet," I told him. "What's your name?"

"Desmond." He tugged his shorts up. "I can run fast, I promise."

I heard Faith's team laugh at something she told them, and when I glanced over my shoulder, she looked so beautiful when she laughed, I forgot what I was saying.

I didn't want Faith to be my type. Not at all.

Because she was not something I should've been noticing. Not the way she treated the kids or the way she'd treated me since I arrived with an attitude I'd carried through my entire morning, not her fingers against the skin of my neck or how she seemed to be completely self-assured, even carrying about such beautiful features.

Maggie called my name, and I snapped my attention from Faith back to my pint-sized teammates. We called the play and stuck our hands in the middle. I had to take a second because with all of them staring up at me, it was like getting glimpses of myself at that age. Theirs was the kind of neighborhood, the kind of childhood I'd had. Except I'd had nowhere like this to go to.

Desmond gave Maggie a look. "Aren't we supposed to be doing something?"

"Sorry," I told him. "Just ... blanked out for a second. All right, on three," I told them. "One, two..."

Everyone paused. Maggie looked at me, and I looked at the kid next to me.

"What are we supposed to say on three?" Desmond asked.

I smiled. "It's okay. We'll get it next time."

After we'd lined up, Faith sidled herself in front of me, assuming I'd take the throw again. She bent her knees in readiness, eyes narrowed and lips curled in a smile.

Maggie called the play, and I spun around Faith, sprinting toward the end zone, with every single person on their team chasing me. From the corner of my eye, I saw Maggie toss the ball to Desmond, who clutched it to his chest like it was made of gold, and he took off, his legs churning furiously.

I raised my arms in victory, yelling as he crossed the end zone.

The LIE

Jogging to him, I swooped him up and tossed him in the air while our team screamed and jumped.

Faith, joined by Keisha, watched with big smiles as I high-fived everyone around me. Faith pulled out her phone and asked us to pose for a picture. Desmond and Maggie flanked me, their skinny arms wrapped around me while I kneeled in the middle of all the kids.

Keisha handed me a Sharpie. "Would you mind signing the ball? We'll keep it in the classroom on our special shelf."

"Aw, man," Maggie said. "That was my favorite ball."

"Can I send the center a few more to replace it?" I asked.

Keisha nodded immediately. "We'd be so grateful, thank you."

"What else do you need?" I asked, scrawling my name over the surface of the ball.

When I looked up, Faith watched with a careful smile. Fuck if I didn't love that smile, and the fact that I'd put it on her face.

Keisha took the ball when I handed it to her. "Any sports equipment that can be shared by all the kids gets used the most. Bats, balls for any sport, gloves, jump ropes. You name it, they love it."

"You got it," I told her.

She gave me a warm smile. "Thank you, Dominic. The kids will talk about this all year long." Then she turned to Faith. "Speaking of big events, I got the invite for the Black and White Ball."

Faith smiled. "Can you come?"

Keisha nodded. "Wouldn't miss it. I'll dust off my fancy dress." She smiled at me. "Faith sponsors a table at the Team Sutton fundraiser and invites different program directors from the places that have received annual grants from Team Sutton. It's one of my favorite events every year."

"It's our primary fundraiser," Faith explained. "A lot of the team shows up, and we do a silent auction among a few other things."

"And this is your big year," Keisha said, nudging Faith with her elbow.

She tucked a piece of her hair behind her ear. "It's just a quick speech."

"Stop being so modest." Keisha shook her head. "You'll be an incredible director, Faith."

Faith eyed me under her lashes, carefully studying my face. And I couldn't blame her with how I'd acted.

Before I could say anything or study Faith's reaction further, Maggie tugged on my hand. I crouched down to her height.

"What's up?"

She inhaled, visibly gathering her courage. "Thank you for letting me be quarterback."

"You're welcome." I could tell she wanted to hug me, but I held my hand up for a high five instead. If this little girl with the big arm and huge eyes hugged me, I'd be a goner. Maggie tapped my hand with hers.

"The boys never let me throw the ball," she said quietly.

"I bet they will now." I ruffled her hair. "Don't forget to set that back foot, okay? Keep your elbow in."

She grinned. "I'm gonna play football someday. You watch."

Her words pierced straight through a tiny opening in my ribs, and I felt the slow hiss of air leave my body. "I believe you," I answered quietly. As she took off on the playground, I wanted to escape from that schoolyard and not look back. All of it, even the good parts, had me feeling strangely raw. The slightest touch to that area, and it would bleed for days before it could start healing.

When I stood, I felt Faith's gaze on me. Keisha was still talking to Faith about the fancy dinner where she'd be center stage. Then Keisha glanced down at her watch.

"Oh, fracksticks, I have to get back to my office for a meeting."

My eyes zipped to Keisha's face. "What did you just say?"

She laughed. "Stole that off Faith. She always says it."

Faith shrugged, giving me a strange look as I stared at her. "I'm

The **LIE**

around too many kids on a weekly basis. If I don't find creative ways to swear, I'd get myself fired really quick."

If I thought I'd felt raw before, it was nothing compared to how I felt now. I'd never heard that phrase *anywhere* except from one person. My heart thudded erratically as I stared at the line of Faith's neck, underneath the dark curtain of hair that covered her shoulders. I couldn't see a golden chain, but with the way the neckline of her shirt fell, that wasn't too surprising.

"I-I have to go too," I said.

Faith gave me a tentative smile. "I hope it wasn't too bad. I know the kids would probably love to see you again."

But I couldn't bring myself to answer.

I nodded, brushing past her to the chain-link gate that separated the schoolyard from the parking lot.

I could hardly pull my phone out fast enough, scrolling to the messaging app and clicking on Turbo's profile picture. There wasn't a single piece of hair showing in the picture, nothing I could compare definitively to Faith. Just the line of her neck. The curve of her jaw.

When I raised my head, Faith was standing in the playground, staring after me, shading her eyes from the sun.

And she stood that way as I cranked my truck on and backed out of the spot, my heart pounding and my mind racing.

If Faith was Turbo, Turbo was Faith, then I'd been the biggest asshole in the entire world to the one person who'd made life bearable for me. And I wasn't sure what to do with that until I knew if it was true.

Chapter NINE

Faith

Dominic's exit—not to mention his amazing visit with the kids at the center—could hardly get a foothold in my head before my phone rang from the office. I found a quiet bench in the sun and picked up the call.

"This is Faith."

"Did you see the email?" my assistant asked. Kim's breathy excitement had me smiling, even if I had no clue what she was talking about.

"No, I'm out by Keisha. We had a player visit come up last minute."

She paused. "That wasn't on your calendar."

"I know, I forgot to tell you," I answered with a wince. I'd only been the official director for less than a year. Sometimes, I forgot that I was supposed to be updating someone on where I was. "Allie asked me to facilitate this one personally."

"Ahh."

"Yeah."

"Either he's a troublemaker or he's looking to write a big check."

I laughed. "The former."

"Who is it?"

Her tone wasn't mean, but it hit that low, excited pitch, the kind you heard when someone was digging for some juicy gossip. Not only that but I was still puzzling through what I'd witnessed and how great he'd been with the kids, considering he was about as friendly as a cactus. Talking bad about him didn't feel right, in some way.

"Kim," I said gently, "you called about an email?"

Her demeanor flipped like a switch. "Right. Sorry." Kim cleared her throat. "We got three big donations today, not even connected to the dinner, and we can fund all the requests that came through for the next six months."

I grinned. "That's great. Even the community theater project?"

"Even that."

We'd honed our mission at Team Sutton to focus on after-school programs for kids in elementary and middle school in lower-income areas, where the extracurricular activities were just too expensive. The skills the kids learned from such things as playing in sports, participating in plays, and getting some extra help with their reading had lasting impacts on the rest of their life.

"They need a huge renovation to that gym to be able to start the program," I said, putting my phone on speaker and flipping over to my email so I could review the donations. Two were from players on the Wolves and one from a well-known actress who had moved to Seattle a couple of years earlier. I'd have to reach out to her and send a thank you because her check had a *lot* of zeros.

What a weird, weird job I had.

Kim's voice interrupted. "Are you coming back to the office this afternoon?"

"Yeah, I'm heading in soon. I need to follow up on a few of the new fund requests because they forgot to include their estimates from vendors."

"Faith," she chided. "That's not something you need to do anymore. Maybe when you were an intern."

"I know, I know. Thank you, Kim."

I could hear the smile in her voice when she answered. "So you'll still be able to make the three o'clock meeting?"

I covered my face with my hand because I'd totally forgotten about it. "Remind me of that one again?"

She laughed. "To finalize the silent auction items for the dinner. We may need to reach out to former donors for some more. I think your dad is coming too."

"Right. That meeting." With a glance at my watch and a mental GPS route of how long it would take me to get back to the Team Sutton offices, I blew out a slow breath. "Yeah, I should be there in plenty of time."

"See you soon, boss," she said and hung up.

With my phone still in my hand, I saw a notification from Nick and smiled. When I clicked on it, I saw it had come through just before Kim had called.

NicktheBrickLayer: How's your day going? I need someone to have a more exciting day than mine.

TurboGirl: Not bad so far. Got to do the fun stuff this morning. Now I have to go do the boring meeting stuff.

He started messaging, and the sight of the dancing dots had my heart rate picking up. We so rarely connected in the moment.

NicktheBrickLayer: You know, you've never actually told me what it is you do. You were still in school when we "met."

With a loaded exhale, I squinted up at the bright sky. He was right. I'd never told him on purpose. There was this account, the one that didn't hold a single hint as to who I was, and there was my official Faith Pierson—director of Team Sutton—account, one carefully curated by the PR team at the foundation. I'd never had anything to do with that one, which suited me just fine, but with Nick asking me like this, it felt like I was … lying.

How did Tom Hanks make it look so easy in *You've Got Mail*? Probably because he was Tom Hanks. And when I got reactions like the open hostility from Dominic Walker, it only served to make me that much more wary to be honest.

Tapping my thumb on the side of my phone, I mulled over what I could say.

> **TurboGirl:** I work for the organization my stepmom started. I was young when she married my dad, so I was always at the offices. It was a natural fit for me, I guess. After college, I kinda took over the office. Most people would look at it as a boring desk job with lots of paperwork and meetings, but I like what we do.

> **NicktheBrickLayer:** But this morning wasn't boring?

> **TurboGirl:** Got to play a little football actually. My team lost, but we gave it our best try.

The dots came up again and then disappeared. That happened two more times. When I glanced at the clock to see how long it was taking him to respond, I realized I'd been sitting for too long.

"Oh, fracksticks," I whispered. *Nick would have to wait,* I thought as I shoved my phone into my bag and took off toward the parking lot. I'd still make the meeting in plenty of time as long as the traffic wasn't too bad on the way back to the office.

Stabbing my key in the ignition, I cranked it over … and nothing.

My car wouldn't start.

I pulled it out and stared at it like it would give me an explanation, then tried to start it again. Nothing.

"Oh, come on," I groaned. I sent Kim a text and told her I might be late and got out of the car. My jacket came off first, then I tugged a hair tie out of my console and jammed my hair into a messy ponytail while I walked around to yank open the hood of my car.

I pulled open my phone and dialed my dad's number. He was in the thick of helping with recruitment—looking for free agents just like Dominic—for the upcoming season at Washington, but he picked up on the first ring.

"Hey, Turbo," he said, but his voice sounded distracted. "What's up?"

"My car won't start." I peered at the engine. "I think it's the battery, but I don't know for sure."

"Shit. Are you at the office? Someone could give you a jump, right?"

I rubbed my forehead. "No, I'm out at Keisha's community center. I don't exactly have jumper cables in my car."

Silence from my dad had me wincing. "Where'd they go?"

"I took them out because I had all those buckets from the car wash event. I think they're sitting on my kitchen counter."

"Faith." He sighed. "This is one of my family rules. Always keep—"

"Jumper cables in the car," I finished. "I know. I'll go in and see if Keisha has some. I just wanted to let you know I might need a new battery since this happened last week too."

"You sure you don't need me to come get you?"

"No, I just didn't want you to freak out if I'm late for that meeting about the foundation dinner. Kim said you'd be there."

My dad sighed again, a sound that had me grinning because I heard it all the time. Between me and my twenty-year-old sister Lydia, it was the thing we heard most, actually. And if I was the do-gooder princess (according to one cranky football player) then my younger sister was the one who would actually cause my parents to lose their minds. She lived to cause trouble.

"Well, let me know if you change your mind about the help."

"Love you."

"Love you too," he answered gruffly.

Just as I was tucking my phone back into my pants pockets to go ask Keisha for a jump, the familiar sound of a loud truck had me pausing. Because I'd heard that truck leave the community center parking lot not that long ago. Shading my eyes from the sun, I watched Dominic Walker pull back into the lot.

His eyes were covered by black aviator shades, and when he slowed next to my car, it didn't matter that I couldn't tell where he was looking because I felt his gaze like he trailed a finger down my spine.

How had I described him earlier? A dangerous animal.

When he shut off the engine and got out of his truck, he didn't say a word as he approached even though he removed the sunglasses.

Because he was so much taller than me, I had to tilt my chin to look up at him. Dominic was so big, everywhere. His shoulders, the length of his arms, the span of his chest, and his hands. He was just ... impressive.

"Forget something?" I asked. Why was it hard to get those words out? My lungs felt sucked clean of air, nothing to support my ability to speak easily.

He still didn't respond, but I saw his eyes snag on the gold chain that laid flat on my chest, the pendant tucked against my skin.

His chest expanded silently, and I found myself holding my breath. My shoulders were bare because I'd taken off my blazer and pulled my hair back.

"Need a jump?" he said in a rough rumbling voice.

My heart skipped at the implication. I hadn't been ... jumped in a good long while. It wasn't even a good jump at that. And my palms went a little sweaty when I tried to imagine us. Doing that. Except I didn't date football players because ... rules. Important rules for important reasons that I tried very hard to remember when he looked at me like that.

"What?" I asked, voice breathy.

He raised one eyebrow sardonically. "The car?"

I blinked. "Yes. I think I do."

Dominic gestured to my vehicle. "Cables?"

"On my kitchen counter," I said sheepishly.

His eyes narrowed, but he didn't say anything. When he ambled to the back of his truck and opened the silver lockbox in the bed, I rubbed the back of my neck. He still hadn't said why he came back.

And suddenly, I found myself quite desperate to figure out why.

Chapter TEN

Dominic

B
EING NEAR HER, WITH ALMOST A HUNDRED PERCENT certainty that she was Turbo, my hands could hardly stop shaking as I pulled the jumper cables from the lockbox in my truck.

Tell her, tell her! the angel on my shoulder screamed.

Briefly, I glanced at where she was waiting by the hood of her car, but keeping that glance brief took all the discipline I'd honed as an athlete. I didn't want to look at her in short windows and small glances. I wanted to devour every inch of her with thorough study, this woman who'd become one of my closest friends in the past few years.

It all made sense. Every piece of it.

Faith Pierson was a helper. She wanted hands-on ways to give, to do, to serve. And it reminded me of the very first conversation we'd had, where she replied to a comment I'd left on the Woodland Park Zoo social media account, asking about the koala. She wasn't even an official volunteer if I remembered correctly, but her friend worked there, and she helped out on occasion.

This woman, who organized flag football games for little kids, when she probably should've been sitting behind her fancy desk, had a heart the size of Mt. Rainier.

My eyes pinched shut as I thought about all the things I'd said to her and the ways I'd sneered. My fist curled around the jumper cables as I braced myself to walk back in her direction.

If she was Turbo, I didn't deserve to breathe the same air as her. So many levels separated us, and it wasn't even just her upbringing versus mine. Faith was a good person, and I was the guy who always listened to the dude with the pitchforks and horns as he whispered to my subconscious. Tear down all those good things around me before I could possibly get hurt.

At that moment, the embarrassment was just as potent as it had been in the Washington locker room. It made my tongue freeze instantly, words cramming up in my throat like a traffic jam. What could I even *say*?

She was waiting, hands on her hips, hair up-swept and her eyes shrewd with study.

"Why did you come back again?" she asked.

My lips tightened into a line. "I, uh, needed to check if I forgot something."

The lie was ... sort of not a lie.

I did want to come back to check on something. On her. Sitting in my truck, two minutes down the road, I'd hardly thought it through when her reply came through that she'd spent the morning playing football.

In no less time than it took me to take a breath, I'd peeled out of the parking lot and turned my truck back toward the community center.

It's her.
It's her.
It's her.

And the second I saw her, still as beautiful as she'd been earlier, but somehow more beautiful because she was also the other version of her that I knew, my heart kick-started in a way I'd never experienced.

For the first time in my life, I imagined how I'd greet her if she actually felt happiness at the sight of me instead of immediate wariness. I'd slide my hands into her silky, dark hair. I'd tip her face up to mine, crowd her against the hood of her car, and slide my lips across hers. I'd taste the line of her pink mouth until she opened wide, and I could use my tongue and feel her hands on my back.

But the second she gave me that look, that Little Miss Sunshine look of *oh shit, now what,* the image dissipated like smoke. Because Faith Pierson wasn't excited to see me. She might've been my type before I knew who she was, but I was clearly not hers.

Because I'd been the world's biggest asshole to her. For no reason other than the family she was born into.

While she watched, I hooked the jumper cables up to her car, and thought about what I should—or could—say.

There was no way to tell her who I was, not yet. And as I caught a whiff of her bright, fruity shampoo as she leaned in closer, I knew I didn't want to be done with this interaction. It was too fast.

I straightened, removing the clips from her battery.

She looked at the engine and then back at me. "I think those work better when they're attached."

Swallowing my impulse to laugh, I lifted my chin at her driver's seat. "I want you to try starting it again. Let's make sure it's the battery, not the starter."

Faith pinned me into place with those big eyes of hers, and the questioning look in them had my throat going as dry as the fucking desert. Not just questioning what I was doing but also questioning me. And I couldn't blame her.

So far, I'd given her absolutely no reason to trust me.

"My battery had issues last week too," she said, making no move to get into the car.

"Can you just try?" When her lips twitched, I added, "Please."

"Well, look who found some manners today," she mumbled. As she climbed into her car, which probably cost more than my parents' house when they bought it, I caught the edge of a smile on her pretty face.

Again, the sight of that smile did insane things to me. It was the kind of rush I only usually got playing football. Making a great catch. Scoring a touchdown. And now, I could add *making Faith Pierson smile* to the list.

While I waited, she turned the key in the ignition, but there wasn't even an attempt for the engine to turn over. She lifted her hands.

"Did you hear the click?" I asked.

She nodded.

"It's your starter, not your battery."

Her face scrunched up in an adorable grimace, and holy fuck, I was thinking words like *adorable grimace*.

How quickly the tides had turned.

"Well, I guess I didn't want to go to my meeting this afternoon anyway," she said, climbing out of the car and joining me as I closed the hood.

"I can take you to work."

Her dark eyebrows, somehow just as expressive as her big eyes, popped up in surprise.

"You'd drive me across town?" she asked, clearly skeptical.

Leaning my hip against the front of her car, I gave her a slight grin. "Thought about making you walk, but… I think your mom would really hunt me down after that."

Faith tucked a piece of hair behind her ear, a gesture I'd seen her do a few times now.

Her hair looked so soft. If I rubbed that piece between my fingers, it would feel like silk. And just like that, all I wanted to do was bury my nose in it, pull her scent into my lungs, and stand next to her car in the afternoon sun and listen to her talk about all the things we normally messaged about.

Already, I knew so much about her.

She loved her parents and was still getting used to her promotion at work.

Given a choice, she'd work with animals or kids, getting dirty and sweaty every single day because it brought her joy.

She hated french fries—which was a crime in my mind—but she loved eating cereal for dinner, which we had in common. And none of those things could help me right now when she still couldn't understand why I'd want to be nice to her.

Like I could tell her the truth. That she was the only bright spot in my life after Ivy died. That she was the only woman with whom I'd shared anything real with.

Every other woman in my life had been there for a meaningless interaction, one they'd move on from just as quickly as I had. And in front of me was the one person who understood who I was underneath all of that.

And she had no fucking idea it was me.

The end of her hair snagged on her necklace as she pulled her hand away, and she winced.

I couldn't help myself as my fingers started tingling with the need to touch her. I stood and faced her. "I've got it," I said quietly. "You don't want to break the chain."

Faith stilled as my finger brushed the side of her neck. Carefully, I slid my finger underneath the dainty gold links, pulling gently until the charm was free from underneath her shirt.

My heart thrashed behind my ribs as my gaze caught on the delicate curl of the top of the snail's shell.

It was her. Unequivocally.

I'd found her without even trying. Without even really wanting to risk finding her, of ruining that one perfect friendship in my life.

And when her chest rose and fell on a shaky inhale, I realized that I wasn't the only one affected by this. Faith was staring at my throat, not even attempting eye contact. As I gently untangled her hair from the chain, I allowed myself one moment to enjoy the cool, slippery softness of it against my skin.

"There," I said quietly.

Faith stared up at me, her mouth slightly open, confusion stamped all over her pretty features. "Thank you."

I hummed, studying the charm again. If I risked anything else, it would be nothing as bold as what I'd just done.

Child's play, considering what I wanted to do to her.

It wouldn't take mere hours in a bed with her because it was so much bigger than sex. Days. I'd need days or weeks of undivided time with Faith. To see her wake up, know what she looked like when she got out of the shower, to feel the texture of her skin against my tongue and wind my fingers through hers as I held her down, to curl my body around hers to see how we fit together as sleep took us.

Maybe I should have been scared at how quickly my feelings toward her could shift from disdain to unfettered desire. But there we were. And even if Faith was confused by the shift in my actions, she felt it too.

Something palpable existed between us, something strong enough that I felt like I might be able to grab onto it with both hands. She opened her mouth to say something, and I found myself holding my breath to hear what it might be.

"You guys are still here?" Keisha's voice broke between us, and Faith blinked rapidly.

In my head, I cursed at the intrusion, but maybe it was for the better.

"My car won't start," Faith said. "Dominic was checking it for me, but I'm going to need to have a tow come get it later."

"I'm heading back toward Kirkland," Keisha said. "I've got a meeting in about an hour. Want me to drop you off somewhere?"

I held my breath as Faith gave me a quick glance under her lashes. "Yeah, thank you, Keisha. That would be great."

"I guess I'd want to ride with someone besides me too," I said dryly.

And I couldn't blame her. Not really.

Faith gave me a small smile. "I appreciate your help, though. Thank you for offering."

"Anytime," I told her. The way her cheeks flushed a sweet pink color, I knew she heard the double meaning.

The two women walked back to Keisha's car, and with my hands in my pockets, I watched them get in.

Something dark and powerful filled me, something that made the devil on my shoulder whisper into my ear. Could I win her like this? Could I win her over as me? With the bad attitude and awful start, with the tattoos and the way I'd stormed out of her mom's office.

Faith gave me one last curious look through the windshield, and when the sun glinted off the golden chain laying against her neck, I knew which voice I'd listen to.

Chapter ELEVEN

Faith

"**W**HAT DO YOU MEAN YOU DON'T WANT TO GO WATCH? We always watch the first few days of these mini camps together." My dad, standing across the kitchen island, crossed his arms and gave me that look that he was so good at, that I hated so much. "It's tradition."

I fidgeted with my necklace. "I just … can't I skip this year? I've got so much to do at the office today."

His eyes narrowed. Allie walked out of their bedroom, and he softened long enough for her to give him a soft kiss. She gave me a look of her own. "You're not coming to camp? It's tradition."

Oh, what could I tell them that wouldn't be a blatant, full of shit lie?

Any truthful answer would send my dad into orbit. *Well, Dad*, I imagined myself saying, *there's this asshole player who got in trouble on day one, and everyone hates him. He was a total jackass to me the moment we met, but something happened yesterday in that parking lot, and that something different was sexier than about eighty percent of the times I'd actually slept with someone. And now I don't* want to be faced with him again because I caught myself dreaming about him last night. It was definitely an NC-17 rated dream, involving a truck bed and jumper cables and a thin gold chain in his big, big hands.

So no, I didn't want to go watch the mini training camp.

I didn't want to stand on the sidelines while he did physically impressive things that made me want to break my rules about dating football players.

Which was why, for the first time in like, ever, I wanted nothing to do with the Washington Wolves.

When Allie cleared her throat, I had to blink my thoughts away from my face because my parents were staring at me expectantly.

"You know I love going to the first couple of mini camps," I told them, speaking slowly, so I didn't tell any bald-faced lies. And it was true—I'd been at every one since the age of like six. Maybe even younger. Back when I'd sit on the sides, watch my dad line up against the new players for some friendly scrimmages. It was Washington tradition, and I loved it.

The team had been in my blood even before Allie came into our lives.

But not once had a player wearing one of those red and black jerseys ever made me feel the way Dominic did in that parking lot. Guys in Camp One—who wanted in Lydia's and my pants simply because of who we were—were the easiest to overlook. They were the reason it was one of my family rules. I'd made the rule because of a guy like that. Players in Camp Two—the ones who saw us as asexual beings that they'd never touch in a million years—never even attempted to get a reaction out of us.

But I knew now, Dominic didn't fit into either of those.

Dominic Walker had not looked at me like I was asexual anything. No, he looked down at me like I was the juiciest, most delicious thing he'd ever seen, something sweet he wanted to devour.

If Keisha hadn't walked out, I would have taken him up on his offer. I would've broken my rule, and there was no way for me to lie about it, even to myself. It was the most un-Faith-like thing I could have done, and something was really freaking scary about that.

My dad spoke, and yet again, I had to yank myself from the horrible, horrible direction of my brain.

"We talked about this last week, and you said you cleared off your morning at work." The stubborn set of his jaw had Allie smiling slightly. We both recognized it.

"I did say that, didn't I?" I hedged. The hem of my T-shirt was wound tightly around my finger, another nervous gesture I hadn't even realized I was doing. I focused my energy on that one small spot of white cotton. We all wore our Wolves gear, my dad in a long-sleeve T-shirt with dark jeans, Allie in a tank and black blazer, skinny black pants and red shoes, and I was in my white fitted T-shirt and jeans with holes at the knees. Wardrobe alone, they should have called me on my bullshit when I'd shown up for our traditional pancake breakfast before heading over to the practice facility.

"At least come for an hour," Allie suggested. "If you've got responsibilities at the office, we understand." She gave my dad a pointed look as she said it.

He sighed, dropping a kiss on her forehead as he moved to refill his coffee. "You two always gang up on me."

I snorted. "Are you suggesting Lydia's always on your side?"

He tilted his head. "Fair point."

Allie glanced at her watch. "Speaking of your sister. Can you go down to her room and tell her we need to leave soon? She slept here last night."

"She's twenty. She can read a clock just fine."

My dad gave me a look.

"Fine." I sighed. As I left the kitchen and skipped down the stairs to find Lydia's room, I had the strangest feeling that my younger by six years sister would probably handle this dilemma better than I ever could. From the moment she was born, she seemed to have the male species wrapped around her finger.

No one looked at her like she was asexual, even the guys in Camp Two. They just didn't try to do anything about it. Maybe because the parent we didn't have in common genetically—Allie—had blessed my younger sister with the bombshell looks she'd been famous for in her early twenties.

Lydia's room was immaculate, which surprised me as much as anything else, because normally it looked like her closet had puked up all over. From her old bathroom, I heard the soft sound of her laughter. When I carefully pushed open the door, I shook my head at what I saw.

She was taking a video in front of the mirror, turning her body at various angles to show off her short denim shorts, her skintight Wolves tee that she'd cut off to show her stomach. On her legs were knee-high black boots.

Once she ended the video, her demeanor relaxed, and her blue eyes found mine in the mirror.

"Oh my gosh, you are alive," she said.

I smiled. "Been busy, sorry." Walking into the bathroom, I picked up a tube of bright red lip stain. "That's pretty."

Lydia studied me in the mirror, and when she sighed dramatically, I knew she found my attire lacking. "It would look killer on you, if you'd actually try."

I swept my hands down the front of my body. "This is me trying, little sister. I just don't need to show the world my efforts."

"This?" She held up her phone. "This is how I make my living, thank you. One post wearing these boots will probably pocket me about ten G."

"Good Lord," I muttered. "I'm in the wrong business."

"Or," she pointed out, "you're not leveraging your background in a way that could benefit all your charities." She kissed the air next to my cheek, exiting the bathroom in a cloud of beautifully curled blond hair and cleavage that would have Dad sighing heavily at the sight of her.

"My charities don't need me to post my outfits in order to earn money."

She stopped at her dresser, adding a stack of gold bracelets around her wrist. "How many followers does the Team Sutton account have?"

"I have no idea."

"You should." She leaned back, studying herself in the mirror. "How do I look?"

Unwittingly, I smiled. "Glorious. Dad's gonna have a coronary."

Lydia laughed. "Nah. I think he made peace with it when I crossed two million followers and had that guy show up outside the house waiting to propose."

My mouth fell open. "When was that?"

She shrugged, wiping the edge of her lips. "A couple of months ago."

I crossed my arms over my chest. "Lydia."

She matched my stance. "Faith."

"You need to be careful."

"I know, I know. I watch what I post now about locations, trust me." She gave me a wicked smile. "Not that I need to worry about today. Surrounded by big, strong, muscley men." She shivered. "I love this family tradition, even if your dating rule precludes you from having too much fun."

"Is that why you're so dressed up?"

"Yes."

With a smile, I shook my head again. "Why do you make it sound so simple?"

Lydia picked up her purse and shrugged again. "Because it is. I just like looking. Nothing wrong with that."

That was the difference between my sister and me. She loved looking. Loved flirting, even if she didn't really do anything about it. And I wanted to hide behind giant stacks of paper because one guy made me want to break my rule.

"What's that look?" she asked, studying my expression with a shrewdness I didn't expect. I must have hesitated just long enough because she gripped my arm and emitted a high-pitched squeal. "Oh holy shit, what happened? Who is it?"

I pulled my arm from her grip. "Who's what?"

"Spill. Now." Lydia's eyes were bright with excitement, and I couldn't help but smile. Even this, she made it look so easy. Honestly, if she took over Team Sutton, she'd probably triple our donations by sheer force of will.

"Girls," Dad yelled from upstairs. "We have to go."

She tugged my arm again. "Ignore him. We have plenty of time. Faith, you spill right now because you never have good stories."

"I have good stories," I protested.

Lydia's eyebrows lifted slowly. "Yes, I heard all about the baby kangaroo, which was super sexy and everything, but you are a boss-ass bitch with a master's degree and great legs and giant brain, and you get absolutely no action, which saddens me."

"Ugh," I groaned. "Okay. There's this new player who's kind of… a jerk, I guess. Or I thought he was. But he had to spend the day with me at the community center yesterday."

"Dominic Walker?" she asked.

"How do you know that?"

"I watch *SportsCenter* every morning. He's a total wild card, but damn, he's good. He's almost impossible to defend because of how tall and fast he is."

Somehow, her immediate knowledge of him made me … edgy. Jealous. Because I had one single sort of sexy interaction with him. But because it felt good to tell someone, I gave her a brief rundown of what happened in the parking lot.

"Oooooh, yes," she whispered, nodding slowly, "I see that spark in your eye. I am a fan of this for you. He's all hard and tatted, and he would totally push you out of all those comfort zones you like."

"Lydia," I moaned, "there's nothing to be a fan of. He was so rude when we first met. Like, he hated me just because of who our parents are."

She shrugged. Again. Everything made my sister shrug. "He was undrafted when he started in Vegas, and in college, I'm pretty sure he was a walk-on. He's the kind of guy who's had to work three times as hard to prove himself, so I get it."

"Do you?"

Lydia nodded. "Everyone underestimates players like that. Makes them even more impressive when they can dominate their position."

I gave her a long look. "You sound like Mom right now. It's freaky."

She gave me a sunny smile. "Thank you. Someone has to take over the team someday." Again, with the light, unconcerned shrug. Only the people who knew her best knew that those shrugs hid an incredibly intelligent brain and ruthlessly loyal heart. "Might as well be me, right?"

I slung an arm around her shoulder as we walked upstairs. "Sister, I would never doubt your ability to do it."

"So you're not going to be weird and ignore him or anything, right?"

"Ignore who?" Allie asked, meeting us at the top of the stairs with a smile. "You two look so pretty."

Dad came out of the kitchen and froze when he saw Lydia. "Lydia Alexandra," he started. Allie pinned him with a look, and he rolled his lips between his teeth and took a deep breath. "You look beautiful."

I choked on a laugh. Lydia walked over and patted him on the shoulders. "Thanks, Dad. I can see how much that cost you."

"I hate this tradition," he muttered, under the sound of Allie's laughter.

We piled in the car after Lydia snapped a couple of pics for her social media accounts, and as we neared the practice fields, I felt my stomach roll into writhing, nervous knots. The sounds of the players echoed in the practice fields, along with the happy chatter of families and office staff.

Before even the official start of training camp in mid-summer, these small mini camps signaled the real start of the season for those of us that were fully entrenched in the Wolves organization.

People milled around, all decked out in red, black, and white. Former players chatted with current, and Allie went over to speak to her best friend Paige, who was surrounded by a couple of Logan's younger sisters. Logan and Paige's son Emmett, now towering over them at the age of twenty-one, had grown into his broad-shouldered frame and looked more and more like his dad as he aged. I smiled in his direction and couldn't help but notice that his eyes flicked over to my sister and her glorious boots when he waved.

I should call that the Lydia Effect, because he wasn't the only one glancing longingly in her direction. More than one player gave her quick glances, hopeful that the owner they loved and respected so much didn't notice. Or my dad. But to Lydia's credit, she hadn't left my side yet, her arm wrapped through mine.

Veteran players tossed the ball back and forth, while rookies stretched on the turf. And unwittingly, I found my eyes searching among them for Dominic.

"There he is," Lydia said in a hushed tone, gripping my arm in a painful vise when I started to move my head. "Don't look. He's staring at you."

I laughed under my breath. "He's probably looking at your boots."

"Oh no, my darling, clueless big sister. He is looking at you like you are an entire meal, and he hasn't eaten in weeks." She bounced on her toes. "You leave this to me."

I gripped her arm. "Don't you dare go over to him."

"What do you take me for, an amateur?" she asked. Lydia carefully plucked my hand off her arm and patted it condescendingly. "Trust me."

And off she flounced, leaving me with my mouth hanging open. Carefully, I hitched a piece of hair behind my ear and risked a glance in the direction she'd been looking.

He was wearing dark shorts and a fitted white shirt, a black jersey slung over his muscular shoulder. And his eyes were right on me.

When he noticed my gaze, his lips curled into a crooked grin.

Slowly, I blew out a breath, because that was just about the most potent grin I'd ever seen in my entire life. He could weaponize it and take over the entire free world, if he wanted to. And something about being on the receiving end of it was wildly disconcerting.

Pretty soon, I'd need a new rule. No extended eye contact with Dominic Walker.

It wasn't good for my heart rate.

Coach called his name, and his attention was pulled away.

Once it was, I could do other things, like … breathe properly. Think rationally.

This was so, so bad.

I made my way to the sideline, where my dad chatted with Logan Ward.

He held his arm open, and I gave him a side-hug. He spoke quietly when he leaned down. "Aren't you glad you came?"

With a glance around—if I ignored the potent presence of Dominic—I could answer honestly. The energy was infectious, warm and happy. This was home, it was our life. "Yeah, Dad. I'm glad."

Logan watched us with a smile. "Someone thinking of skipping this year?"

My face felt warm. "Just have stuff waiting for me at the office."

Dad's hand tightened on my shoulder again. "Faith has more than doubled the reach of the Team Sutton grants since she took over. We're dispersing funds to schools and day programs in fifteen states now. She's the best thing to happen to that place."

Logan gave me a wry grin. "Don't you love when your board members are unbiased about your performance?"

A loud, hysterical-tinged laugh burst out of me, drawing the attention of some of the people gathering around us. He meant it as a joke, but unconsciously, my gaze flitted quickly to Dominic because it was exactly the kind of thing that made him dislike me in the first place. How many twenty-somethings could make statements like that and have it be true?

None that I was aware of.

I cleared my throat. "I meant to reach out to Paige and see if she'd reconsider taking a seat on the board," I told him.

Logan glanced over at his beautiful wife, who was telling a story to Allie and one of Logan's sisters—I couldn't tell who it was—and had them laughing loudly. "She should. Emmett's almost out of the house now, and I think she's going to lose her mind when we don't have any kids under the roof." His eyebrows rose in concession. "Though, the girls have more than enough kids to keep us busy."

"Emmett's almost done with college?" I asked, placing a hand on my chest. "Oh, that makes me feel old."

Logan laughed. "Makes *you* feel old?"

Dad lifted his chin in Emmett's direction, where he was tossing a ball with one of the rookies. "He's starting at Stanford again this year?"

Logan nodded. "Paige can't stop telling everyone she knows."

I watched him drop back and throw a perfect spiral to Mack, one of our rookie receivers. "I'm assuming he's going to enter the draft."

My dad whistled when Mack stretched out to catch it, the ball exactly where it needed to be.

"Oh yeah," Logan assured us.

"Maybe he'll end up at Washington someday," I teased. "We can really keep this place in the family."

My dad laughed.

From the corner of my eye, while the two men continued chatting, I caught a glimpse of Dominic. He'd finished talking to Coach, and was stretching his long arms over his head. The motion brought the hem of his white shirt up, and the glimpse of hard squares of muscle had my mouth going dry. Splitting down the middle of those muscles was a dark line of hair. That didn't make my mouth go dry. It had my entire body lit like the Fourth of July.

His gaze rose, connecting to mine with a forceful clash that did more than make my throat go dry. It had all my fight or flight systems ramping up into overdrive. That same desire to hide from whatever this was came back with a roar.

I was not the kind of person who wanted the attention of a man like Dominic.

Yet, as I refused to drop my gaze, and he seemed to do the same, I wasn't sure hiding was an option anymore.

Chapter TWELVE

Dominic

Everywhere, there were people laughing and talking and enjoying the atmosphere. An event like this never would've happened at my old team, a gathering of people who wanted nothing more than to celebrate an unofficial start to the season, months before training camp kicked off. It was a reunion of sorts, and not just current players.

All around the practice field were legends from past Washington Wolves teams, some that had won trophies, and some that hadn't. Hall of Fame players. Legendary quarterbacks and receivers and linemen, their families, all decked out in red and black.

The fact that I'd been off to the side by myself wasn't lost on me, another disparity between me and the rest of my teammates. There were other current players without families present, but I had to guess that their families didn't live within thirty minutes of the practice facility. Taking in the atmosphere, the buoyant energy that crackled through the air, it was like a blade through the ribs when I thought of how much Ivy would've loved this. A few younger kids ran around, playing tag, throwing a ball back and forth, on the shoulders of whichever player they came with, and if she'd been alive, my sister would've been almost sixteen. Too big to ride on my shoulders. But at the age where, knowing her, she would've been trying to out-throw every single boy there.

My jaw was tight as I watched two college-aged kids do exactly that. Someone passed in front of me, and I blinked at the confused look on his face.

"Fuck," I whispered under my breath. I probably looked like a raging jackass. In reality, I was trying to wrap my mind around the fact that I hadn't even thought to invite my parents to be a part of this. My dad probably wouldn't have taken the day off for it. My mom, either. But I hadn't even asked.

No wonder the other players didn't want me around. There I was, in the middle of a giant party, glaring at anyone who came too close without even realizing.

A fragile ceasefire existed in the locker room since my conversation with Coach Ward and James. Only a couple of guys gave me looks of outright disdain, but most of them left me alone while we were still in these early days of solidifying what this year's team looked like.

That was the kind of stuff I should have been thinking of and planning for. But instead, I thought of Faith. It was impossible not to.

In the middle of everything—the sun that held court while everything shifted around its orbit—was Faith and her family. They were royalty here, and it was obvious. Even some of the most recognizable names in football history hung back, waiting their turn to talk with her parents, and she and her sister knew every single one of them.

All night, I'd tossed and turned, unable to banish her from my thoughts.

Unable to sleep, I'd scrolled through my phone as I laid in my quiet, starkly decorated apartment, trying to separate what I'd known of her for the past few years from what I knew now.

Like me, Faith had never outright lied in our chats online, and I took a lot of comfort in that. Now that I knew who she was, one particular conversation stuck out to me, so I scrolled back to find it. It was just after I'd started playing in Vegas but hadn't ever actually told her that I'd moved away from Texas. From what I knew now, it was just after she'd taken over at Team Sutton and worried that maybe leadership wasn't for her. According to our history, Faith thought Nick was a college grad who'd worked construction to pay his way through to a business management degree, something that could've been used in a million different ways.

For all she knew, I still built houses.

As I read through a few things, it was easy to smile at the glimpses I saw of her as Faith in the messages sent back and forth. Splices of our interaction in the parking lot ran through my mind in the middle of all that. The silky feel of her hair. The skin on her neck. The way her pupils dilated at my nearness. I loved that she was the same girl who came to me with all the normal day-to-day bullshit that weighed on her.

> **TurboGirl:** Don't you ever worry about disappointing people, though? If you tell them you may not be good at this thing everyone expects you to be good at?
>
> **NicktheBrickLayer:** Hell no.
>
> **TurboGirl:** LOL. It's seriously that easy for you?
>
> **NicktheBrickLayer:** Yes and no. I'm a hard worker, so if I don't feel like I'm good enough at something, I'll be the first one to show up in the morning and the last one to leave at the end of the day if it means I get better.
>
> **NicktheBrickLayer:** But I don't do that because of what

people might think of me. It's a slippery slope if you do, Turbo. And if I'd let them tell me how to live my life, I wouldn't be where I am.

NicktheBrickLayer: If you don't think this job is a good fit for you, don't do it. But if it's just fear holding you back, then work your ass off to be better at it.

TurboGirl: Just like that, eh?

NicktheBrickLayer: You didn't tell me you were Canadian.

TurboGirl: I'm not, but that's beside the point. Eh has a LOT of wonderful uses in everyday vernacular.

NicktheBrickLayer: Turbo, we get one life. That's it.

TurboGirl: I knowwwww. I know. I think I'm so used to my life playing out in expected ways, that when something trips me up, I don't know how to get over it quickly. Come on, you remember how I was after I broke up with assface.

NicktheBrickLayer: Ahh, yes, the control freak tendencies.

TurboGirl: Hush. I'm not a control freak … I just, there's so much craziness in certain aspects of my life that I like knowing the OTHER parts will play out in ways I can… I don't know if I'm saying this right…

NicktheBrickLayer: Ways you can control?

TurboGirl: *middle finger emoji*

NicktheBrickLayer: I don't know you well enough yet, but thank you for the offer.

Having her in the same room, where I could watch the way she moved, talked, and laughed, was intoxicating enough, but adding in all the layers of her personality that I knew to be true … I could get drunk off it. Telling Faith that I was Nick would have to come eventually, that much was clear. But as I looked around us, that time wasn't now.

Dominic Walker was something she absolutely felt like she couldn't control, even if she did a damn good job of managing me when I was at my worst. And it was that, her ability to climb right under my skin as Faith, that had me wanting to see if she'd let go of some of that restraint.

To my right, I saw the rookie approach tentatively. This time, he came without a bottle of tequila in hand.

"Walker," he said in greeting.

I nodded. "How's it feel to be on the field when you're sober?"

He grimaced, scratching the side of his face. "Better. That was … stupid."

"Probably right." I tossed the football, and he caught it. "You get in a lot of trouble?"

"A bit." He tossed it back. "Just got into my head, you know? The whole picture of what we're doing here. This is the shit you dream of when you're a kid." With wide eyes, he glanced around the facility, at the people gathered around us, and shook his head. "Look at who's in here, man. These are legends. Their names will never be forgotten, even decades after they're done playing the game. And I don't think they were dumb enough to get trashed on the fifty-yard line."

"Probably right about that too," I said dryly.

The rookie went still as a statue.

"Oh shit," he whispered. "Lydia Pierson is walking over here." His eyes got big, his voice edged in panic. "What do I do?"

With a wry grin, I studied Faith's younger sister as she left a conversation with a couple of people near us and strolled purposely in our direction. Where Faith had dark hair and dark eyes, Lydia was all blond hair, blue eyes, and curves that would make a man weep. The only similarity I could see, as she came closer, was in the shape of their lips and the arch of their eyebrows over big eyes.

"Just ... talk to her," I told him quietly.

But unfortunately for the rookie, as she got closer, Lydia pinned those big blue eyes in my direction. I crossed my arms because something about the speculative look on her face had me feeling like I was a bug on display. Pinned in place so she could pick me apart.

The only reason I didn't hate it was that in my mind, it meant her big sister must've been talking about me.

"Gentlemen," she said, bright red lips curling in greeting. "I'm Lydia."

She held out her hand to the rookie, who took it so eagerly that it had me rolling my eyes. "J-John Cartwright," he said.

"John Cartwright," she repeated. "Rookie out of Florida, right? You're a receiver."

His face split into a massive smile. "Yeah, that's me."

She raised her eyebrows. "Impressive senior year you had. I was surprised you didn't go higher in the draft, but I guess that's for Washington's gain."

That rookie could hardly form words. It was pathetic.

I sighed. "I'll leave you two alone."

But before I could walk away, she held her hand out to me. "And you are?"

"Don't have my bio memorized?" I laid a hand on my chest. "I'm devastated."

"Are you?"

"No." I shook her hand. "Dominic Walker. My senior year wasn't as impressive as his, which is why no one drafted me."

Lydia hummed. "Well, that settles something I needed to know."

Something about the gleam in her eye had me on edge, but I couldn't pinpoint why.

"John," she said in a low voice, "can you do me a huge favor?" With a light touch to his arm, she leaned in and said something into his ear, too low for me to understand. But his eyes flipped to Faith's direction just as she found a seat on one of the sidelines. My brow furrowed, and I tried to hear what Lydia said to the rookie.

He grinned when she pulled away. "I'm on it," he said, all confidence now. The stammer was gone, and he gave her a quick nod before jogging away, right toward Faith.

I glanced at Lydia, feeling a touch of very masculine desperation at what had just unfolded. "What'd you ask him to do?"

Lydia didn't look in my direction, watching carefully as the rookie approached her sister. Faith looked up at Cartwright in surprise but gave him a sunny smile when he crouched in front of her. I didn't want her to give him a sunny smile.

"I told him to ask my sister out on a date."

"What?" I barked.

She gave me a droll look. "My, my, quite the overreaction, considering the story I heard about your first meeting."

I rubbed the back of my neck, watching helplessly as the rookie said something that made Faith laugh.

When did he become so fucking funny?

"Maybe I was a little…" I paused, considering my words carefully. "Quick to judge her."

"You think?"

Tearing my gaze away from the car wreck unfolding in front of me was hard, but I managed a quick glance at Lydia's tone. "Why'd you tell him to ask her out?"

"Faith needs to get laid."

It actually took a second for the statement to register because she answered so quickly, so evenly. I rubbed my chest. It felt tight and heavy. Was this how it felt to have a heart attack?

"And you just ... send some random asshole football player over to, what? Ask her for a quick screw in the bathroom?"

She rolled her eyes. "Obviously not. Faith is not the screw-in-the-bathroom type. She also doesn't date football players. But my sister is so focused on doing things for others that she completely ignores her own needs." She tilted her head, giving me some meaningful eye contact. "If you catch my drift."

"Yeah, I catch your drift," I snapped.

But my snapping did nothing except make Lydia grin widely. This was the kind of shit that had my temperature gauge skyrocketing. There was no slow shift in my mood, no gradual color change as I heated up inside. The idea that that stupid, tequila-toting rookie was making her laugh and asking her out and trying to get her to break some anti-football player rule had my skin on fire. And as I tried to decide how to maneuver the rookie as far away from Faith as fucking possible, she tucked her hair behind her ear and gave him a sweet smile that had me moving before I'd made a conscious decision to.

When I got closer, I heard the rookie say something stupid about his college stats in a stupid voice that made me want to punch him in the stupid face.

"Hey, rookie," I barked. "You're needed elsewhere."

He stood and held out a hand to help Faith out of the chair she'd been in. The grateful smile she gave him had my eye twitching.

I could count on one hand the times in my life I'd felt jealous of anyone. Actually, I could count on one *finger* the times in my life I'd felt jealousy.

Right now. Because of her and this idiot.

"Am I?" he asked.

Where'd *this* guy come from? He was giving me a slightly

challenging look that had me crossing my arms over my chest and facing him head-on.

"Yeah."

He gave me a considering glance and then winked—*winked!*—at Faith. It was like he wanted to get punched in the nuts. "I was just about to ask Faith if she wanted to join me for dinner tomorrow, so I think whatever it is can wait."

"She can't," I said.

Now it was Faith's turn to cross her arms over her chest and give a challenging look. "Can't she?" she asked.

I might've had a self-destructive streak a mile wide, but the caveman approach wasn't going to get me far. This was not a woman who wanted me to barrel through any of her reservations. So I took a deep breath and managed a softer tone.

"Did you forget, sunshine?"

At the nickname, her cheeks went a little pink, a lot attractive. "Forget what?"

"You promised to go out with me tomorrow night," I said gently. My tone might've been gentle, but I held her gaze steadily to let her see exactly how serious I was.

"Did I?" Her answer was quiet.

So often, I made decisions based on a churning in my gut and didn't stop to consider the ramifications. But this wasn't a churning or a slow build to a reaction. This was exactly where I was supposed to be, talking to the girl who did something to me even before I knew who she really was.

To her gently spoken question, I nodded, taking a step closer, until the rookie had no choice but to back away from her. I lifted my hand and went to tuck a piece of her dark hair behind her ear, but I stopped just before touching her.

Too many eyes.

Too many important eyes.

But by her shaky inhale, she knew what I was about to do. She knew, and she didn't back away.

The air between us trembled from that almost touch, and in an instant, I had the bone-deep certainty that when we kissed, she'd rock me to my core. Faith Pierson was a game changer, and nothing about it bothered me.

The rookie whistled under his breath. "Sorry, man, didn't realize."

My eyes never wavered from Faith's. "Now you do. Go away," I told him.

As he did, she exhaled a quiet laugh. "You are..." Her voice trailed off incredulously.

"Taking you out tomorrow night."

"Incredibly cocky," she replied. "And I don't date football players."

I tilted my head to the side. "Why not?"

That stopped her short. Faith's mouth popped open.

"Someone break your heart, sunshine?"

I knew who had. I'd heard all about him when we first started talking. And I wanted to see if she'd admit it to me.

She blinked rapidly a few times. "I just don't."

I licked my bottom lip, and her eyes locked onto that tiny spot. "Come on, there's got to be a better reason than that."

Faith inhaled, snapping her gaze away from my mouth. "I'm pretty sure I don't owe you any explanations, hotshot."

A part of me wanted to gently tease her about those control-freak tendencies again. Say something that Nick would've said to her.

"What if I promise not to talk about football?"

Her lips curled slightly, then she rolled them together to stop the smile from spreading.

Risking one step closer, I moved in so that her shoulder just barely brushed my bicep. "One chance. See if that rule needs to be broken."

Faith exhaled a shocked laugh, but again, she didn't pull away. "Why should I?"

With a quick glance to make sure no one was watching us, I ducked my head down so I could speak into her ear. "Because I think you're just as curious as I am about what this is between us." My voice, low and hushed, ruffled the hair on the side of her head. And when I finished speaking, I caught the way she shivered. "Come on, sunshine," I urged. "Won't you explore it with me?"

Faith pulled back, and her eyes studied my face. She gently licked her lips, and I fought the urge to do the same, to see how they tasted.

I'd never felt this sort of desperation with a woman before. It was reckless to spend too much time with her without telling her the truth. But I had to know if she'd take this step with me as Dominic, had to know if we could connect in more than one place, as different versions of the same people.

"One date," she said quietly. "And it better be good."

Because my body blocked us from view, I trailed a finger along the inside of her wrist, the curve of her palm, and her fingers curled helplessly.

"It will be," I promised.

Faith Pierson didn't know it, but I was exactly the right man for her, and I was about to prove it.

Chapter
THIRTEEN

Faith

Twenty-four hours later, my fingers curled up again when I dragged my own finger on the same spot that Dominic had so gently touched. Who knew that the wrist was a hidden erogenous zone? Not me.

When I looked down at my fingers, I couldn't help but replay the words he'd said, the way he'd looked at me, and most importantly, the reactions that both of those things had set off in my head.

Big firework-type reactions.

Like *only achieved through battery-operated assistance* reactions.

Reactions that I couldn't stop thinking about as I lay in my bed the night before. Alone. In the dark.

My attempt at sleep had been choppy at best, tossing and turning, kicking at the sheets when they were too hot for my body. More than once, I'd clutched my phone, trying to get the lady balls to text him and cancel the date.

The date. Honestly. Lydia had simply given me a smug-ass smile when we left the mini camp.

"Why are you pissed?" she'd asked. "He did exactly what I meant for him to do. That's why I sent the rookie over there first."

"I know, Lydia," I hissed when Dad gave us a strange look. "The rookie told me what you told him."

She grinned. "Why not be honest? All he needed to know was that I'd owe him *big* if he made Dominic jealous."

"Gawd, your forthright tendencies are going to get you into trouble someday, little sister."

Lydia booped the end of my nose. "I think the words you're looking for are *thank you*. Because now you have a date with a man who is just..." She shivered. "Exactly what you need. You never should've made that no dating the players rule anyway."

"Please, you know exactly the kinds of guys I was trying to avoid. We've known way too many of them."

She gave me a sisterly look. "You've known *one* too many. And we've known ten times more that are like Dad. You can't keep people labeled in neat little categories, Faith. It leaves no room for happy surprises."

At my desk, replaying her words, after replaying my reactions, from replaying his talent at throwing me off-balance, I knew there was nothing else to do except buckle up and be as ready as possible for this one single date I was allowing him.

I muttered a curse word and picked up my phone, hitting the button to call Tori. She picked up on the first ring.

"Well, look at who it is. It's a miracle. To what do I owe the pleasure, Miss Pierson?"

I rolled my eyes. "I saw you this morning at the apartment."

"That hardly counted. I was half asleep because your overthinking kept me up all night. I could hear it through the walls every time you tossed and turned."

Blinking, I sat back in my chair. "Really?"

"Those walls are thin, no matter how astronomical our rent is." She sighed. "What's up, buttercup?"

"Since you're off today, can you do me a huge, huge favor and bring me some clothes?"

"You looked cute when you left this morning," she protested. "What's wrong with wearing what you've got on?"

As I blew out a hard breath, I pushed back from my desk and stood to study myself in the mirror hanging on the wall next to the door of my office. The reflection that stared back at me looked … fine. If I was going grocery shopping.

"I look just like I do every other day of the week."

"You're wearing the pink shirt and the jeans that make your ass look incredible, right?"

Turning slightly, I looked at the aforementioned body part and shrugged. "I guess."

Tori laughed. "I swear, you are chronically incapable of recognizing your own hotness."

"Lydia got those genes in our family. Lucky for her that Allie is the most gorgeous woman in the entire world."

"Stop that now," she instructed. "I've seen pictures of your mother, and she was beautiful. You've got the best kind of beautiful, Faith, because it doesn't make you unapproachable. You're like … one of those flowers that's so sweet and pretty that people stop to smell it and take pictures, then *bam*, you realize too late that the flower is a dangerous man-eating plant because it lulled you into a false sense of security. And now it killed you, and it's too late."

Covering my face with my hand, I groaned. "Please stop talking. Can you just bring me a different shirt and some date shoes?"

"Sure." She let out a gleeful squeal that had me pulling the phone away from my ear. "Do I get to choose the shirt and the shoes?"

"As much as I may come to regret this, yes." Spinning lightly in my chair, I studied a picture of the Washington stadium. Specifically the logo at midfield. Without his little initiation exercise, I wasn't even sure I'd have ever met Dominic.

Without warning, a dull thud of disappointment hit me in the chest.

I was excited about this one single date that he'd probably screw up.

The only time I ever got excited to interact with any man was Nick, and I hadn't even thought to check my messages the night before when my brain was spinning with thoughts of my upcoming date.

Kim popped her head into my office. "Molly Griffin is here to finalize her auction items for the dinner. She wanted to know if you were available for a couple of minutes so she could say hi."

I gave her a thumbs-up. "Tor, I need to go. Just ... don't pick anything too fancy or skanky looking."

"Killjoy," she muttered. "He makes millions of dollars at his job, Faith. Don't you think he's going to go the *Bottle of Cristal-wow you with his connections at the fanciest club try to dry hump you in the corner with loud, dirty music playing while all the cool kids do drugs around you* route? You should dress appropriately if that's the plan."

"Blech. I hope not."

"Okay. I'll shoot for a happy middle. He'll want to rip your clothes off with his teeth, I promise."

"That's not—" But I was speaking to no one because Tori hung up. "Great," I muttered. The possibilities of what she could bring me, hidden in the dark corners of my closet, made me shudder.

"Now that's a happy face," a friendly voice called from my office door.

If anyone understood what it was like to be as enmeshed into this strange little Washington Wolves club as I was, it was Molly and her sisters. Raised by their brother, Coach Ward, and his wife, Paige, they'd grown up on that field just like I did. Molly took it a step further, marrying a former defensive player, Noah Griffin. He'd just retired a couple of years earlier.

With a smile, I stood to greet Molly with a warm hug. "Missed you at mini camp yesterday," I told her.

"Our six-year-old puked all over my shoes right before we walked out the door, so... kinda wrecked the idea of a family outing." Pulling back to study me, Molly shook her head. "First, it's amazing how you get older and more beautiful, and I somehow have not aged a day past twenty-five."

We laughed, and I gestured for her to take a seat across from my desk. "Kim said you're dropping off your auction item?"

She nodded. "Noah and I decided to join forces on this one. It's our take on a surf and turf, but we're calling it *log cabins and red carpets*. A weekend in our cabin in the Black Hills, and a red carpet experience for our next *All or Nothing* premiere," she said, referencing her job working with the Amazon production.

"Ooh, love it." Taking the envelope from her outstretched hand, I pulled out the single sheet of paper that held all the details and gave her a huge smile. "Thank you, Molly. This is perfect."

Leaning forward in the chair, she turned a picture of Lydia and me at a Wolves game, making silly faces at the camera. "I can't believe you're old enough to be running this place. I remember when Allie took over all those years ago. You were so little." Carefully, she returned the photo to its original place and took an approving look around my office. "This looks good on you, Faith."

"Thank you."

Her gaze softened. "So why'd you look so frustrated when I walked in?"

"Ahh." I cleared my throat. "My roommate is bringing clothes for a, a date I have later, and I don't know if I trust what she'll pick."

"Ooh, who's the guy?" When I hesitated, she clasped her hands over her heart. "Please, indulge someone who's been married for years and hardly remembers what the dating world was like."

I sank back in my chair and gave her a considering look. Because she was more than a decade older than me, it wasn't like

The LIE

Molly was someone I was close to. But with her upbringing and the man she married, she just might've been the perfect person to walk into my office.

"How did you…" I paused. "Did you ever worry about dating a player? Like it was too much."

"Too much in what way?"

I gestured to my office. "In every way, I guess. We were practically born with the Wolves logo tattooed on our foreheads, and I work for the foundation that's tied to them, and my parents are there every day, and"—I shrugged—"putting my love life in that same category feels like … it feels like it's too much. If I can even trust that all he wants out of it is … me."

I hated putting that fear into words, but I couldn't leave it out. It was always lingering just out of reach.

Molly took a deep breath. "Is it really in that same category, though?"

One of my eyebrows rose slowly, and she laughed.

"Okay," Molly said, "so he plays for Washington. I know that much."

My face was hot when I nodded.

"Have you ever dated someone on the team before?"

My nose scrunched. "Not for Washington, no."

She heard something in my careful answer. "On another team, though?"

"In college," I said. "Let's just say it wasn't a good experience. So it's never been hard to put everyone on the Washington roster out of my head."

"So … he's not like the guy from college, though, right?"

I breathed out a laugh. "Not at all."

"So what's the problem?"

"It's always seemed too complicated. Allie owns the team, and my dad is *my dad*, so he's crazy overprotective when he thinks about Lydia and me dating someone like my ex. But I've never found anyone the normal way, you know? In the grocery store buying the same ice cream or something."

"Listen, in every single facet of life, there are keepers, and there are guys who should come with warning labels. It doesn't matter if they play football for a living or if they're a doctor or a teacher, or you met them somewhere normal. You and I know better than most that there are solid, loyal, loving men who do this job. My husband is one of them, your dad and my brother are too. All three of my sisters married athletes. And the amazing thing is that they get it. Noah knew exactly what kind of crazy was involved in my family, in this life, because he comes from this world too." Molly smiled. "Can I get a hint of who it is?"

"Not yet," I hedged. "I don't even know if we'll go on more than one date. He's not exactly … I wouldn't have picked him for me, at first."

She hummed. "I know a few couples like that. Nothing wrong with someone unexpected. It kinda sounds like you're just over-thinking a rule that's been in place for a long time."

"It's possible."

"It only takes one person, Faith. Just one person who makes you want to risk something big, simply for a chance with them. I know that's how it was for Noah and me."

Her words held more than a ring of truth and were prophetic enough that I couldn't ignore them. Already, I'd felt that unnameable, overwhelming tug to Dominic, even before he asked me out.

Well, it did have a name.

Want.

There was no other way to say it, and it was absolutely pointless to hide it. I wasn't the type to throw caution to the wind, but he made me *want* to. If he'd touched me more than that one finger along my wrist, I might've kissed him right there in the middle of the field. But there was still so much about him that I didn't know and wasn't sure of.

Yet from what I'd seen, he was worth the risk.

"Judging by the look on your face, I think you may have the answer of whether he's that person or not."

I set my hands over my cheeks. "I can't know that before the first date, Molly."

"Can't you?" she asked lightly. "As far as I know, there's no timeline of what's right or wrong. It might come completely out of nowhere. But if you feel it, then go for it. You'll know soon enough if him being in this world with you is too much or not."

It was exactly what I needed to hear.

"Thank you," I told her. "Your timing today was ... impeccable."

She stood to give me a brief hug. "Good luck on your date tonight. Do you know where he's taking you?"

"No. Hence the clothing situation I find myself in."

Molly laughed. "I like that he wants to surprise you. You and I are planners, Faith. We need someone who's not afraid to knock us off-balance."

As I watched her go, I turned those words over and over in my head. In general, I was a pretty easygoing person ... except when I wasn't. I liked knowing what to expect. I liked feeling competent in what I was doing. And when those things were removed from the situation, off-balance was a great way to describe it.

I just had to know Dominic could help steady everything if I was.

My phone buzzed, and I picked it up off the desk, assuming it was Tori about my clothes.

But when I saw Dominic's name instead, it was like he clipped a jumper cable around my nervous system. A quick turn of the key, and I felt the effect everywhere. Again, Molly's words rang in my head. *It might come out of nowhere.*

"No shit," I whispered.

Dominic: I'll pick you up from your office at 5:30.

Me: I thought we were going to meet somewhere? For all I know, you could be a serial killer and your whole plan is to lure me into your truck so you can chop me into a hundred pieces out in the woods somewhere.

Dominic: First, that's incredibly morbid and terrifying. Second, I never said I wasn't going to pick you up. You assumed, and you know what they say about assuming, sunshine.

Me: Fair. I also assumed we're going somewhere public?

Dominic: Well … I could hardly dismember you if we did.

Me: …

Dominic: Yes. Sort of.

Me: Can I just get one tiny hint of what you've got planned?

Me: I'm not very good with surprises.

Dominic: As a wise man once said, surprise is the greatest gift life can grant us.

I sat back in my chair, jaw hanging open. The tattooed man who got drunk on the fifty-yard line just … yup, a quick Google search confirmed it.

Me: I'm sorry … did you just quote BORIS PASTERNAK to me?

Dominic: Even reprobates like me had to go to college, sunshine.

Me: So you won't give me a hint then?

Dominic: See you at 5:30.

There was no denying that he had me intrigued. And confused. His sudden change of heart toward me still caused some head scratching, but I'd give him an actual chance. Especially after my talk with Molly. If he could manage to, as he said, give me the gift of surprise, maybe I'd figure out why this man—with his hard shell, chip on his shoulder attitude and surprisingly gooey center—suddenly decided I wasn't the enemy. And why I wanted to jump his bones with a terrifying intensity. With a deep breath, I shot off a text to Tori.

Me: Tori?

Tori: OMG don't tell me to pick something boring, I'll scream.

Me: Nope. Pick something I'd never dare to pick for myself.

Tori: ON IT.

Chapter
FOURTEEN

Faith

"**W**ELL?"

Tori's expectant expression had me biting down on my bottom lip to stem my smile because torturing her was a genuinely enjoyable life experience.

But when I caught a glimpse of my reflection in the wall mirror of my office, the grin broke free. Tori raised her fists in the air, her face comically frozen in a scream of victory that had me laughing.

"I never would have picked it," I told her, adjusting the teeny tiny strap of the cheetah print bustier-style top that was slicked tight to my midriff, tucked inside the dark ripped jeans. My boobs—not normally the type to give second-glance-worthy cleavage—were pressed together and quite glorious, if you asked me. "But," I continued, "I still have no idea what we're doing, what if this is way too…" I gestured at the ladies, all propped up and pretty.

Tori laughed. Then she held up a finger and started rooting around in the bag of goodies she'd brought with her. When she straightened, she held out a small black ball of material that had me raising my eyebrows.

"This is the key," she said, with a serious voice and serious eyes.

I pointed at the wad in her hands. "That right there?"

"Yes." As she extended it toward me, she took a deep, dramatic breath. "You must wield it carefully."

It was light in my hands, but when I held the material from the top and let it unfold in front of me, I blinked a few times before meeting her eyes cautiously. "It's ... a cardigan."

Tori rolled her eyes, gripping me by the shoulders firmly so she could stand behind me. "Put it on."

"The basic black cardigan?" I shook it. "We're talking about the same thing, right?"

Her expression went grave. "Remember when I went on the date with that med student from UDub, and we barely made it out of his car because I drove him so crazy?"

"Yes."

"We almost did it in the car ten minutes after he picked me up, Faith."

My eyebrows popped up. "And why are we recapping this?"

"It was the cardigan."

Helpless laughter spilled from my mouth. "Oh my *gosh*, Tori."

"I'm serious! Try it on."

With a sigh, I slid my arms into the cardigan. When I had it over my shoulders, Tori shifted in front of me to button one of the large mother-of-pearl buttons. She stood back, and I gave my reflection a surprised once-over.

Okay, she wasn't wrong.

It hung down past my hips in a way that my waist was hidden, but my cleavage wasn't. The jeans and nude strappy heels made my legs look a mile long. Then she turned me to the side.

"Now, this is the magic," she said. "Drop your shoulder just an inch or so."

I did as she asked, even though it felt stupid, and the cardigan slid fetchingly down my shoulder, exposing the bustier top. Even half covered up, I looked sexy. But ... not in a way that made me uncomfortable. That whole *I will own and show my killer body* sexiness was Lydia's thing, not mine. I loved that for my little sister, but it had never been my thing.

This, however, *was* me. Tori nodded in satisfaction when she saw the expression on my face change. "See what I mean? This cardigan, Faith Pierson, you treat it with caution."

With a soft laugh, I pulled it back up onto my shoulder. "Noted."

"You ready?" she asked.

A nervous exhale slid through my pursed lips. "I guess. I'm not used to dates like this. As much as he pissed me off when he said it, Dominic was not wrong. I usually date nice guys."

"Yeah, I remember the guy who showed up in pressed khakis," Tori said, her face in a tight, disgusted grimace. "I think Mr. Tattoo is a wonderful choice for you to loosen up a bit."

And like her words had conjured him, my phone lit up on the corner of my desk, and his name appeared on the screen. Tori leaned over and smirked as she read the message.

"Oh yeah." She handed me the phone. "I like this."

"*If you're up for a challenge tonight, sunshine, I'm ready whenever you are,*" I read. "What a cocky shit."

Tori laughed. "He knows how to build a mood, that's for sure."

"Ahh, but I have the cardigan. Apparently, I'm bringing a mood of my own."

She set her hands on my shoulders. "May it treat you well tonight, my child." With a smile, she shooed me out of the office. "You go. I'll pack up my stuff and tell Kim to lock it up after me."

"I'll see you later," I told her.

"Wait, I need your car keys."

I paused. "Why?"

Her grin was pure evil. "I took an Uber so I could drive your car home and force a drop-off scenario with Mr. Tattoo."

The LIE

Fishing them out of my small purse, I glared mightily as I handed them off. "You owe me for this, Victoria."

She blew me a kiss.

No one was in the front of the office when I left, and I was glad of that. My parents might have some raised eyebrows if they knew I was going out with Dominic, and the last thing I needed was any well-intended Team Sutton employees to send Allie or my dad a text like, Saw Faith get picked up by that tall, muscular tattooed guy!

And they would've commented because when I pushed the front door open, he was like every teenage fantasy come to life, even if I'd never fantasized about something like this.

His truck, clean and gleaming in the sun, was parked in the closest spot to the building, and Dominic was leaning up against the passenger door. If it hadn't been for the slightly crooked smile on his face, he would've looked so incredibly dangerous. His arms were crossed over his chest, which was covered by a black button-down shirt. The sleeves were rolled up, so his inked forearms were exposed. The shirt was unbuttoned at the top, and another dark swirl of ink covered the tanned patch of his chest that was visible. Like me, he wore dark jeans, but on his feet were heavy black boots.

This man would cause every overprotective dad in America to lock their doors and double-check the windows in their daughter's rooms because he looked like sex. He looked like something sinful and decadent.

And when he pushed his sunglasses up onto the top of his head so he could cast a leisurely gaze from the top of my head to the bottom of my strappy-sandal-clad feet, I actually, physically felt like I'd burst into a puff of pheromones.

I hadn't even done the *casually expose my shoulder and all the good cleavage thing* yet, and when he straightened, smile spreading, I wanted to build a shrine to the cardigan.

"Sunshine," he said, setting a hand on his chest and giving me a slow shake of his head, "you look incredible."

I smiled. "Thank you."

After one last lingering glance, he made a quiet, appreciative humming sound, like he'd just eaten something delicious. The sound hit me square in the solar plexus—a veritable punch to the chest—because I couldn't help but imagine that same sound against my lips. Dominic popped open the passenger door and held out his hand to help boost me up into the tall truck. After a quick, nervous swallow, I slid my fingers against his rough palm.

Gaze steady, he helped me up, then he brought my hand to his lips, dropping a soft kiss onto my knuckles.

It was unaccountably charming and so sweetly unexpected that my face burned hot as he carefully closed the door.

Dominic climbed into the driver's seat with ease, his long legs and broad frame settling into the truck while I tried very, very hard not to look like I was ogling every friggin' inch of him.

"Do I get a hint now?" I asked.

He turned the key, the engine roaring to life as he flashed me a white-toothed smile, broader than I'd ever seen from him outside of when he played football with the kids at the center.

This version of him, even though I'd been in his presence for about two point two minutes, was so infectious, I could feel his energy soak into me like a sponge.

"Hmm." He pulled the truck out of the parking lot, heading away from the highway. So we weren't going downtown. "If you're even a little bit as competitive as I think you are, you'll like what I have planned."

"*That's* my hint?"

He laughed quietly. "No sports. But I still need to see your skills."

I found myself leaning forward in my seat, watching the scenery, waiting to see where he'd turn the truck next. The ride was quiet but not uncomfortable, and I found that I liked it.

"Dinner first?" I asked. "Or after I kick your butt in whatever this unnamed competition is?"

He took a left, slowing the car as we approached a parking lot with a few large warehouse-style buildings set back off the road. "One-stop shop tonight, Miss Pierson."

I squinted as we approached the building farthest back, giving him a surprised look. "An arcade?"

For the first time since I exited the building, Dominic looked nervous as he assessed my reaction. "An arcade."

The parking lot was empty. "There's no one here."

He shut off the truck and hopped out, jogging in front of the vehicle to grab my door before I could get out. Again, he held out his hand, and this time, I didn't hesitate to wrap my fingers around his. Stepping carefully out of the tall truck, I gave him a quick smile.

"Are you sure it's open?" I asked.

Without responding, Dominic set a big hand between my shoulder blades and guided me toward the entrance. His total refusal to tell me anything had me vibrating with anticipation, and I wondered if he could feel it seeping out of my body where he touched me.

He dropped his hand just long enough to pull open a door. "After you," he said.

It took a second for my eyes to adjust to the room because it was dark with bright flashing lights and loud dinging, random bells and whistles from the various games filling the massive space. In the center was a circular table, set with a clean white tablecloth, two place settings, and two empty wineglasses.

I gave him a shocked look. As I did, he produced a bucket from a small side table next to the door that I hadn't seen. When I took it from his hands, it was filled with tokens.

"Where shall we start?" he asked.

"You rented out the whole arcade?"

Carefully, Dominic lifted one of those big hands and tucked a piece of hair behind my ear. His eyes burned so bright with heat, but he did nothing except lightly drag the tip of his finger along the shell of my ear. "Can't have any witnesses if you annihilate me, now can I?"

My answering smile was huge and immediate. Because it was exactly, perfectly, precisely the kind of first date I would've planned.

It took every shred of self-control not to grip his face in my hands and stamp my mouth over his. Let him slide his tongue into my mouth to see what he tasted like.

The thought was so unexpected, so potent, that I had to wonder if I was losing my mind.

"Where shall we start?" I asked.

Dominic pursed his lips, glancing around the arcade. "I think I can take you in skeeball."

"Ha," I said. As I started in that direction, I let my shoulder move *just* so, and the cardigan slid down my arm. With a quick glance at him, there was no escaping the way his eyes were frozen on the tiny strap holding up my bustier. His tongue darted out to wet his bottom lip. And I curled my lips in a victorious smile. "You have no idea what you just started, hotshot."

Chapter FIFTEEN

Dominic

After the slaughtering that took place at the skeeball game, my only defense—as a professional athlete whose *job* it was to have good hand-eye coordination—was that she could have only beaten me because of how badly she had my head spinning.

More than once, when it was my turn to throw the small wooden ball up the ramp, she'd move or shift in a completely innocent way, or she'd laugh at something I said, and all over again, I was struck dumb.

Faith Pierson, much to my surprise, *showed up* for our date. There was no hint of reticence and no part of her held in reserve. And it wasn't like going on a date with a groupie because I'd done that too. In college, it was stupidly easy to find someone to spend an evening with if you were a football player. It got even worse in the pros.

They draped themselves over you, whispering more and more outrageous things in your ear, in the hopes that you'd give them an hour of your time, a release, and a good story to tell their friends. All of it—while not without some flickering moments of pleasure—was so fucking empty.

In this big building, filled with games and lights and noises, was the least empty I'd felt in years, and it was because of her. Her smiles, so broad and happy, her laughter, which was unrestrained when she found something really, really funny, and her energy, which crackled around us like a force field.

"You're not even trying," she said around helpless laughter.

I blinked because with the useless bright blue plastic gun in my hand, she'd just kicked my ass in a military video game. "Yeah, well, I had no idea how violent you were when I asked you out."

Faith slid me a look, dark eyebrow raised, and it had my own smile spreading. In fact, I'd smiled a lot since we arrived. And in general, there wasn't a single person in my life who'd describe me as an overly happy person. But being around her like this was as intoxicating as anything I'd ever experienced.

It was hard to remind myself that she didn't *know* she knew me as well as she did. But I could glance over at her—holding out that plastic gun attached to the machine with a big black cord, standing like she was Lara Croft—and know that this was the same woman who told me she cried every time she watched Animal Planet. That she never mastered a round-off back handspring even though she desperately fantasized about being a gymnast when she was little. That her favorite book is *Little Women*, but she hasn't read it in years because it always made her so sad.

That was Turbo. And Faith had no idea that I knew those things.

But the sight of her smiling at me, laughing freely at this perfect evening we'd experienced, was a high I didn't anticipate.

Her game finished, and she blew across the top of the gun like it was emitting a curling tendril of smoke.

I held my hands up. "I can't compete," I told her.

Faith slid the plastic gun back into the holder, turning slowly to rest against the game as she faced me. That sweater of hers was driving me insane. Every time she moved, it would shift off her shoulders, the sexiest fucking game of peek-a-boo I'd ever seen.

"So why the arcade?" she asked.

I tucked my hands into my pockets to keep from sliding them around her hips. "When I was a kid, it was my favorite place to spend a Saturday. My parents didn't have much," I admitted, "but if I pulled my fair share around the house all week, my dad would give me a buck or two, and I'd save every single one to go to the arcade around the block from where I grew up."

She gave me a sweet smile. "I bet young Dominic was a troublemaker at a place like this."

"I was a troublemaker in all ways," I told her. "The owner used to kick me out on a regular basis, actually."

"What was your favorite game?" She mimicked my posture, tucking her hands into her own pockets. Briefly, I saw her gaze linger on my mouth.

For the first time all night, I hesitated before answering. Because of our conversations as Nick and Turbo, she knew the answer to that question. About taking Ivy to the arcade and teaching her how to play pinball. She was terrible at it, unable to connect the lever to the small silver ball at the right time, but she loved to watch me play.

That building closed years ago, but the shell of it still remained with dingy, faded letters on the marquis. Turbo knew that too, because before it closed, I told her how I'd bought the pinball machine and had it sitting in my parents' basement. Someday, I'd have a home for it, but my sleek Seattle apartment with floor-to-ceiling windows and ugly black furniture with no personality wasn't it.

"My favorite game is whatever one I can win," I said, the easiest answer I could think of without blatantly lying. I didn't want to lie to Faith.

But I couldn't help the tremendously sweet feeling of victory that she was like this with Dominic, not Nick.

"Typical athlete," she answered with a slight roll of her eyes.

"You'd know."

Faith sighed. "My dad is as competitive as they come. Most people who play the game are. Otherwise, they wouldn't be very good." She looked around the building. "But it seems like a hard way to live life if you ask me. It's probably why I never wanted to follow in his footsteps. Aren't we so much more than our wins and losses?"

"Sure," I answered. "But we all seek out the wins and losses, just in different ways. Look at your job. You have definable things that tell you whether you're doing what you should be, or what needs adjusting. It may not have a scoreboard like mine, but we all compete, day in and day out."

She studied me carefully as I spoke, but it was hard to judge the look in her eye as we stood in a shadowed corner of the arcade. "That's true. Maybe that's why I…" She paused.

"What?"

Faith tucked a curled piece of hair behind her ear, a habit I understood because I wanted to do it constantly too. Maybe just because it allowed me a small piece of her until I knew she was ready for more.

It took her a moment to answer, but when she did, she tilted her head into the light, and I saw decision in those dark eyes. "I can't believe I'm telling you this, but I think that's why I struggled at first when I was promoted. I didn't understand that competitive piece of it after being in the trenches of the day-to-day work for so long." Her shoulders lifted in a dainty shrug. "Then I took over, and I had to figure out how to do things my way. It was hard at first, but I think I'm settled now. And I love it."

There was caution in her big brown eyes, and I knew what a risk it was for her to admit it to me. The guy I'd been in Allie's office, the worst of all my worst impulses and insecurities, would've held that admission over her head like a weapon. Admitting to feeling unsure in a job that had been handed to her because of who she was.

"You don't like uncertainty, do you?" I asked.

The LIE

Her mouth curled into an amused smile. "Who does?"

"Lots of people thrive in situations even when they have no fucking clue how it'll play out. They're the people who jump out of planes and off bridges and climb mountains without a rope."

"Yeah, and they have some screws loose, if you ask me." She made a self-deprecating noise. "But I guess that's why I've never been the exciting Pierson sister. I love Lydia, and I love that she goes after what she wants like she does, but it'll never be me. I think maybe I used to be that way," she said quietly. "But even if I'm not, even if my life is less exciting than people assume it is, I'm okay with that."

Carefully, I reached out and used the edge of my thumb to tilt her face back in my direction so I knew she couldn't look away. Her chest rose on a sharp inhale, another reaction she couldn't hide.

"I don't think that makes you less, in any way," I told her. "I think you're pretty fucking incredible, actually."

Instead of smiling or thanking me for saying it, the graceful arches of her brows bent in a confused V over those expressive eyes.

"What?" I asked. My thumb still touched the soft skin of her chin, and I let it fall at the look on her face.

"Why did you ask me out?" she whispered. "You hated me when we met that first day. And no matter how I turn it over in my head, I'm trying to figure out what changed your mind."

The absolute forthright honesty made me grin because it would've been so easy for her to keep that thought to herself. How many people would've laid out such a vulnerable question on a first date? No one I knew. And in the back of my mind, I knew it was the perfect time to tell her who I was. To be just as vulnerable with her while we had this private arcade and no one to interrupt us. The angel on my shoulder was practically jamming his wings into my brain, trying to unscramble that impulse to follow this date through without being honest.

But I swatted it away because of exactly how she was looking up at me.

Faith Pierson wanted me to kiss her.

And I very much wanted, as Dominic Walker, to be the one who gave her whatever she desired. So I answered as honestly as possible, appeasing both impulses as best as I could.

"I misjudged you," I told her. "And it would've been unfair to hold your background against you because I sure as hell hate when people do that to me."

Again, it was written all over her face that she believed me, in the softening of her posture and the light in her eyes. Practically melting in my direction, Faith stood from where she was still leaning against the game, but instead of walking away, she took a step closer.

"And in the vein of honesty," I told her quietly, "you should probably know that I want you, Faith Pierson."

Faith sucked in a quick breath, eyes huge in her face.

Lifting my hand, I slid my fingers down a soft curl against her cheek and pushed it back. Her eyes fluttered shut, and just as I tilted my head down, anticipating that moment of first contact, imagining how sweet and soft her lips would be when they opened under mine…

But that was the exact moment the machine behind us went rogue, and a blaring whistle signaling the start of a new game had her eyes flying open.

Her smile spread widely, and I blew out a hard breath. Faith sank her forehead against my chest with a soft laugh, and I laid a hand along her back when the warm press of her body touched mine.

A throat clearing behind us interrupted the moment further. A deferential employee stood by the table.

"Is there anything else I can get you two?" she asked.

I shook my head. Instead of sitting at the table to enjoy the dinner, we'd carried pieces of pizza around the arcade while we played.

"Thank you," I told her. "Is our time up?"

She gave me a polite smile. "Yeah, we have to start closing."

With a glance outside, it was the first time I noticed the skies were dark. Faith had stepped back, tugging the sweater up over her shoulder, I noted with a small smile. The moment was officially broken.

Faith picked up her purse from the table and gave me a wry smile when she must've read the frustration on my face. "She has great timing, huh?"

"Yeah." But I held out my hand, and Faith took it without hesitation, sliding her fingers between mine as we left the arcade. The air had cooled, and with her free hand, she pulled her cardigan around her slim frame.

So easily, I'd be able to warm her, surround her with my entire body and let the heat from what was inside me keep her comfortable. But I also knew I couldn't take this night like I normally might have. She was different. So very, very different, and so much more important than any previous interaction I'd had with a woman.

She climbed into the passenger seat, and as I shut the door, I saw her let out a slow breath. The tension wasn't one-sided, and the mood hadn't been completely dispelled by our interruption. She gave me the address to the apartment she shared with her friend, and in the quiet of the cab while I drove, the anticipation seemed to climb with each mile, each excruciating minute.

It was thick, laden with what had happened at the arcade, how close we'd come. There was no shortage of images playing through my head as I brought us closer, each fantasy building on what came before it. By the time I neared the address, I'd imagined pressing her against the stupid arcade game and sliding my hands underneath those impossibly tiny straps, hiking her thigh up against my side so I could press myself between her hips.

I'd imagined her crawling over my lap when I got into the driver's side of my truck, her clothes somehow not a part of the equation anymore. I'd imagined her letting me lay her down in the back seat of my truck where we'd struggle to fit properly. But with her legs tight up against my waist and my hands braced on the door behind her, we'd be able to move.

Faith wanted me just as much as I wanted her, and that was a powerful thing rolling around in my head. Maybe she was imagining the same types of things, maybe not.

If she looked at my lap right now, she'd know exactly what I was thinking.

I was in pain—acute and skin-tingling—but because I saw how tightly she was gripping her fingers together, I could bear it, simply because I wasn't alone.

"This is it," she said, breaking the throbbing silence between us. The building was tall and stately with ivy crawling up the brick exterior. It looked warm and welcoming, expensive as hell, but not unapproachable, unlike my own place just ten minutes closer to downtown.

I pulled into a spot and got out to open her door. There was a locked entrance, and as I cleared the hood of the truck, I saw a uniformed doorman standing behind a large desk, watching me openly. He'd know Faith, of course, but from where she exited my vehicle, he couldn't see us.

When her feet were on solid ground, Faith slid to the side so I could close the door, but she made no move to walk away.

Her sweater had fallen off that shoulder again, and with my pointer finger and thumb, I plucked gently at the collar. "This is … evil."

Faith burst out laughing, her eyes shining. "Is it?"

I lifted an eyebrow. "You know it is."

Instead of answering, she licked her lips. "I had a really great time, Dominic."

"So did I." Carefully, I slid the offending sweater so that her shoulder was covered, allowing my thumb to graze the line of her thin strap and the soft, soft skin just next to it. And for a moment, the edge of my finger touched the gold chain of her necklace, which made my heart thud erratically in my chest.

Faith's hand landed gently on my chest. "I'm glad I broke my rule."

I grinned. "I'm really good at being a bad influence that way."

"I'd invite you up," she said, "but my roommate is home."

She knew I wanted her. I'd told her. But still, this was the closest she'd come to verbalizing that she felt the same. And it triggered a devilish impulse to tease it out of her just a bit. I might not be the asshole she'd originally thought, but she was fucking right when she said I was a troublemaker.

I eased closer, sliding my fingers down the palms of her hands until her fingers curled around mine. Her breathing picked up speed, her chest rising and falling rapidly. Jaw clenched, I pulled those hands up toward my face and pressed a soft kiss to the inside of her wrist. Just for a moment, I let my nose drag against that same spot, letting out a quiet hum of appreciation at the scent I found there.

Against my truck, she looked ready to combust, pupils dilated and cheeks fetchingly pink.

That was when I stepped back. "I hope you'll let me take you out again," I said as her hands fell limply back to her side.

Her mouth fell open, and she blinked a few times. "What?"

Adopting an innocent expression, I gestured to her apartment.

Faith's eyes took on a determined gleam, her hand shooting out to fist into the material of my shirt so she could tug me closer. With a husky laugh, I stepped against her, sliding my hands up the line of her neck into the soft fall of her hair.

She went up on tiptoe as I descended to take her mouth with mine.

Absolute perfection, I thought as I sucked on her bottom lip and let the heat of the kiss roll in waves over us.

It was no tentative first kiss, nothing like I'd planned to do or imagined on the ride over. Immediately, I tilted my head so I could take it deeper, taste her lips and tongue with a bold sweep of mine.

She moaned, pulling my shirt in an even firmer tug, tongue twirling around mine.

This was a wild current of lips and teeth, of moans pulled from the gentle line of her throat. I could kiss her forever.

Faith was an equal participant in this most delicious exploration, and as my hands tightened into her hair, her fingers spread open on my chest. We pressed against each other, the cab of my truck a solid wall for me to feel and feel and feel.

The sweet smell of her filled my nostrils, the soft push and pull of her lips on mine filling my veins with a roaring sense of power, of want. This was unfettered attraction, the likes of which I'd never experienced before her.

And what made it so much better was her reaction. The edge of her nails as she curled her hands up around the back of my neck, the way she tilted her chin up when I slid hot, open-mouthed kisses down the line of her throat. The shoulder of her sweater got shoved the hell to the side again, so I could bend at the knees and suck at the skin where that damned strap had taunted me all night. I wanted to leave a mark there, where it was smooth and flawless. And the way she arched closer, rolling her hips against mine, I thought she wanted me to do the same.

"Holy shit," she breathed, practically climbing me as she tried to slide higher against my truck.

I could do everything, anything to her, fighting the clawing desire against the confines of my skin. But I wanted more from her than a quick, bright flare of relief. Finding her mouth again, I gentled the kiss, moving it into something different. This felt more luxurious, like I wouldn't have to worry that I'd have another chance, another taste. A soft pull at her bottom lip had her sighing. Curling my hands around her back so I could feel all of her in my arms, I was able to pull away after a few sweet, close-mouthed kisses.

Faith smiled against the last kiss. "Yes, you can take me out again," she murmured, hands gripping my shirt at my waist.

I pulled back, blowing out a breath at the sight of her all rumpled against my vehicle.

"Tomorrow?" I asked. It sounded eager, but I didn't give a flying fuck.

Her eyes were bright and happy as she breathed out a shaky laugh, and the power of the satisfaction it gave me was almost unholy.

"I have dinner with my family tomorrow night," she replied, smoothing her hands up my chest like she couldn't pull her hands away. It was a feeling I recognized because my palms were curled around her hips, my thumbs pressing into the curve of her waist.

The shirt under the sweater, which I'd only gotten teasing glimpses of, was silky and wrapped tight around her body. I'd crawl in bed later, imagine peeling it off her. She'd taste sweet and soft and warm with it off her body. "What about the night after that?" she asked.

"Yes." I kissed her again, sinking against those sweet, soft lips with a groan. She sighed happily, smoothing her hands around my back while I teased the seam of her lips with my tongue. She chased it, and my entire body lit like a firecracker when she sucked my tongue into her mouth. My hands tightened on her ass, goose bumps lifting the hair on my arms from what that brazen show of her own want did to me.

She wanted me. Dominic.

Faith pulled back with a happy smile. "I expected you to play hard to get and make me wait by my phone for a week."

I kissed the tip of her nose, which made her laugh. "Life's too damn short to play hard to get, sunshine."

Her fingers curled briefly into the material of my shirt again, but she smoothed them out, flattening her palms over my sides. "Most guys don't feel that way."

"News flash," I whispered against the curve of her neck. "I'm not most guys."

Tell her. I heard that voice in my head, hardly above a whisper, but I shoved it down like it had been a scream. When I kissed a line back up to the corner of her delicious mouth, Faith turned into another kiss with a helpless moan. Her hands swept over my shoulders so that she could wrap her arms around the back of my neck, pressing her breasts into my chest. A car passed the building, honking loudly, and neither one of us so much as flinched.

My tongue licked into her mouth as we chased the kiss further, both seemingly unable to end this moment.

I didn't want to end *anything* when it came to Faith.

This was even more than I expected from my night with her. Something bigger, more intense. If Faith had approached our date with polite reservation or even a hint of holding back, it might have been easier to convince myself that I was imagining how fucking incredible things could be between us.

But I wasn't imagining it. And I definitely wasn't alone in it.

When her teeth nipped at my bottom lip, my arms shook from the force of my own restraint crumbling.

It took every shred of discipline I possessed to pull back. But I did.

For a moment, all we could do was breathe heavily, bodies still intertwined against the side of my truck.

"Shall I plan another surprise for the day after tomorrow?" I asked.

She considered that with pursed lips. "I think the better question is can my heart handle you planning another surprise?"

A low chuckle escaped because I knew she'd say something like that. But this girl, she needed someone who'd help her see that it was okay to let go sometimes.

"A good surprise," I promised. My eyes stayed locked on hers, and damn, it would've been so easy to lose myself in her again.

Whatever this was, it was one of the most powerful things I'd ever felt, and based on the expression on her face, she was feeling the exact same thing.

"Well," Faith murmured, her hands sliding down my arms until our fingers linked, "you certainly held up your promise tonight, Dominic Walker."

"Did I?"

Faith smacked my chest. "Don't fish for compliments. You know you did."

With a laugh, I kissed her softly.

There was something intoxicating about kissing Faith when she could hardly stop smiling, like I'd be able to absorb some of that happiness. She was such a high into my bloodstream, it would be easy to end up addicted.

"Talk to you tomorrow, okay?"

She nodded. "Okay."

I kissed her once more, rolling my forehead against hers when we broke apart. As she walked away, I felt my first true pang of remorse that I hadn't told her who I was the moment I realized it. But now that the choice was made, I couldn't ignore that nagging question of whether it would've played out this way, with this intensity, if I had. I couldn't ignore that dark whisper that promised I'd do it soon.

"Soon," I said out loud.

When she opened the door to her building, Faith turned, aiming a small smile at me over her shoulder. I smiled back, recalling what she'd said to me at the arcade.

Faith told me I had no idea what I'd just started. And it was the truth. Faith just didn't realize how little she knew too.

Chapter SIXTEEN

Faith

Dominic: And you have dinner with your family tonight, right?

Me: Didn't we talk about this last night?

Dominic: Did we? Too many blows to the head, I guess. Now that I have you, what are you doing, what are you wearing, and don't spare any details.

As I was just about to enter my parents' front door for dinner, I paused to reply with a happy smile on my face. Before I could even log into my laptop at work that morning, he'd sent me a sweet good morning text, explaining in great detail that he'd thought of our kiss all night and couldn't wait to see me again.

Dominic Walker, unrepentant bad boy and closet romantic. Who'd have thunk it?

Me: Jean shorts, flip-flops and a plain old black T-shirt. Nothing that would cause much excitement.

Dominic: Speak for yourself, sunshine.

Dominic: Is this enough stuff for Keisha's center? I went shopping after I was done in the weight room.

When I clicked on the picture he'd attached, I burst out laughing. Half his face appeared in the shot, and behind him was a pile of bags from a local sporting goods store that could've stocked three community centers.

Me: More than enough. We've got an event scheduled there next week, we could bring it then.

Me: If you're open.

Dominic: If I get more time with you, I'm always open.

Me: Careful, hotshot ... a girl could get used to this kind of availability from a guy who kisses like you.

I hit send, nose scrunched, uncertainty making my belly flip. My flirting skills were about as rusty as an old junkyard car, but whatever I was doing seemed to be ringing all the bells that Dominic Walker possessed. And when I clicked open his response, my cheeks heated instantly. Speaking of ringing bells ... mine were going crazy. And not in a five-alarm fire-warning danger ahead kind of way.

He was setting off every single skin-tingling reaction that I wasn't even sure existed anymore. They existed, all right. All were in working order because I kept having to remind myself that I was feeling all the big, hormonal, physical, heart-fluttering feelings after one date.

Dominic: Sunshine, you have no idea the things I'd like to get you used to. Give me ten minutes and a flat surface and I'll show you.

Me: Only ten minutes? I'm so disappointed.

Dominic: Can you hear my male pride crying out in pain? It's on now.

Me: *devil emoji* Gotta go in for dinner.

Tucking my phone into my back pocket, I'd barely made it inside my parents' front door when Lydia's hand darted out of the half bath and tugged me inside.

"What are you doing?" I hissed as she closed us in the tiny room.

She gripped my upper arms and shook me lightly. "Well?" Her eyes were all big and shiny and excited.

"Well, what?"

Lydia stomped her foot. "How was the date with the bad boy? You didn't call me last night."

"Why do we have to be in the bathroom for this?"

"Because Mom is down in my room looking for some jewelry that I swore I didn't borrow."

I raised an eyebrow. "Did you?"

"Like she would let me wear the Chopard if I'd asked," she said. "Don't change the subject. How was it?"

How was it?

Such innocuous words, such a simple question. Unwittingly, my lips curled into a dreamy smile, and Lydia squealed.

"It was…" I paused, letting out a ridiculous sigh. "Really good."

"How was *he*?" Her eyebrows waggled.

"I wouldn't know, thank you very much. He dropped me off at the door like a gentleman."

"Shut up. *Him*?"

"I mean, we had the most epic makeout session by his truck before I went in," I amended. So, so epic.

Lydia swiped a hand over her forehead. "Whew. Good."

"Can I leave the bathroom now?"

"How epic, on a scale of one to ten?"

My grin had her squealing again. I flashed ten fingers.

"Oh, this is why I need to live vicariously through you, big sister." She sighed.

I opened the bathroom door and walked out with her right on my heels. It reminded me of when she was little, just learning how to walk, and she followed me everywhere before she realized she could get most places faster on her own. "Why would you need to live vicariously through me? I know what kind of guys want a piece of this," I said, gesturing at all her general flawlessness.

"Please. Like I have to explain to you why it's so hard. Either they're fanboys or frat boys, or they want some sort of leg up in this world." She shook her head. "That's why Walker is perfect for you. He doesn't give a shit what people think, he doesn't need a leg up anywhere, and your money doesn't impress him."

I laughed.

Dad walked into the kitchen. "Who doesn't give a shit about your money?"

He dropped a kiss on the top of my head, and I gave Lydia a warning look.

"No one," we said in unison.

He froze where he was looking into the fridge. "Now why does that make me nervous?"

My recovery came quickly. "I was telling Lydia about the last event we have at the community center before the Black and White dinner. O-one of the players is helping me."

Lydia took the baton when I sent her a helpless look. She slid past Dad in the kitchen and wrapped an arm around his broad shoulders. "I was just telling Faith that I think he's a good…" She paused, eyes wide. "Fit for her. I think he likes her," Lydia finished on a rushed exhale.

Okay. So we were doing this now.

Because yes, based on the window of time last night when I considered risking public indecency with Dominic Walker, I thought he liked me too.

In the Pierson family rule book, I'd been the one to add No Dating the Players. Because of He Who Shall Not Be Named. It was such an easy rule to follow. And the first guy to make me want to go there had the rockiest start of any Wolves' player in probably the last decade. Give or take.

An excellent start, all around. I'm sure my parents would be *thrilled*.

Dad turned slowly. "Who's a good fit for you?"

Silence descended like a bomb in the kitchen.

Lydia's eyes widened when I didn't answer. Dad's narrowed.

I sucked in a breath. "Dominic Walker," I said on the exhale.

He didn't look mad, just shocked. And boy, I couldn't blame him. It wasn't like he kept Lydia and me surrounded by a moat, far, far away from the evil clutches of the team. Just the opposite. He trusted us around them because every member of our family remembered what I was like after that relationship ended. My dad had been the one to hold me through my tears the night I showed up at their house.

And he also trusted that most guys on the team knew we weren't dateable material.

Dominic thought I was. Dominic thought I was a lot of things, apparently, based on what I felt pressed hot and hard against my stomach last night. Either he had a metal pipe hidden in his pants for the whole date, or he thought I was very, very … dateable.

Allie walked into the kitchen with a wide smile. She was

removing her earrings when she caught the father-daughter stare off happening across the expanse of the island.

"What did I miss?" She glanced at Lydia. "What's happening? I always miss the good stuff."

Lydia said nothing, simply pulling a bottle of wine out of the fridge and handing it to her. "Just ... pour a glass of that. You'll get caught up."

"A big glass?" she asked under her breath.

Lydia nodded slowly.

My dad sighed, wiping a hand over his mouth. He dropped my gaze long enough to give Allie a kiss. His eyes softened when he did. It was always like that with them and had been from the beginning. Even though I was six when Allie moved in next door to our house, I was old enough at the time to remember the change in him when they got together.

Before her, I was the only one who my dad melted for, the only one who saw behind the armor he erected in order to do the job he did and maintain his sanity. Until Allie.

If my dad couldn't shelve the hypocrisy of the gruff, tattooed football player softening for the right woman, then we might have an issue.

Dad came around the island and took a seat next to mine. The shortening of the distance between us helped ease a little of the coiled tension in my stomach.

He drummed his fingers on the island. "Talk to me, Turbo."

At my childhood nickname, I nudged him with my shoulder. "Not much to talk about," I said, like the *liar, liar, pants on fire* I was. "He asked me out on a date, and I said I'd give him one shot. That's not a crime."

There was also the minor incident of I almost let him screw me against the side of his truck in the parking lot of my apartment but whatever.

Allie's mouth dropped open, a perfect circle of gorgeous red lipstick. "Who asked you out?"

Silence descended, eerily and immediately.

Lydia glanced between our parents. "How about them Wolves, huh? They're looking good this year."

We all ignored her.

My dad and Allie exchanged a wordless glance, some silent conversation happening between them. They'd been able to do that forever and it was *so* inconvenient. Allie's eyebrows lowered in confusion.

Ahh, so their loaded silent marriage language looks couldn't convey names. Very good to know.

Dad motioned for her wine, and she slid it across the expanse of the island. With his arm outstretched, I could study the faded lines of his own extensive tattoos. If I looked hard enough, I could still see the curl of the F where my name was inked onto his body. Lydia's was on his chest, and there was a small A underneath his simple gold wedding ring. That was one place my father could never judge Dominic. Because at one point, the man who raised me was also a 'chip on his shoulder' football player with something to prove.

Not that it would serve me well to remind him of that just yet.

After taking a sip of the wine, he passed it back to Allie. Lydia rolled her eyes and grabbed the bottle again, setting it between them.

"So he asked, or you've already gone out with Walker?" Dad asked.

"Ohhhhhhh," Allie breathed, eyes widening in comprehension. She glanced at me. "Really? Dominic Walker?" she whispered, like the rest of our family wasn't sitting in the same room. "Huh. Did not see that coming."

"Doesn't it concern you a little?" Dad asked Allie. "All I hear from Logan is that the vets can't stand him. If you want to date a player, Faith, there are so many nice guys on the team right now."

I didn't want a nice guy. *He* had been a nice guy once too. Who held open doors and brought me to fancy restaurants and brought flowers on dates and brought me to meet his mother.

Then he wasn't so nice. When he didn't get what he wanted, he wasn't nice at all.

My tongue fairly tingled from the effort it took not to get defensive of Dominic. One date, and I was ready to pull out the proverbial sword.

But instead of doing that, I sent Allie a pleading look. She'd wiped just as many of my tears as my dad had, but she'd never been the overly protective parent. She was the one who trusted us to step out and make our own mistakes. She winked.

Standing from the chair, she walked around the island. Dad widened his legs on the stool, and Allie stepped straight into his embrace.

Lydia and I exchanged smiles because if there was a Universal Gold Medal for the ability to handle Luke Pierson, Allie would win every single day of the week and twice on Sundays.

"I think," she said quietly, hands sliding up his shoulders, "that we have a very, very smart daughter with a good head on her shoulders."

"I don't think she's talking about me," Lydia said in a stage whisper.

Dad breathed out a laugh. When he opened his mouth to say something, Allie gently laid two fingers on his mouth. "And I also think we don't know Walker well enough to say he's a lost cause. Nor do we need to remind Faith of her past relationship."

"No, you don't," I added gently.

My dad looked between me and Allie, reticence stamped all over his handsome features. He'd aged so well, a small threading of silver along his temples and in the stubble he let grow out in the winter. And underneath that exterior, still tattooed and strong, was a dad who just didn't want his daughter's heart broken again.

No matter how hard he'd tried, he couldn't protect me and

Lydia from everything. It was a tough pill to swallow for a guy who always wanted to be the best at whatever he did.

Briefly, they kissed, a sign that he was ceding the battle for now. Allie pulled away, but Dad's hands lingered around her waist until she came in for another kiss.

Lydia rolled her eyes and went to grab a glass of wine for herself. Neither one of us drank very much, but I motioned for her to get me one as well.

By the time my hand was curled around the glass, Allie had extricated herself and gave me a brief squeeze. "You better tell me later," she whispered into my ear.

I nodded, thankful that the subject was dropped, without any explanations. It was weird to be the one at the center of a family topic that was sensitive enough to require careful handling. Normally, that was Lydia's place, which she relished with great enthusiasm. Last time a family dinner required the finesse of a detonations expert, she told Dad she was thinking about partnering with an edible lingerie line.

That had not gone well.

It was the only time in Pierson family history that my dad had yelled at us, with all the full weight of his deep, scary football player voice. And believe me, when your father uses that particular big, scary football player voice to say, *you will not model grape flavored nipple covers for the world to see,* you never, ever forget it. It scarred all of us to varying degrees, but given Lydia was seventeen at the time, she'd wisely dropped the idea.

As casual conversation took over, we gathered around the smaller table in the kitchen, rather than the monstrosity that dominated our formal dining room. This was one of Dad's rules. The Family Dinner Rule.

There was no amount of money in the world that should replace our ability to make our own meals, set our own table, and sit down as a family to eat. Which is why, once a week, we did exactly that. We rotated weeks, on who was responsible for creating the meal, and everyone else was in charge of cleanup.

Tonight, Dad had whipped up grilled chicken and vegetables, with some baby red potatoes on the side. It wasn't anything that you'd find at a five star, Michelin-rated restaurant, but somehow, it was these normal weekly meals that represented my very favorite part of our slightly abnormal family.

My stepmom commanded a sports empire worth billions, and she sat with her feet tucked up underneath her legs, laughing at something Lydia had done earlier in the day. Dad, even though he now owned a few businesses, sat on a few boards in the Seattle area, had traded in his shirt and tie to wear a stained apron so that he could cook his girls dinner. And my social media star sister sat cross-legged in her favorite raggedy sweatpants and torn Wolves shirt, her face bare of makeup and hair in a messy knot on top of her head while she dipped her potatoes in ranch.

Dominic, when he met me, probably never could've imagined a domestic scene like this. And I couldn't blame him. Most people imagined my life to be run by an army of hired staff, where we didn't have to lift a finger. But the truth of our life was somewhere in the middle.

Our entire existence straddled a line between extreme wealth and privilege, while rooted in moments of complete normalcy.

And it was one of those normal family things to notice how my dad kept watching me during dinner. Lydia was showing Allie something on her phone, and I nudged Dad's foot under the table.

"It'll be okay, Dad." I gave him a small smile. "He's not what you think."

"Just be careful," he said, his voice gruff with emotion. "I promise not to go overboard. But it's hard, kid. I've only got one Faith and one Lydia."

"Thank God for that," Lydia interjected. "You'd be impossible if there were more of us."

Allie laughed, and Dad's face cracked into a smile.

It was enough to break the tension over the dinner. I took another bite of my food, my dad took a slow sip of his drink, and then shared a smile with Allie.

He set down the cup with a sigh. "Shit, I can't wait for you two to have kids so you know exactly how impossible this is."

"Are you ready to be a grandpa?" Lydia asked, eyebrows raised.

Dad groaned. "No. Please, forget I said that."

"New family rule," Allie said, raising her wineglass. "No commentary on the girls' love lives unless they ask for it."

Lydia and I shared an incredulous look.

Dad sighed and clinked his glass against Allie's. "Deal."

Lydia added hers to the mix. "Does this extend to my business collabs too? Because I got a *really* great offer the other day from La Perla."

At the pained look on Dad's face, I burst out laughing.

"One thing at a time, Lydia," he mumbled. "One thing at a time."

Dad set his fork down, but before he could say anything else, Allie laid her hand on his.

"I think Dominic, with good coaching and some time, will be a really great asset to the Wolves," she said. Oh boy, Allie was in full-blown owner mode. "But your father is right. The ball is a big night, and he hasn't … he hasn't proved he can handle the important events without making a scene." She tried to gentle her statement with a soft smile. "Just think really hard before you decide that you want him by your side at a moment like this."

Attention on my every move was nothing new. It had been like that my entire life. But it wasn't normally my family looking at me like they couldn't anticipate what I would do or say next.

Lying to them would get me nowhere because if I wanted Dominic there, and he said yes, I'd walk through those doors without a single ounce of hesitation. They didn't know him. In all honesty, I had to wonder who did.

Chapter
SEVENTEEN

Dominic

Sunshine: So ... as it's now 12:01, technically it's the day you're going to take me out again.

Sunshine: Can I ask what my surprise is?

With a grin, I rolled over in bed, propping my head in my hand while I pulled up her contact info. Screw this texting bullshit, I wanted to hear her voice. She picked up almost immediately.

"You're still awake?" she asked.

"Couldn't sleep."

"Why not?"

I stretched out on my back and laid the phone on my chest. That way I could pretend she was lying there with me. "I went to the weight room around six. I don't normally work out in the evenings. Guess it amped me up too much."

"Must've been quiet at that time of night."

That was the point. I liked the idea of no one else there. Solid strategy I had going in the *pre*-preseason. Avoidance all the way. But I didn't want to admit that to her just yet.

"It was," was all I said. "Kinda nice. Other than the lack of sleep that came with it."

"Why'd you work out so late?"

I sighed dramatically. "I wanted to spend time with someone, but she had other plans."

"Rude."

"I was almost asleep," I admitted. "Then a pretty girl blew up my phone because she wants me so bad."

Faith laughed. "Gawd, your ego is ridiculous."

"You're the one who agreed to go out with me," I pointed out.

A miracle, the more I thought about it. She may not have admitted to Dominic why she had her football player rule, but Nick knew. I knew exactly why she did.

"Yesterday before you picked me up, I probably would have told you it was a momentary lapse in judgment."

I waited, because it didn't seem like she was done. But she stayed quiet. "And now?" I asked.

"Now," Faith started, "I'd tell you that it was probably the best first date I've ever had."

My fist raised victoriously in the air, which she couldn't see. "You sound surprised by that."

"I am, I guess." She paused. "And here I am, talking to you at midnight because I didn't really want to wait until tomorrow."

The fact that she admitted it had me closing my eyes again. This was the kind of shit that would be the death of me. If she felt even a fraction of what I did, we were verging on dangerous territory. These were the stories that ended up with Vegas drive-up marriages after meeting two days earlier. The ones that didn't make sense to anyone else outside of that couple.

When I didn't answer right away, Faith made a self-conscious laughing sound. "I'm not really playing hard to get either, am I?"

"I fucking hope not," I told her. "I didn't mean to go quiet. This is … it's different for me. In a good way. I don't date a lot. Haven't had a serious girlfriend since like, high school."

That's when Ivy got sick. Nothing else mattered after that.

"Oh come on," she said. "Really?"

"Really. Broke up when I graduated and moved away to school. Then I had a lot of family shit going on when I was in college. I was too busy with football and working and school." I paused. "Wait, am I allowed to talk about football now?"

She breathed out a soft laugh. "Yeah."

"Good, because that would've made this relationship very awkward, sunshine."

"Are we in a relationship after one date?" Faith asked. "Isn't that … crazy?"

"Crazy for who? I don't want to date anyone else. Do you?"

"No." She sighed. "It's … it's been a long time for me too. I know I didn't answer when you asked, but there was a guy in college."

I pinched the bridge of my nose, because I hadn't expected her to admit it so soon. "Yeah?"

"Honestly, it was stupid how long I was with him."

Asking her any questions about him felt as bad as a lie, so I hesitated. "I don't think it makes you stupid though. You trust people. Nothing wrong with that."

"Two years," she said quietly. "It wasn't even a good two years, when I look back on it. My family could tell he didn't really love me, but I was young. First guy to sweep me off my feet my freshman year. He was a senior at UDub. Played Cornerback."

I hummed. "That's your problem. Cornerbacks are assholes."

Faith laughed. "Are they?"

"That one is."

"You don't even know what he did," she teased.

I winced, because, yeah I fucking did. Or most of it. "If he was bad enough for you to ban all football players, then he was an asshole."

"He was," she agreed. "I didn't see it at first. But when he realized that being with me, knowing my family wasn't going to give him any sort of boost into the pros, it came all the way out." Faith groaned. "I can't believe I'm telling you all this."

"You don't have to talk about it if you don't want to."

"Honestly, it wasn't even what he did. It was how stupid I felt afterward," she said quietly. "What kind of girl stays with a guy for two years and doesn't see just how awful he is deep down?"

"You are the least stupid person I've ever met," I told her.

Faith paused, then spoke on a rushed exhale. "When I dumped him, he got so mad that he cursed me out in front of all his housemates, then said sleeping with me was like fucking a dead fish. Exact quote."

I bolted upright in bed. "He said *what*?" I yelled. "You didn't tell—" I caught myself. She'd never told me that before, and I was … *furious*. "Faith, you didn't believe him, did you?"

She groaned. "I've never told anyone that before. It was so embarrassing."

"*For him.*" Holy hell, my hands were curled tight, and if that cornerback asswipe had been in front of me, I would've wrenched his nuts from his body and shoved them down his throat. "You have nothing to be embarrassed about. He's a wimpy ass fucknut who should be put out of his misery for ever talking to you like that."

Faith made a sound of mild amusement. "My goodness, I'm a little flattered by this anger on my behalf. I still should have known he was capable of something like that, though. Two years, Dominic."

"If you didn't see it, it's because he wasn't showing you who he really was." As my heart rate slowed back to a normal rhythm, I lay back down, trying to wrap my head around that she *had* been willing to give me a chance after that. No wonder she never wanted to dip her toe into that particular dating pool again.

Faith was quiet for a second. "You sound so sure for a guy who hardly knows me."

Licking my lips, I knew if I was going to tell her in this phone conversation, she'd just opened the door. But something held me back. Probably dumb-ass male fear, if I was being honest.

Faith was the first person who saw me. Beyond Walker the Wild, or whatever stupid shit the press said about me. Beyond coaches and bad teams and foolish choices fueled by grief or insecurity. It was the first time since Ivy that I'd felt this kind of ease with someone, and the most selfish part of me was what kept me from telling her.

On the heels of what she'd just admitted to me, I physically couldn't force the words out when she wasn't right in front of me.

No. This wasn't the time.

"I don't know everything," I answered carefully. "But what I do know only makes me want to know more about you, Faith Pierson. That's a pretty rare thing in my world."

"Mine too," she murmured sleepily. "I'm glad you called me, Dominic. I like hearing your voice before I go to bed."

I groaned. "You're gonna change the direction of this phone call real quick if you keep that up."

She laughed. "I've never had phone sex before."

Tilting my chin up, I blew out a hard breath. "Woman," I warned.

"Maybe we ought to have a second date before we try it."

"Can't this count as our second date? We already had the talk about our exes."

"True," she conceded. "You know what I like about you?"

"No. Give me a detailed list and say it slow in that sexy voice you just did."

She could hardly talk around her laughter, and I found myself grinning widely.

Faith was so much braver than I was. Everything about this with her felt fragile, like if I moved wrong, I'd lose it. And I couldn't handle the thought of that so soon after I'd found her.

I'd tell her. And when I did, it would be perfect. Something that showed her exactly how much I listened to her, how well I knew her.

Because I did. Faith had been hurt, and even if enough time had passed that she was willing to take a chance on me, I wanted that confident girl from the first date. The girl who did nothing more than smile at me, and had me wrapped completely around her dainty little finger. Any words he'd ever put in her head would be erased completely.

Not just because of me, but because she knew they didn't belong there either.

She hummed, and in the background, I could hear the rustling of sheets. I swiped a hand down my face because holy shit, the mental images. They were so good. I wanted to be in those sheets with her.

"You don't fool me," she said.

The hand dropped off my face at the change in her tone. "Don't I?"

"I think this whole bad boy thing is an act."

"All the refs who flagged me in the past three years would beg to differ," I answered wryly.

"That's different."

I closed my eyes at how sure she sounded. "Is it?"

"Yup. You might play like you've got a point to prove, but it doesn't mean anything about who you are underneath the helmet. I think you're a big ol' softy," she said quietly. "And for some reason, you don't want to show it."

This time, when my heart sped up, it wasn't because I was mad. Or because I was turned on. I mean, I *was* turned on, but it wasn't just that. It was because I might as well have been standing naked in the middle of that field where I'd started my time in Washington.

How did she do this?

And when did a giant wooly sock get stuck in my throat? I tried to swallow, and it took me another try before I was successful.

"That's the whole plan, sunshine. I can only show my soft side to a few select people. If everyone knew how amazing I was, imagine the chaos that would ensue."

"Then I guess I should feel very special that I'm one of them."

My eyes were pinched shut tightly as I spoke. "What does your day look like tomorrow?"

"I have to work, but my roommate Tori is pulling an overnight because a rhino might give birth."

"Ohhhkay?"

She giggled. "She works at the zoo."

"Ahh." I knew that too, I thought with a grimace.

"But a birthing rhino means I'll have the apartment to myself," she said lightly.

"I love that rhinoceros."

"Do you?"

"More than I ever thought possible." I winced when I caught the time. "I should probably try to get to sleep, but I'll be there at five thirty, and I'll bring something to eat with me."

"Is the food my surprise?" she asked.

"Patience, sunshine. You'll find out tomorrow."

She sighed. "Fine."

"Sweet dreams," I told her.

"Good night," Faith answered sweetly.

It took me a few minutes after she disconnected, where I did nothing but stare up at the ceiling. It was impossible to know whether this was actually the dumbest thing I'd ever done. Even if it was, with her voice echoing in my head as I drifted off to sleep, it was a risk I was willing to take.

Chapter
EIGHTEEN

Faith

AT FIVE TWENTY-NINE, I PACED MY APARTMENT, DOING ONE last check that I'd picked up Tori's clothes tornado that always ended up on the floor by the couch. My hands were jittery by my side, as they'd been all freaking day as I watched the time wind closer to when I'd see him.

"This is crazy," I whispered in a singsong voice. That one phone conversation, after one date, had me flying so high that I was starting to worry just a little bit.

I told him about Charlie, for crying out loud. Told him the one thing I'd never told anyone, ever. And poof, it came out of my mouth just like that. Maybe because we'd been on the phone, it was easier.

But he was making it so easy, somehow.

Which is why I was pacing and my hands couldn't stop twitching, and I had to remind myself that I should not jump him the moment he walked through the door. Because I still had a good head on my shoulders.

Maybe.

In front of the mirror over our small table by the door, I gave another quick glance at my reflection. There was no time for a carefully constructed outfit with magical properties, so Dominic was getting what I'd worn to work: a denim pencil skirt and a simple bone-colored tank tucked into the waist.

The buzz at the speaker by our door sounded, and even though I knew he'd be on time, I jumped. With my hand on my chest, I hit the button.

"Hey, sunshine, a really intimidating man down here at the desk wants to make sure you're expecting me."

With a laugh, I hit the button to speak. "You can let him up, Michael."

"You got it, Miss Pierson," came our doorman's deferential tone.

Dominic must have caught the elevator immediately because I could hardly do any fidgeting before there was a brisk knock on the door.

My poor heart.

It was off to the races at the sound of that knock, and I did the mental pep talk thing again.

No jumping, Faith.

You can control yourself.

You are a capable, strong woman who has self-control.

And I was doing great with all those affirmations until I opened the damn door.

Dominic had a large, reusable grocery bag gripped in one hand and braced himself on the doorframe with his other hand. For a moment, he didn't move, his eyes tracking down my body like I was wearing edible lace or something instead of a perfectly boring, perfectly normal workday outfit.

"Sunshine," he said in a low, growly voice.

"Hotshot." Mine wasn't low and growly, but it was all sorts of breathy and girly, like I was *not* a woman with self-control. "Come in."

I stepped aside, and when his shoulder brushed against me, I closed my eyes.

No jumping, Faith.

You can control yourself.

You are a capable, strong woman who has self-control.

It didn't even register I was still standing there holding the door until I heard his low, amused chuckle. When I opened my eyes, he'd set the grocery bag on the small table where Tori and I ate.

Again, Dominic was wearing dark jeans that highlighted exactly how long his legs were, and a black T-shirt that hugged his chest and shoulders. Ink crawled down his arms. On his head was a solid black baseball hat, backward again, and I could tell based on the dark stubble coating his sharp jaw that he hadn't shaved.

He wasn't trying to impress me—even though he was doing that too—and somehow that made my self-control crumble further.

"How was your day, dear?" he murmured, leaning up against the edge of the table, his legs spread wide.

But it was the look in his eye that had the crumbling self-control disappear in a happy poof.

I strode toward him and grabbed the side of his face, just as his big hands came around to grip my ass. Our mouths melded in a hot, hard kiss. Before I could blink, he'd turned us, licking into my mouth while he boosted me up onto the table. Those hands shoved the hem of my skirt up just far enough that I could split my thighs around his hips. When Dominic fitted himself there, he groaned, a sound that vibrated out of his broad chest and into my mouth with such delicious tremors that I whimpered.

One hand stayed against my lower back, the other anchored roughly into my hair as he directed the kiss. With my head angled to the side, I felt very much like he was devouring me.

And in his capable hands, with that tongue, and his lips, and the sounds he made, I yielded without hesitation. My arms wound around his neck as we kissed and kissed. When I finally broke away with a gasp, it was only because he'd moved his lips to the edge of my ear and sucked my earlobe into his mouth.

"Oh," I moaned. "Oh, I like that."

Dominic pulled back with a dazed look in his dark eyes. "I'm going to find all the ways to make you say that."

I traced my thumb underneath the curve of his lip. "Are you?"

At my touch, he nipped the pad of my finger. The sharp bite of his teeth had me feeling achy and empty, and when I exhaled shakily, he saw it.

"What do you need?" he asked with something dark and intense threading through his voice. "Tell me."

Because I didn't trust my ability to speak, I knew I couldn't tell him, but I could show him. Sliding my hand over his, I moved it from the curve of my ass and helped him push the edge of my skirt higher. Even as his fingers curled into the warm flesh of my thigh, his eyes never wavered from mine.

Then I pushed his hand between my legs.

Dominic needed no further instruction, and his eyes lit dangerously as he leaned forward, bracing his free hand on the table. His big fingers knew exactly what I needed, moving slow and sure until my head dropped onto his shoulder, and I tightened my fist into the material of his shirt. At first, it was all I could do to breathe through the build, but then even that wasn't enough. I turned my head and found his mouth, hot and seeking, that tongue twining with mine as my hips started rocking back and forth.

Then he moved, curled his wrist, and I broke away from the kiss as warmth slid fast through my veins.

I came down slow and quiet.

On my dining room table.

Five minutes after he walked in the door.

"I'll find all of them," he whispered, ducking his head to kiss my cheek. The tip of my nose. My forehead.

With my hands still gripping his shirt, I had to tuck myself against his chest while he held me. Something about this unexpected exchange had my whole body trembling.

"Hey," he said, running a soothing hand along my back, "you okay?"

I nodded. But it still took me a second before I could lift my head and meet his eyes. "This is ... intense, right? It's not just me?"

Dominic's jaw flexed as he slid a hand along the side of my face. "It's not just you."

But concern was etched over his face as he studied me.

"Was it too much?" he asked.

I shook my head, then gave him a soft kiss. "No. Not in a bad way." I smiled when he helped me down from the table. "Just ..."

"Intense," he finished.

"Yeah."

Dominic blew out a hard breath, then grinned in such a boyish, charming way that I about jumped right back on that fracking table. "That's not how I planned to start this date."

Tilting my head to the grocery bag, I asked, "Something a bit more tame?"

"Oh, we're not having a boring dinner, sunshine. We're living on the edge tonight."

I moved to the side while he pulled the bag toward him. And simply because I wanted to, I slid my arm around his waist, tucking myself under his arm while he rooted around in the bag. Amazing how easy affection felt after a greeting like *that*.

He produced a box of Hershey's chocolate.

I stared at it. Then stared at him. "What's that?"

"Can you take it, please?"

With a confused smile, I did, then watched him unfold a big plaid blanket and lay it in the middle of the room. With his back to me, he rummaged through the bag and took out a small box. That went onto the middle of the blanket, followed by pillows from our couch. Dominic tucked a giant bag of marshmallows under his arm, then gestured to the blanket.

"My lady," he said.

I sat, still clutching the chocolate in my hands. That was when I noticed an assortment of other sweets. Peanut butter cups. White chocolate bar. Dark chocolate with toffee. And two stacks of graham crackers.

"A s'more picnic?" I asked.

"I'd planned to do this out in the park behind your building, but…" He gestured at the window, where rain pattered gently against the glass.

My grin split my face wide. "I love it. We're going to get a sugar high, though. You know that, right?"

"That's the plan." He leaned forward and gave me a sweet kiss.

From the box, he pulled a small silver canister that set on top of a square black rock. With the flick of a lighter that he pulled out of his pocket, we had our own little flameless fire.

I glanced at him wonderingly. "You're setting the bar very high, hotshot."

"Does that mean I can stay after dessert and kiss you some more?"

Nodding, I leaned in again and gave him one that was a bit longer than the last.

"How was *your* day?" I asked while he loaded up two small sticks with marshmallows.

"Oh, you know how it goes," he said, eyes fixed on the marshmallow as he rotated it, "lots of weights. Lots of sweat. Watched some film for a while."

"What film?" I ate a marshmallow plain, then added another one from the bag onto my roasting stick.

"Wolves versus Green Bay, two years ago."

"We lost, right?"

He nodded. "By a field goal at the end. Green Bay's defensive scheme makes it harder for tight ends to slot into that receiver role."

"Scared of their linebackers, are ya?" I teased.

Dominic emitted a little growl, which had me laughing.

"Did Torres give you that homework?"

He shook his head. "Just wanted to start taking some notes. We play Green Bay week three, want to find some holes in what they do."

I studied him because it was more interesting than roasting my marshmallow. Something had been eating at me with this new little journey of discovering the many sides of Dominic Walker. And instead of tiptoeing around it, I decided to embrace whatever crazy foundation we were building—the intensity and the connection—and just go for it.

"Can I ask you something?"

Dominic raised an eyebrow. "Every time you start with something like that, I feel like you're about to psychoanalyze me."

I smiled. "I'm serious. If I ask you a question, will you answer me honestly?"

He pulled the stick away from the flame, giving me his full attention before he replied. His eyes searched mine for a beat. "Yeah. I'll answer honestly."

I held out my pinky. He took it without hesitation, curling his much larger one around mine.

"You weren't the one who puked out on the field, were you? It was the rookie, Cartwright."

His eyes widened, his mouth popping open just slightly.

"I knew it," I breathed. "Why'd you tell Allie it was you? She should know."

"Shit," he muttered under his breath. Dominic exhaled heavily, still holding my gaze. "That's not your story to tell, young lady."

"Don't young lady me." I smacked his shoulder. "Why would you lie about that?"

Dominic sat back and watched me evenly.

"Tell me," I encouraged him. "You are a hard worker, hotshot. You love what you do. I can see it. The more I get to know you, the less that whole thing makes sense."

But he didn't want to. And I didn't want to push too hard. But something was going on in that locker room, something that weighed on him, especially when I thought about what my dad had said and what I'd seen at the car wash event.

The vets were wary of this new guy—Walker the Wild. But honestly, I didn't think he was all that wild. He played aggressively, but in the right atmosphere, that edge would smooth out. Nothing I'd seen of him made me believe he'd drink so much his first night here that he'd get sick on that field. But for some reason, he let them believe it.

When he stayed quiet, I allowed myself a moment of disappointment that he wasn't telling me the full story, but we would get there. I could feel it. He and I were at the start of something good, and it was okay if some things about it progressed at a more normal pace.

But he must have seen that disappointment on my face.

"It was the rookie's idea," he started. "He had the tequila in his bag."

I set my chin on my hand and listened.

"I only had a couple of shots all night. Hardly enough to get buzzed, but he drained half that bottle. When they flipped the lights on..." He gestured from his mouth.

"Got it." At my tone, Dominic grinned crookedly. My favorite of all his smiles. "That's when my mom showed up," I added.

He nodded slowly.

"Why...?" My voice trailed off. "I don't understand."

Dominic swallowed, slicking his tongue over his teeth before he answered. "After that disaster of a press conference, I already felt so ... out of place. And because they immediately expected me to do something stupid." His jaw clenched. "Everyone did. Might as well let them believe it, if it let the rookie start with a blank slate."

Carefully, I set my roasting stick down, and staying aware of where the flame was, I crawled over until I was straddling his lap. My hands looped loosely around his neck, and I waited for him to move his eyes from the line of my tank top before I spoke. His big hands slid up my upper thighs, exposed by the position I was sitting.

"I won't tell Allie," I promised.

"Thank you."

"But you shouldn't keep this to yourself. It's not your responsibility to bear someone else's mistakes, Dominic. You know what you told me yesterday? That I didn't see the jackass was a jackass because he didn't let me?"

Oh, Dominic didn't like being compared to *him*.

I held up a hand, then laid it over his heart. "You know what I mean."

Dominic raised an eyebrow in concession. His fingers traced the hem of my skirt.

"You have an amazing opportunity here, and it's not too late to let them see the good. Even if chaos ensues because everyone is obsessed with you once they do," I finished lightly.

Dominic's gaze burned into mine, but it took him a long moment to speak. "How did I find you?" he asked roughly.

I grinned. "I think I'm the one who found you, hotshot."

He wrapped me up in his arms, holding me tightly, before he rolled us to the soft blanket for a deep, seeking kiss. It was a long time before we came up for air, and with rumpled hair and kiss-swollen lips, we ate our sticky, sweet dinner between stories about our day.

Whatever this was, however crazy it might have been, I knew there wasn't a single rule book I wouldn't light in flames just to make space for him in my life.

WASHINGTON WOLVES

Chapter
NINETEEN

Faith

TurboGirl: Oh my GOSH, I'm so sorry I missed your last few messages. I think I looked and mentally responded but then didn't actually respond.

NicktheBrickLayer: It's fine. I had to book some emergency therapy sessions to deal with my abandonment issues at you leaving me on read, but…

TurboGirl: Ha. Ha. Says the guy who went two weeks last year without responding to one of my questions. I thought you hated me.

NicktheBrickLayer: Yeah, I remember that. I'm sorry. Beginning of September was … insane for work, so. Not that it's an excuse. You done with work already? I think someone must've snuck out of the office.

TurboGirl: I did. Just a little.

TurboGirl: But I really am sorry I forgot to respond.

TurboGirl: I can't even blame work. I've just been busier than normal outside of work. By the time I make it home, I usually face-plant into my bed.

NicktheBrickLayer: What a visual. What's been keeping you so busy? Good stuff?

As I shoveled a dripping spoonful of cereal into my mouth, I stared at his message but couldn't will myself to respond. It felt odd to talk to Nick about a date. He knew about Charlie. Not all the details, but I'd been so fresh off that breakup when I started messaging him that he knew a lot. And honestly, it was the only time in three years we talked about our love lives. When we first started chatting, he'd been vehement about not having time for a girlfriend with school and working full time. This suited me fine because dating was the last thing on my mind when I went for my master's.

But for some reason, not telling him about Dominic felt wrong too.

As I thought about Dominic, I found myself smiling. We were building a small little library of memories the past few days. In a surprisingly old-fashioned turn, Dominic Walker insisted we do "normal date" things and not "greet you on the table with my hand between your legs" things.

We'd taken a private cooking class where we learned how to make homemade pasta.

He helped me walk dogs at the shelter around the corner from my apartment.

We drove an hour outside of Seattle because I told him I'd never been to a drive-in theater, where we snuggled in the bed of his truck to watch *Breakfast at Tiffany's*.

A lot of kisses in there too—a lot—but in the past five days,

Dominic had kept his hands out of my pants, and I honestly wasn't sure I could take much more of it.

Getting to know him was great, and I knew he was doing it because of my reaction after what happened in my apartment, but I was also *dying*.

I wanted his hand back between my legs.

I wanted my hand between his.

And I wanted us naked while we were doing it.

He was thinking about it just as much as I was, and if we didn't make all those happen soon, I honestly could not be held liable for my reactions.

So yeah, I smiled when I thought of the man. Every single time.

And if someone, just by the thought of them, made me smile, then they deserved to be talked about.

TurboGirl: Very good stuff. I, umm, I'm kinda hanging out with someone new.

As I finished the rest of my Cinnamon Toast Crunch, I watched with fascination at the typing bubbles that started. Then stopped. Then started again before disappearing.

NicktheBrickLayer: New friend, huh? Like a friend who would borrow your casserole dish or a friend who touches under the bathing suit lines?

Unwittingly, I smiled again. Out of respect for Nick, I answered carefully. But even as I typed, I could feel the desire to share bubble up like a pot on boil.

TurboGirl: Maybe he's both. Though he doesn't seem like the type who needs a casserole dish.

NicktheBrickLayer: So he didn't try on your date?

TurboGirl: We've actually been on a few dates.

NicktheBrickLayer: …..

TurboGirl: Did he try to borrow my casserole dish? Nope. Not even a hint at needing my 9x13. Talk about a disappointment.

NicktheBrickLayer: You know what I mean.

TurboGirl: I do, but I'm not the girl who kisses and tells.

NicktheBrickLayer: Ah, so it's that kind of friend.

He went quiet after that, and it felt … odd. As I tipped the cereal bowl up to drain the milk, I glanced at the clock on the kitchen wall. We had an event at Keisha's starting in about forty-five minutes, and I had yet to change.

Well, I didn't *have* to change, but knowing that I'd be seeing Dominic—and who knows what else after the event—I wanted to feel like I had in the magic cardigan without actually wearing a magic cardigan. As much as I appreciated his attempts to "do this the right way" or what the frick ever, I was ready to do something else the right way, and if a strategic outfit would help me with it, then I definitely wanted to take the time to change. But despite the press of the clock ticking closer to when I needed to leave, I took a deep breath and messaged Nick.

TurboGirl: He is that kind. I really, REALLY like him. He's kind of … unexpected. You know I haven't really wanted to date after what's-his-name.

TurboGirl: Sorry. Maybe you don't want to hear about this. Tell me to stop if you don't.

NicktheBrickLayer: Don't apologize, Turbo. We're friends, right? You've always listened to me when I needed it. I'm always here to return the favor.

TurboGirl: Okay. I'd hate to make it weird, so don't feel like we can't talk or something, just because I'm dating someone.

NicktheBrickLayer: We've moved to dating, eh? That was quick.

TurboGirl: I DON'T KNOW, Nick! He was so rude to me the day we met, so by all rights, I should've written him off immediately. He's not like any guy I've ever been attracted to, and honestly, I don't even care anymore because he's got my head spinning so badly. Nothing about it makes sense, but I'm excited about it. About him.

NicktheBrickLayer: Being excited is always good, and sometimes people act out for a whole lot of reasons we don't understand. Who knows what he's going through that you don't see.

TurboGirl: You're so smart.

TurboGirl: We had a "relationship talk" after our first date, and it was moving pretty fast at first. But the last week, he's been like, absolute perfect manners and totally respectful and messaging me sweet things.

NicktheBrickLayer: What a dick. How dare he.

TurboGirl: LOL.

TurboGirl: No! It's not bad. I just … I LIKE him, you know? And we've had opportunities, I just want to make sure things don't get too respectful, you know? If this guy ends up putting me in some "you're too good for me, blah blah, now you're friend zoned" classification, I might light his truck on fire.

TurboGirl: Omg. I'm sorry. I shouldn't be word vomiting to you about this, but my roomie isn't home, and I'm supposed to see him in about an hour, and I'm kind of in my head about it. I would have SLEPT WITH THIS GUY on our first date, Nick, and I have never ever felt like that.

NicktheBrickLayer: Did he …

NicktheBrickLayer: Sorry, accidentally sent too soon. Did you tell him you wanted to sleep with him that night?

TurboGirl: I didn't invite him up because Tori was home, and I don't know … it FELT like it was too fast, even if I really, really wanted to.

TurboGirl: We could've the second night too, but I kind of freaked out because of how intense it is with him.

NicktheBrickLayer: What made you freak out?

TurboGirl: Blech. I don't know. After Charlie, I never thought I'd be one of those girls who'd get SWEPT UP, you know? I thought I'd be cautious and careful and make sure that whoever I was with was a good guy who was with me for the right reasons.

The LIE

TurboGirl: And instead, I let him in my apartment, and three minutes later, I shoved his hand up my skirt. Every good intention I have goes out the window as soon as I see him, and now that side is just … on pause or something?

TurboGirl: Gah, I'm sorry, this is too much.

NicktheBrickLayer: No need to apologize. I think a hand shoved up the skirt is always a solid move, pretty clear on what you want.

TurboGirl: Indeed.

NicktheBrickLayer: But if you want more, I have a feeling he wouldn't say no.

NicktheBrickLayer: Guys like a girl who takes initiative, so if you're feeling it tonight, be clear. Can't imagine him turning you away. Not if he has a brain in his head.

TurboGirl: Says the guy who's never seen me, LOL.

NicktheBrickLayer: I've never needed to see your face to know all the important things about you, Turbo. You're a good person, you have a huge heart, you're funny, and you're smart and thoughtful. Any man would be lucky for a chance with you.

My eyes pricked with unexpected tears. It was the nicest thing he'd ever said to me.

TurboGirl: Don't you dare make me cry before I have to get ready.

NicktheBrickLayer: It's true. You're amazing. Even if you take forever to answer my messages now. He must be a worthy distraction though.

TurboGirl: He is. I promise.

Nick didn't message after that, and with a pang of sadness, I knew this was the inevitable shift if either one of us started dating.

TurboGirl: But thank you for listening to my rambles. Your friendship is so important to me, Nick.

TurboGirl: Gotta go get ready. <3

Without waiting for a response, I took a deep breath and set my phone down. For some reason, making that decision felt like clearing a hurdle that I'd erected for myself. With it behind me, it didn't feel so big anymore.

Maybe it was as simple as Nick had made it seem. I wanted Dominic, and what he'd shown me without the armor. When he wasn't putting his fists up in a defensive position, I absolutely loved what I saw.

Standing in front of my closet, I caught a glimpse of the garment bag that held my two dress options for the Black and White Ball. With a smile, I imagined arriving with my hand curled around Dominic's elbow.

Putting the dresses and that night out of my head, I took a deep breath and focused on the task at hand. The day was still warm out, the sun shining brightly, the kind of early summer day that made me love Seattle quite desperately. It wasn't all gloom and rain, despite the reputation.

My hands trailed over the hangers until I stopped on a simple cotton sundress in light blue, with a small, delicate pattern and capped sleeves that would still be appropriate for a work event. It skirted my thighs, ending a respectable distance above my knees, and when I paired it with bright white sneakers, I still felt like myself.

I kept my hair pulled off my face, added another coat of mascara, and a quick swipe of my perfume over my wrists.

Before I started my car, now with a working starter, my phone dinged with a text.

Dominic: About to head out to the center. You're still coming, right?

Me: Just getting in the car.

Me: You think I'd ghost you?

Dominic: Just looking forward to seeing you, sunshine.

Me: You too, hotshot.

For the entire drive to the center, it was impossible to wipe the smile from my face. When I arrived, the schoolyard had been transformed by the Team Sutton staff. Long tables were set up under arches of brightly colored balloons. Staff and a few players from the Wolves mingled with families from the neighborhood. Before my promotion, I would've been one of the people setting up for hours before a single person showed up. Things were a little different now, but I was glad I could still find the time to help out.

Just as I got out of my car, I heard the sound of Dominic's truck pull into a spot just behind where I'd parked. Through his windshield, he stared me down, eyes covered with those aviator shades again, but a crooked grin on his face had me biting my bottom lip. Leaning up against my car, I tucked my hands behind my back to wait for him.

He hopped out of his truck and ambled in my direction, those long legs of his covered in dark denim, his broad chest and shoulders wearing the hell out of a bright white T-shirt stamped with a small Wolves logo over his heart.

"Look at you," he murmured as he approached. "Am I allowed to greet you the way I want to right now?"

His nearness, his unapologetic display of his attraction had me breathless for a moment. After a quick glance over my shoulder to make sure no one was watching, I nodded.

Dominic planted his booted feet just outside of mine and slid his big palms over my waist, thumbs brushing my hip bones.

"How was your day, sunshine?" he whispered against my cheek, his lips brushing my skin.

"Good." Was I panting? What was it with this guy and the sides of vehicles? "I have to say," I said in a tremulous voice, flushing hot from the way he dragged his nose over the spot just under my ear and his hands tightened around my waist, "I didn't expect this kind of forthrightness from you when your teammates might see your mushy side."

He kissed the side of my neck. "No?"

"No." I trailed my fingers underneath his shirt, feeling the hard squares of muscle. "Thought we'd be all respectful distances and no touching in public."

His nose pushed into my hair, where he inhaled deeply. "I'm not feeling too respectful tonight, actually."

I laughed. My fingers curled into the waistband of his jeans, his skin hot against mine. "It was the drive-up movie that pushed you over the edge, isn't it?" I teased.

Dominic pulled back, dipping his chin so that his gaze locked with mine. "I find it much better to just be up front about it when I want something."

I curled my fingers around the hot skin of his forearm, and the muscles underneath rolled deliciously. Nick's words from our earlier conversation rang through my head.

With Dominic's dark eyes still searching mine, I took a deep breath. "And you want me?" I asked.

He licked his bottom lip. "Yeah, Faith. I do."

I pushed up on the balls of my feet, which brought me flush against the strength of his body. I nipped the edge of his jaw, and he hissed in a sharp breath. "Good," I whispered against his lips, which still hovered a millimeter away from mine. I placed a soft kiss against his delicious mouth. His lips curved into a smile, and it wasn't until he did that that I realized I was smiling too.

He didn't deepen the kiss like I expected him to. Instead, he wrapped his arms around my back, folding me into a tight embrace. I burrowed my face into his chest and inhaled a lungful of his addictive scent. What was *happening*?

This was crazy.

Too fast.

No one would believe me if I told them what types of feelings he was stirring up inside my body.

And all of it felt exactly, perfectly right.

Like he could read my thoughts, his arms tightened imperceptibly, and his chest expanded when he took a deep breath into the hair at my temple.

"You okay up there?" I teased. "You really must've missed me."

Dominic pressed a kiss to the crown of my head. "I'm just glad you're here," he said.

I smiled up at him as we pulled apart, again feeling more than a little dazed by the immediate chemistry in our greeting.

His eyes held such intensity, but to my utter surprise, it didn't scare me or overwhelm me.

"You look like you're thinking some serious thoughts up there," I commented lightly. I slid my palm against his stubbled cheek. Dominic closed his eyes at the touch, and the rush of tenderness at his expression was just one more reaction I hadn't expected.

When he opened his eyes, I thought he'd say something, but

after a moment, his expression changed back into that crooked smirk I was coming to love so much.

"Just happy," he said as he stared down at me.

This man. The things he was doing to my heart. "Good," I told him.

"Come on," he said with a grin, "someone has to help me carry all these bags. I need to go show up my teammates."

WASHINGTON WOLVES

Chapter
TWENTY

Dominic

"YOU SURE IT'S NOT TOO BIG FOR ME?"

My little quarterback, who hadn't shot a cannon into my junk today, palmed the ball dubiously. Her hand was so tiny, the sight of her fingers between the white laces did uncomfortable things to my heart.

"Nah, you'll grow into it," I told her.

Maggie gave me a gap-toothed grin as she tossed it into the air. "Did you buy anyone else their own football?"

I held my pointer finger up over my lips. "Our secret for now, okay, kid?"

Everyone else was busy digging into the summer activity boxes that had been distributed over the past two hours and the surplus of sporting equipment I'd purchased. The line of kids coming to the tables with their parents had been longer than I expected, but the smiles and gratitude from all of them had made the time pass quickly. We took pictures and chatted with the families, and not once had I felt like an outsider. So many of the boys, too big for the shoes on their feet or wearing shirts that didn't quite fit their frame, reminded me of my own upbringing.

Faith and I had stood shoulder to shoulder the entire event, but none of my teammates seemed to notice the way my hands lingered on hers when I handed her something, or the flush in her cheeks when our eyes caught.

My Faith Pierson high was as dangerous, as addictive as any substance on earth.

If she had any idea of the kind of power she held over me, she could absolutely crush my heart. Sitting in my apartment before I left, I knew what I risked by asking about her date as Nick. But the sight of her unfiltered honesty had only strengthened what I knew to be true.

She was the kind of girl you wrecked your life over. Because as long as she was in it, even the carnage left behind would be better than just about any life without her.

Every date. Every moment I was spending with her, we were building something. She knew it. I knew it.

Even more surprising was how much I liked the time spent putting each block into place. Each date where we did nothing more than kiss, where I simply got to know her better, and she was able to do the same.

When we arrived together, arms laden with bags of sports equipment, Keisha hugged me like I was family.

One of our defensive linemen, Roberts, eyed all the bags in my hands. "Suck-up," he said with a smile. "Why you gotta show everyone up, Walker?"

His good-natured teasing had something tight easing in my chest. Faith smiled over at me when she heard what he'd said. A secret smile, and I fucking loved that we had things that we could share secret smiles over.

In fact, his teasing wasn't the only slight smoothing in the path with my teammates. It was the first event I'd been at where the few teammates present had greeted me with cautious smiles and fist bumps.

Press took some pictures. Asked some questions.

Nice questions this time. I was able to talk a little bit about the time I'd spent at the community center in conjunction with Team Sutton, and not a single reporter asked me about flags or penalties or Walker the Wild.

And when the line trickled out, the activity boxes distributed, Faith was meeting with some of the Team Sutton staff, so I found myself wandering over to where Maggie was flipping through one of the activity books that had been in the box.

"There's good stuff in there," I said.

She glanced at the coloring books, art supplies, the reading books, and other educational items carefully packed by the foundation's workers. Then she shrugged. "I guess."

"You don't like doing crafts and shit?" I asked.

"You're not supposed to swear in front of us."

With a wince, I made sure no one was around us. "Sorry, kid. Sometimes I forget about that."

"You must not be a dad. Dads usually remember that."

The thought of me as a parent was terrifying, but the simple way she'd deduced the truth had me laughing. "I'm not. You can get me in trouble with Keisha if it makes you feel better."

For a moment, Maggie peered thoughtfully over by where Keisha stood next to Faith. Then she shrugged. "Nah. If I tell her you're a bad influence, she won't let you around us no more."

"Any more," I gently corrected. "And that's good. She should be protective of you guys."

Maggie spun the football. "I don't think a lot of football players would buy a girl a football. They always get us softballs or volleyballs or something. It's stupid."

Again, she reminded me of Ivy with that challenging glint in her big eyes, and I had to breathe through a few heavy memories before I could answer her.

Hospital beds.

Tubes.

Holding her hair back while she fought the nausea from her treatments.

My fingers started tingling a little, a sure sign of an anxiety attack, which were only ever tied to thoughts of my sister.

Maggie tossed the ball in the air but misjudged the height, and I was forced out of my head to catch it for her. The pebbled leather brought me back down to earth, and as I handed it to her, she gave me a small smile.

"Girls should be able to play whatever sport they want," I told her, images of my sister swimming slowly through my brain. "And if any players come here and say you can't play football, you send me a text, and I'll beat the shit out of them because they're assholes."

For a second, Maggie did nothing but blink up at me, her eyes wide with shock. I winced because my threat was all sorts of inappropriate.

"That's..." she started.

"Too much?" I asked.

"So. Cool," she breathed. "I'm gonna go tell my friends!"

As she sprinted off to find them, I swiped a hand over my mouth because that probably wasn't the smartest thing I could've done. Story of my life. I was always doing things I shouldn't have done. Shouldn't have said.

Or in today's case—things I *should* have said, but just ... couldn't find the right moment. From where I sat on the step, I had a clear line to watch Faith interact with the people who worked with her.

Worked for her, I corrected mentally. The leadership position was something she wore so naturally. Whoever was talking to her at any given moment, she listened attentively and never dominated the conversation.

It was so odd that the physical version of Turbo, standing in front of me, was somewhat of a novelty to me, but still, I was so fucking proud of her. That novelty, though, I had to get my impulses in check because I was one hug away from telling her something insane like I was falling in love with her. But the second she was in front of me, I could hardly help myself.

She wasn't perfect, that much I knew, but fuck if she wasn't as close to it as I'd ever met. And if I told her that, I'd sound insane.

She was thinking all of that too, how fast this was, even if it was real.

Those types of thoughts were all I could blame on why I didn't notice my QB approach and sit next to me on the steps. Because Faith and I had arrived just as the event was starting, and James had been on the opposite end of the tables, it was the first I'd spoken to him all evening.

"Walker," he said, stretching his long legs in front of him. "Didn't expect to see you here."

It made me laugh under my breath. "Trying to make those good choices you talked about."

Trying was the operative word. Didn't claim to be perfect.

James nodded, a smile playing around his lips.

"I'm going to invite you somewhere," he said. "And you'll probably want to say no, but I want you to think about it."

"Invite me where?" I asked.

"Small offensive retreat I hold every year at my place in Mendocino. There are seven of us."

My eyebrows popped up. "You want me to come?"

He laughed, a rich, deep sound. Faith glanced over in our direction, and I gave her a tiny wink.

"Yeah, Walker, I want you to come. It's a good chance for me to get to know my receivers and running backs, tight ends if they can stop being grouchy enough to let me."

The reproach was gently handled because somehow, it didn't raise my hackles. "When is it?"

Another smile. "We leave on Sunday morning. Five days, four nights on the ocean. We work out, cook, toss the ball, just get to know each other before the season really starts."

I blew out a hard breath. "What time?"

He pulled his wallet out of his back pocket and handed me the card of a private airfield. "If you're there by eight, I'll know you're coming. There's room for you on the plane. But this is a serious opportunity, Walker. I ask the guys to leave their phones in their room during the day, no distractions. This is about forming a unit on that field, and if you can't set your personal stuff aside in order to do that, then I'd rather have you stay back, and I'll just pray we click once the season starts."

Swallowing proved difficult because I had to choke down the way I'd started off here in light of his generous offer. It was a massive opportunity, something that would allow me to forge a bond with the guys who lined up next to me every Sunday once the season started. If this was what happened behind closed doors, it explained why Washington always had some intangible chemistry among their players.

And I thought about what Faith said. They'd never see past the bullshit if I didn't let them.

He stood, shoving at my shoulder. "Hope to see you there, Walker. I promised my wife I'd be home for dinner."

Faith waved at him as they passed, but I was gratified to see the way her smile changed once I was the only one looking. The blue dress she was wearing swished around her thighs, and the fact that she'd paired something so subtly sexy, so feminine with her white sneakers was driving me out of my fucking mind.

When she took a seat on the step next to me, there was a

respectable distance between us, and I had to grip my hands together to keep from sliding my palm up the long length of her bare leg.

"Have fun?" she asked, eyes forward.

I glanced at her before doing the same. "Yup. Wasn't bad."

"Saw you give the football to Maggie. You know she's going to idolize you for life now, right?"

"Why do you think I did it? She's the only one who's ever managed to nail me in the balls with a football. I want her on my good side."

Faith laughed, a sunny smile spreading her mouth wide, and a dimple popped on the side of her face.

I leaned back on my hands, and we sat quietly for a few minutes. "You're really good at your job, sunshine."

Her face softened in surprise when she looked over at me. "Thank you."

"Everyone likes you. But more than that, they respect you." I gave her a quick look. "Takes a special person to be able to pull that off."

She blinked rapidly, and I realized she was tearing up.

She laughed under her breath. "Don't worry, I'm not going to burst into tears."

"I don't care if you do."

Faith turned at that. "Most guys panic at the sight of women's tears, especially if they're the cause. That's not you?"

"Hell no." I turned too, and our knees brushed. Neither one of us seemed to care that there were people around, that someone might see our body language. "If I do something to make you cry, good or bad," I told her quietly, "you can bet your ass I'll stay right here until you feel better."

"Who *are* you?" she asked incredulously.

I grinned.

"I'm serious." She shook her head. "Sometimes, I can't believe you're the same guy I met that day in Allie's office."

Like it had been with James, it was difficult to stick my past actions under the spotlight in the face of her generosity. The words of explanation about Nick and Turbo still crowded my mouth, but I kept them leashed for now. But this honesty was something I could give her. "I misjudged you because of my own past. My own issues." I held her gaze. "And I'm sorry. It wasn't fair."

Faith stared at me with something behind her eyes as she listened. Her reaction wasn't immediate, and I liked that. There was no disputing how I'd acted, no brushing it off. And when she did speak, it wasn't what I expected her to say.

"Will you be my date to the Black and White Ball on Saturday?"

It was the second invitation that had my eyebrows popping up. "The big fundraiser?"

She nodded. "You'll need a tux. I know it's kind of short notice, but…" She paused, letting out a slow breath. "I'd really like it if you'd come with me."

I edged closer on the step. "Isn't it like, a big, public, fancy-ass deal?"

Again, she nodded. Her pinky stretched out on the concrete and brushed against mine. Our hands were blocked from view, and I slid the tip of my finger over hers, dragging it over the soft skin of her hand.

"And you want *me* to come with you?" I asked. Emotion had my voice coming out a little rougher than I anticipated.

But I couldn't fight the tidal wave of victory at the realization. It was exactly what I'd wanted when I didn't tell her who I was. To know that even with all the ways I'd fucked up at first, she was willing to take this giant step with me into the spotlight.

Faith turned her hand and wove her fingers between mine. "I want you to come," she affirmed.

"I, uh, I'll have to leave early the next morning." I leaned into her, dropping my voice slightly. "If it's a late-night type thing."

Her eyes sparkled happily at that. "Leave for what?"

"If I go," I hedged. "I might not. James just asked me to this offensive retreat thing at his place in California."

She smiled. "He invited you?"

"Crazy, right?"

Faith shook her head. "Not at all."

"I have an early morning tomorrow too," I told her. "I'm not used to updating someone on my trips. Sorry."

"It's okay. What's on the calendar?"

"Some Gatorade thing in Chicago. I'll just be gone for one night. They're gonna strap me up to machines and do those tests to make sure I don't die while I'm working out and drinking all the stuff they pay me a lot of money for."

Her laughter was loud. A few people looked over at us, but Faith didn't pull away.

All around me, walls were crumbling at an alarming rate. "I should pack a bag or something tonight, I guess," I murmured.

Her eyes glowed when she spoke. "Do you want some help?"

My breath caught at her offer, at the look in her eyes. As Nick, I'd practically dared her to do this, to make it obvious that she wanted me. The devil on one shoulder crowed obnoxiously in victory. Even the angel was silent because I think even that self-righteous asshole wanted me to take her home too.

"You don't have any other plans tonight?" I asked.

Faith dipped her head, her hair falling over her shoulder in a way that made me want to fist my hands in it and tug it tight while I sucked at her skin. When she lifted her gaze, she was thinking the exact same thing.

"Just you," she answered simply.

"I really want to kiss you right now," I spoke low and fast.

She breathed out a laugh. "I can tell."

"I live about fifteen minutes from here. I'll text you the address." I stood and held out my hand to help her up.

"Do you want me to pick up something to eat?" she asked.

"I have food at my place." It wasn't an outright lie. I had milk, three beers, a package of cheese, and bananas that were too green. But in my pantry was probably six boxes of cereal.

Faith nodded, tucking a piece of hair behind her ear. Did she have any idea what she was doing to me? She couldn't possibly.

We stood just a bit too close as I pulled out my phone and sent the address to her. And because I couldn't stop myself, I crowded into her for just a moment so I could lean down and whisper in her ear.

"Drive fast, sunshine," I growled.

Chapter TWENTY-ONE

Dominic

MY LEAD FOOT WAS POINTLESS. I ARRIVED AT THE ENTRANCE to my building a solid five minutes before Faith was able to find parking at the hotel lot across the street. Times like that, where all I wanted to do was be inside and not dealing with parking or downtown or people getting in the way of finding parking downtown, I started making plans to sell the ugly apartment that I didn't really like and move somewhere ... else.

With my own parking. And no people. So I didn't have to wait for her.

Oh, how the mighty fall, I thought. A handful of dates and I was ready to uproot where I lived to make it easier for her to come over.

A group of tourists passed, a few of them tilting their heads together and gesturing in my direction. But because they didn't stop, I didn't smile.

When I was waiting out front like this, something that didn't happen often, I kept a hat tucked low on my head, combined with my sunglasses, and I only got a few curious stares as people passed.

The people in my building left me alone for the most part, and for that, I was grateful, especially now.

Faith emerged from the hotel parking garage, a wide smile on her face as she jogged across the street during a break in the traffic.

"Jaywalking is illegal you know," I told her.

She hopped nimbly up the curb and joined me on the sidewalk. "Is that a deal breaker?"

With a quick scan of my key card, I opened the shining glass door to hold it open for Faith. "Might be, sunshine. Can't have you bringing down my reputation with your lawless ways."

Her laughter was light and happy, echoing through the space in a way that I'd probably remember every time I came back to my apartment.

As we walked through the impressive entryway, I nodded at the doorman and pushed the button for the elevator. She glanced around at all the shining marble, the water feature in the two-story entryway with floor-to-ceiling windows. My building was just down the street from Pike's Market, and I could tell by the way she was looking at everything, she was trying to figure something out.

"What is it?" I asked her.

The elevator doors slid open, and she walked in first, tucking her hands behind her back as she leaned against the wall. "It doesn't fit you."

"No?" I punched the button for my floor. Instead of crowding against her and taking her mouth like I wanted, I matched her pose and stood opposite of her in the elevator. "What makes you say that?"

Her brain fascinated me.

"It's so shiny," she said. Faith trailed a delicate finger along the bright chrome railing, and it was impossible not to imagine her doing that on my stomach, teasing me like that where I was so hard that it was painful. "And you," she continued, a warm smile on her face, "are not."

"I'm not shiny," I mused, pushing from the wall to brace my hands on either side of her hips on that railing that she was touching like it was a personal test to my restraint. "I'm not sure how I feel about this assessment."

Faith tilted her head up. "You need exposed brick, big beams of wood," she whispered. "Not shiny rocks that gleam perfectly."

I dipped my head and caught the edge of her jaw with a soft, sucking kiss. She pulled in a quick breath. "Brick, huh?"

"Some-something with character," she whispered, trying to turn her head so her mouth would snag mine.

Lifting my head, I locked gazes with her just as the doors opened. "Something hard."

Her grin was wide and pleased, her eyes lit with scandalized pleasure. "That too."

Side by side, we walked down the elegant, dimly lit hallway, and her astute observation about the building triggered a strange reaction somewhere in the pit of my stomach. How was it, after such a short amount of time, that she somehow knew me so well?

Again, that voice in my head screamed itself raw that I should be admitting I was Nick and that I knew she was Turbo while we were alone with no one to disturb us.

"Why did you pick this building?" she asked as I fished out my keys.

I grinned over my shoulder. "This is really bugging you, isn't it?"

"What kind of place did you have when you played in Vegas?"

Once the door was unlocked, I pushed it open and laughed under my breath. "Basic. Looked exactly like every other house in my neighborhood. It wasn't all that fancy, but I paid cash, and it was mine. That was all I needed to know."

Her eyes tracked over the black leather furnishings, the prints on the wall that someone else had picked, and then shook her head when she saw all the gleaming granite in the kitchen.

"Well, now I see how shiny everything is," I mumbled. "Thanks a lot."

Faith laughed. "What do your parents do again?"

I paused by the island because ... what had I told her as Nick? It was getting hard to balance them in my head even though she had zero reason to suspect I was him. Still ... it made me want to proceed with caution.

Or tell her the truth. She wandered slowly, the delicate tips of her fingers trailing over each shining surface.

"My mom is a medical assistant." Leaning against the island, I watched her make her way into the living room and look out the wall of windows in the direction of the famous Ferris wheel overlooking the Sound. "My dad works in concrete."

"Where do they live?"

My gaze tracked every movement of her body, each careful step, each detail she seemed to absorb in my apartment, like she was trying to ferret out clues. Having her here, like this, was a big fucking step. We both knew it.

"About twenty minutes from here."

She turned, eyebrows raised. "You're from Seattle? I don't think I knew that."

The roof of my mouth was bone-dry. Each small puzzle piece was clicking into place, forming the edges of a picture she couldn't yet see. "Grew up with Wolves' posters on my wall and everything."

She smiled. "Did you?"

"I should probably admit that your dad was my favorite player."

Faith kept her slow wandering around the family room, studying books on the chrome and glass shelves. "You have excellent taste."

My eyes tracked down the length of her body. "I do."

Over her shoulder, she gave me a prolonged look because she heard the tone in my voice. I wanted her to.

Leaving her position by the windows, she approached me,

hands clasped demurely in front of her. "There's nothing in this place that looks like you," she said. "It doesn't give me a single hint about who you are."

When she stopped walking, I could've reached out, slid my hands over her hips, and tugged her close, but I didn't. It took a Herculean effort, especially with the way she was looking up at me, anticipation making her eyes glitter in the bright overhead lights of my shiny, shiny kitchen that I now hated.

She was right. The apartment was soulless and empty. Nothing about it made me feel comfortable. The fact that it was the first place to give me true privacy with her was the only thing that made it salvageable.

"It's stupid, now that I think about it," I told her, hooking a finger around the edge of her wrist and giving her a slight tug. She came willingly, hands sliding up my chest. I widened my stance, so she could fit neatly into the space between my legs. "My big return to the place I grew up. Thought I needed the nicest address to go with it."

Her smile was bemused. "I hate to break it to you, hotshot, but I don't think anyone cares whether you live here or not."

She was right about that too. It proved absolutely nothing. Impressed no one. Especially not this woman in front of me, who would've been just as happy in an old building with brick and wood and character that felt like me. No matter what was happening in the locker room, I realized that I didn't actually care to impress any of them. All I'd wanted was to feel welcome. The reason I didn't was because of all the shit I'd pulled, no matter what my intentions had been.

The one who made me feel welcome was Faith because she pried back the Walker the Wild persona, simply because she could tell it wasn't real. Or that it wasn't all that I was.

In front of me, Faith smelled so sweet and clean, and my whole body vibrated unsteadily, want rushing fiercely through my veins. Everything about her was warm and giving, and more than anything,

I wanted to see how that translated in bed. All the places she'd smell sweet and clean like she did now. All the places she'd be warm and soft, where I could pull her into my mouth, feel her with my fingers and hands.

She'd take me. And I couldn't wait to know what that felt like.

"I know they don't care," I admitted, plucking her hand from my chest so that I could gently suck one fingertip into my mouth. I rubbed my tongue along the pad of her finger, and her breath caught. "I hate that I still feel like I have something to prove, even if they're not watching."

"W-why do you think you do that?"

"Sometimes, I get these awful impulses," I told her quietly, "a devil on one shoulder, an angel on the other. I can see them clear as if they were real."

Faith listened quietly, her eyes wide and patient. Her gift, what she'd given now in both versions of herself, was understanding and acceptance without the chains of judgment. I wondered if she understood how rare that was. She was the most inherently trustworthy person I'd ever met, and still, I couldn't bring up the words of honesty that I knew I owed her.

"The day I signed the paperwork for this place, I couldn't even tell you why I listened to one over the other." I met her gaze. This was my admission of guilt, even if I wasn't saying every single thing I should have. "In your mom's office, I was so pissed off at how everything was turning out that first day. I think you know which impulse I followed then too."

"What did they tell you that day?"

I hummed. "That someone like you could never understand what I'd been through, the things that ended with me in that office. That you'd look at me in the exact same way that all the rich scholarship boys did in college, like I didn't deserve a spot on that field."

Even talking about it now, which I hadn't planned to do, I could feel those same prickles of anger, at myself, at the impulses I told her about that led me to shove just a little too hard on the field, to rip my helmet off and get in someone's face when they talked just a bit too much shit behind the safety of their protective gear.

But instead of boiling over, it simply set my blood to a low simmer.

Nothing I'd said made her back away. Nothing I'd admitted darkened her eyes or filled her face with pity.

"I don't really understand why you were willing to give me a chance after that," I said, my palms skimming up the curve of her waist until my thumbs brushed the bottom curve of her breasts. "Most people don't once they see what they want. What they think is the truth."

Her body arched slightly into my touch, the skin under her thin cotton dress warm and supple. I couldn't wait to use my tongue there. "Do you still feel like you need to prove something to me?"

The million-dollar question. Wasn't that why I'd done all of this? Clawed my way into a position where I'd earned her favor, where I felt worthy of it. Every step of my career had been exactly like this. I did the thing no one expected of me, the thing they'd dismissed upon the first glimpse.

Did I feel like I needed to prove more to Faith?

I shook my head. "Not anymore."

Faith's pink lips curled softly, and I couldn't wait any longer.

Cushioning her bottom lip between mine, I sucked gently until it pulled a soft gasp of air from her mouth. My hands slid down her back until the curves of her ass were under my fingers. She was pressed tight to me, my hips bracketing either side of hers, and against the softness of her stomach, I was so, so hard. Ready to rip and tear, to lay her out on that horrible shiny surface like she was a feast prepared only for my enjoyment.

She arched her back, winding her arms around my neck. Our kiss turned quickly from soft, sweet sips to dark and wet and sucking.

The slide of her tongue against mine had my grip tightening, the line of her dress riding up over her hips as I tugged it upward. Underneath her dress was lace, so fragile as I curled my fingers into the hem surrounding her hips.

Her fingers shoved up underneath my T-shirt, raking the sharp tips of her nails against my stomach, and it was that sweet edge of pain that had me tug her underwear to the side until she broke away from our kiss with a shocked gasp.

"You're so beautiful," I told her, ducking down to suck along the skin of her shoulder. Frantically, I pushed at the short sleeves, but they didn't bare her to me like I wanted. Faith shoved away from me, hair and eyes wild, and for just a second, I braced for her to stop me, to tell me she couldn't, that she didn't know what she was doing here with me.

But then she gripped the edge of her dress and tugged it over her head.

Underneath was a simple lace white bralette, the matching underwear that I'd almost ripped clean from her body. I stood from the island, giving my shirt the same treatment, dumping it in a pile on the floor next to her dress. With her eyes wide, Faith traced the design tattooed on my chest, an ivy-covered cross.

Heart beating viciously in my chest, I gripped her hips in my hands and started walking her backward toward my bedroom.

"Is this the rest of the tour?" she teased.

My voice came out a growling, angry command. "Later. Much, much later." I took her mouth, pressing her against the back of the couch when I couldn't go another inch without tasting her again. My bed was too far away. She met me with equal fervor and then some, her fingers digging into my skin, her tongue searching and hot and wet. My hands filled with warm flesh underneath the innocent-looking bra, and she trembled in my arms when I tugged it off.

She toed off her shoes while I struggled with my belt and shoved off my jeans because there were way, way too many clothes between us.

I fisted my hand into the soft, silky length of her hair and slanted my mouth over hers, again and again, while her toned thighs wrapped around my waist. All that was between us was the scrap of white lace.

My thumb moved in tight circles on her chest, and she whimpered into our kiss.

"You feel so good," I breathed against her kiss-ravaged mouth.

"Take me to bed, Dominic," she begged. I bent at the knee and boosted my hands underneath her ass to carry her. It would've been so easy to take her there on the couch, but yes, a big bed was good.

The bed dominated the center of the room, and I stopped at the edge, let her legs unfold slowly until her toes touched the floor. Our mouths moved over each other. Her hands were sliding over my shoulders and back while mine tangled again in her hair when I sucked her tongue into my mouth.

She slid out of my grasp and backed up to the mattress, her legs closing together demurely. It drove me *crazy*. I prowled over her, pushing her knees apart with a rough hand, my tongue licking a line up the center of her chest, stopping to circle her breast, to blow lightly along her chest until her body shook.

Faith tugged her underwear off, and I reached into the nightstand for a foil packet.

For a moment, clutching the small square in my hand, I stared dazedly at her sprawled over the pristine white bedding. There was no way she was real, no way that somehow, I'd done enough good in my life to deserve someone like Faith laid out like this for me.

For years, she'd been my best friend. And now, she was every fucking fantasy come to life as she arched her back, sliding her nimble fingers around me until my chin dropped to my chest.

I covered her hand with mine and directed her until I had to yank those slim, strong fingers off before this ended way too soon.

"What are you waiting for?" she whispered, sitting up to kiss along my chest, finding my mouth open and waiting and greedy

My hands were clumsy, shaky in my haste to cross this line with her, the most important person in my life.

Tell her, tell her, tell her.

I blocked out the voice with a vicious snap of an iron door in my brain because, at this point, stopping just might kill me. And in the way she moved against me, the way she pressed desperately into my hand when I brought her to a moaning, body-wracking peak, it might kill Faith too.

Forehead pressed against her, her thighs snapped tight to my sides, I did nothing more than breathe her in when I carefully pushed forward, inch by delicious inch.

She fit me so perfectly.

Everything about her—the way she kissed, the way she filled my hands, the way her body responded to mine. This was no first time, no matter what our history said. I'd fight the truth of it until my knuckles were bloody because this woman wasn't new to me. She couldn't be, not with how good it was.

I wasn't sure if I believed in reincarnation, but if I'd ever lived another life, it was one spent with her.

With each roll of my hips, each shift of hers, sweat gathered at the base of my spine and dotted her chest. I licked it off, and she cursed under her breath when I locked her hands down on the bed with mine.

"More," I urged her, moving furiously between her legs until the bed creaked ominously.

"I can't."

I bit down on her bottom lip. "Come on, sunshine," I growled. "Give it to me."

Her teeth sank into the flesh of my shoulder, my skin absorbing her moans when I changed the angle of my movements.

There.

The angle, the speed, and her, everything rolled and burned

together under my skin until I shouted her name with my head tossed back.

She sobbed through a shuddering finish, and I sank against her body.

I gathered her to me, pressing soft kisses along the sweet lines of her face.

And when Faith's mouth curved into a pleased smile, I knew how completely and utterly wrecked I would be if she ever left me.

Chapter
TWENTY-TWO

Faith

"You haven't packed yet," I murmured drowsily. But instead of getting up, I tucked my hands under the pillow and buried my nose straight into it, the smell so fricken addictive that I worried I might steal the thing and take it home with me.

Dominic hummed low in his chest, bracketing me with his muscular thighs as his hands slid along my naked back.

It was truly amazing how relaxed one felt after two orgasms and a back massage from someone with really, really good hands.

"I'll throw some stuff together in the morning," he said.

"It is morning."

"Shhh, we're not worrying about what time it is right now." Dominic leaned down and trailed kisses down the length of my spine. "I don't need to leave until seven, which is at least another five hours."

After our first round, he'd fed me cereal in bed, then tugged me on top of him for round two. I liked round two a lot because

Dominic Walker was just as demanding from underneath as he was when he was on top, and it did good, good things to me.

It was my very first experience with the kind of sex that could make you feel crazy, make you want to push yourself beyond the worst of exhaustion, simply to have more.

With unerring accuracy, he pressed his fingers into a knot on my shoulders that had my hips tilting from the pressure it released.

"Holy fracksticks," I moaned. "Where did you learn that?"

"Just doing what would feel good to me, I guess."

"Don't ever, ever stop." I blew out a hard breath when he released another knot.

He gentled his movements, and I tried very hard not to pout when he slid back under the sheet and tugged me from my position on my stomach so that my arm was draped over his chest, my breasts pressed against his side. I set my chin on his chest and studied his face as he closed his eyes and let out a contented sigh.

When would this gentle side of him stop surprising me?

"You know," I said quietly, "I misjudged you too."

Dominic's eyes opened, that gaze locking onto mine.

My fingers traced the edge of his bottom lip, a dangerous weapon in its own right.

He propped a hand under his head so he could see me a bit better. "How's that?"

I kissed his chest, marveling at the softness of his skin over all the hard, hard muscle. "Even though we had such a good visit at the center that first time, I knew you weren't as horrible as our first meeting suggested." I paused to kiss him again, so he knew I was teasing. "Even with that, I was so sure I knew what would happen when you asked me out. I've known so many football players in my life. More than I can count."

"Uh-huh, let's not talk about them right now."

His surly tone had me nipping his chest. He pinched my butt, and I laughed.

"I would've bet everything I owned that you were going to take me to some obnoxious club, try to grind on me to terrible music, maybe cop a feel in the car and then pout when I wouldn't sleep with you on the first date because you took me to an obnoxious club to grind on me in the dark."

Dominic's chest shook with silent laughter. "How incredibly vivid your imagination is."

"I know." I shook my head. "You've surprised me, Dominic Walker. In the very best way. I'm glad you asked me out."

He turned us so that we faced each other, our legs tangled underneath the sheets. His affection was so easy, so unrestrained, and he studied my face while he tucked my hair behind my ear.

"Faith, I—" he started, his eyes searching mine.

There was a look on his face that had my heart thumping, my tummy going weightless with anticipation. I was feeling some crazy things too, falling in love things, but I wasn't sure we were ready to say them.

Carefully, I set my finger over his lips. "We have more than tonight."

His brow furrowed for a moment, and I took that finger off his lips and smoothed it over the adorable lines.

"Is it the devil and the angel again?" I teased.

The expression on his face faded into a smile. "Always."

With a devious hum, I shifted over top of him so that I was sprawled fully over his chest. "What is the devil telling you right now? What impulse shouldn't you follow?"

I was so intrigued because I'd never known someone like Dominic, who was so open about his bad habits when most people tried to hide them.

But instead of smiling, like I thought he might, or teasing me right back, like I'd hoped, Dominic looked torn.

I touched my lips to his. "What is it?"

"I wish I didn't have to leave tomorrow," he said, rubbing his thumb along my bottom lip. "I'd rather stay here with you, eat cereal in bed, go out to eat, go buy you flowers at the market."

"We can still do all those things when you get back."

"Maybe I won't go to the retreat," he said. "I won't even get to see you before the ball, then I leave again right after."

Dominic was staring straight up at the ceiling now, but his hand rubbed soothing circles on my back, almost like he was reassuring himself that I was still there, still real.

"You have to go," I told him.

His eyes found mine. "Is that an official girlfriend order?"

"Yes." I leaned down to kiss him softly. He tried to deepen it, but I pulled back when his tongue slicked over the line of my lips. "James never would've invited you if he didn't think it was important." I laid my head down on his chest and tried as best as I could to wrap my arms around him. "Whatever impulse is telling you this won't work, that they won't get over this, that you're doomed to be at odds with your team." I felt him tense underneath me, but I kept going. "You need to push that down. You've got too much good in you to keep hiding from people, Dominic."

He rolled us, rearing up over me with eyes so dark, so intense, that I felt a stirring of desire kindle somewhere under my skin.

"I'm not hiding," he said, low and dangerous.

My hands smoothed up his chest. "Not from me, you're not. From everyone else." He slid a hand up my leg until he pressed my knees wider, wider, and my breath hitched at how bared I was to him. "Y-you have nothing to hide."

"Not everyone is like you, sunshine." He curled his fingers between my legs, and my back snapped up in a helpless arch.

My hands scrambled to find purchase in the wrinkled sheets as he pulled out my pleasure like it was warm, pliable putty, stretching it impossibly far before it snapped back in a sharp, hot rush over my body.

Body trembling, I came down as he kissed over the lines of my ribs and pushed his palms up the length of my arms. This was the kind of connection I never actually thought was real. Cracked-open hearts while his body did unspeakably wonderful things to mine.

I never wanted it to end.

"What are you afraid of?" I whispered as he slid up my chest and licked the flat of his tongue over my sweat-damp skin.

He lifted his head, gaze searing and intense. Dominic sat up between my legs.

With his teeth, he tore open another foil packet, and I shivered at the look in his eyes. He wanted to stop me from saying what I was. But he didn't.

"There is so much good in you," I managed as he started moving forward, so slowly that my jaw clenched.

"No, there's not." He snapped his hips. Hard enough that I might bruise. I threw my head back from the force, bracing my hand on the wall behind my head.

"You're so good," I gasped. He did it again, and I wasn't sure what I said after that. Wasn't sure it was English, or that he could understand. His control blew my mind because he moved so steady with such sharp, unwavering intensity. I'd never walked the tightrope for this long before. Every time I was about to pitch forward over the edge, he'd slow. Then build, and build, the crest just out of reach. "Dominic," I begged in a keening voice.

And instead of torturing us further, the man with the dark eyes and the big heart surrounded by such high, high walls, he unleashed himself on me. He exorcised whatever demons he'd heeded for so long. His gaze on mine was naked, hiding absolutely nothing of what he felt for me.

In that look, I knew he'd adore me forever. He'd move heaven and earth to protect whatever we were building, and it took every ounce of self-control not to tell him I'd fallen in love with him.

He must have seen the same thing in mine because he braced

a palm on the bed next to my head and wrenched my leg tight up against his chest.

By the time he finished, with his arm curled around the back of my neck, hand gripping my shoulder now, I was sobbing in relief. My toes curled helplessly at what he'd pulled out of me. Nothing else could be wrung from my body after that. I was limp, spent, sweaty, and deliriously happy.

Without a single word, but with so much tenderness, he cleaned me up. Then he curled his big body around mine, and I fell into a deep, dreamless sleep.

Chapter
TWENTY-THREE

Faith

When I woke up the next morning, it was to an empty bed and a note he'd left on the nightstand.

Good morning, sunshine. Given you were comatose when I got up, I decided to let you sleep. I won't have my phone on me during the day but help yourself to whatever you can find in the fridge and lock the door when you leave.

I'll see you Saturday.

It was impossible to keep the grin off my face as I stretched my sore, sore body out in his bed. Without anyone watching, I was able to tug his pillow up to my face, clutch my arms around it and inhale greedily.

If this is what good sex felt like, it was no freaking wonder it had the capacity to ruin people's lives when they chased after it.

One night spent with Dominic Walker was a revelation, and I did not say such things lightly as a pragmatic person. Not just what had happened with us physically but it was almost like he'd lost any ability to hold his armor up anymore.

It made me wonder how he managed to keep it up for an entire football season, what kind of people he'd been surrounded by that he was able to. The guy I'd been getting to know, who was sweet and thoughtful, openly affectionate, and had a clear soft spot for kids, seemed to be a different person than the guy who walked through the doors of the Wolves training facilities, who suited up on the sidelines with his teammates.

Sitting up in his bed, I studied his bedroom because I'd been a tad distracted when we entered the night before. Like the rest of his house, it gave no clues to his personality. Nothing that I could use to get to know him even better.

"I hate this apartment," I said out loud.

Tugging the sheet over my shoulders, I got out of bed and wandered to the closet. When I pushed open the door, I laughed out loud.

The room was huge, a closet that Lydia would've filled in a heartbeat, and Dominic was using less than a quarter of the space. Jeans were folded neatly on a shelf next to some white-labeled storage bins. Shaking my head, I gently studied some of the clothes that hung on matching black hangers. There was nothing showy, nothing that he'd dropped hundreds and hundreds of dollars on.

The fancy shiny apartment filled with a regular guy who didn't quite know how to fit the space.

A black leather jacket caught my eye, and I grinned, imagining him wearing it. It was well-worn and well-loved, and because I couldn't help my smitten self, I tugged it off the hanger and brought the jacket close to my chest.

Yes, I was smitten. It was the only way to describe all the flittering, fluttering things happening inside of my body. It reminded me of the first few days of high school, where every guy you locked eyes with was a potential crush and every conversation held opportunity, except you couldn't quite see where it was going to go.

It was something I'd lost after Charlie. I didn't want to lock eyes. Didn't want to see potential crushes. And with a smirk, I knew just how far I'd come because, in the past twelve hours, there'd been no dead fish anywhere in that bed.

There was one bad-ass Faith Pierson, though, who drove a guy like Dominic Walker out of his damn mind. It was a powerful feeling, especially as I strode naked through his closet, covered by nothing but the sheets we'd thoroughly used.

Even without him around, the effect he had was staggering. The smell of leather, and him, surrounded me, and I fought against the sensation that I missed him.

Not once had I met a man who could bulldoze his way through every single reservation I might have, every single logical next step I thought we needed. I was in his closet, wrapped in his sheets, sniffing his clothes, and missing him.

And because no one was watching and no one could judge what I was doing, I hugged the jacket to my chest.

The sound of crinkling paper had me pulling the jacket away. In the inside pocket, there was an envelope, and just past that, the worn edge of a picture.

As I saw the edge of the picture, dark hair held back by a pink barrette, I thought of what Dominic said about opposing forces telling you what you should and shouldn't do. We all had experiences with that, right?

But it wasn't an actual person with horns or wings. It was just our own internal compass telling us which instinct we should listen to. Maybe his compass was calibrated differently than mine because of his upbringing, the things he went through, but something about being in his closet, surrounded by his things, I found myself following the impulse that I might normally have ignored.

The picture came out with a gentle tug, and at the sight of her face, I felt a strange thump in my stomach, a stirring of recognition that took a moment to filter through my brain.

It was a school picture, the same boring gray background that we'd all had at some point in our lives. She couldn't have been much more than six in the picture because her big smile showed all the perfectly neat little baby teeth she wouldn't have lost yet at that age.

Her eyes were big, heavily lashed, just like Dominic's, and for a moment, I wondered if it was his daughter. She wore a tie-dye shirt, and that recognition again, it rang like a bell somewhere in the back of my head.

When I flipped the picture over, I understood why.

In big, childish writing, with her y written backward, was scrawled *Ivy Lee Walker, 6 years old*.

When he'd adopted the koala, the name he sent, where the In Honor Of that still proclaimed it hers at the zoo, read Ivy Lee. I'd always assumed it was her last name, not her middle name.

My heart raced, thoughts and realizations tumbling through my head in a big sloppy mess.

How was this even possible?

I'd seen her picture once before. It was one of the only photos Nick had ever sent me, on the anniversary of her death, about a year after we'd first started chatting.

But by the time he sent me one of his little sister, she'd lost her hair and had wrapped a tie-dye scarf around her head. But it was—undoubtedly, unequivocally, illogically, impossibly—the same little girl.

"Holy shitsticks," I breathed out. I whipped around, staring at the rumpled bed like it would explain itself to me after what had happened.

But of course, there was no one there to help me figure out why or how.

All the different conversations I'd had with both of them melted together in my head, which was impressive because I was still standing naked in Dominic's closet. I scrambled to the kitchen, where my purse had ended up on the floor. It was lying underneath my dress, and my cheeks were flaming hot as I kicked that out of the way. My phone had a few texts from Tori, telling me to enjoy my night, and then another one from Dominic, which he must have sent just after he left the apartment earlier that morning.

When I clicked on it, my breath caught because he'd taken a picture of me sleeping. It was like peeping through someone's window at a scene I wasn't meant to see. Something intimate and sexy. Dominic must've crouched next to the bed with his camera up close to my face.

The sheet appeared nowhere in the shot, so while I looked like I wasn't covered, he'd managed a shot where nothing showed that I didn't want captured on his camera. My mouth was slightly open, lips pursed, and my lashes long and dark against my cheeks as I slept. All the dark hair around my head looked tangled and mussed, and in the bottom of the frame, the shadow my cleavage showed where my arm covered my breasts.

And then I saw the text that accompanied it, and my breath caught for an entirely different reason.

> **Dominic:** Don't say I don't ever ignore my baser instincts because seeing you like this, it was almost impossible not to touch you, to wake you up the way I wanted to.

> **Dominic:** I'll be back in twenty-six hours, and I'm not even pretending I wanted to be gone that long right now. I'll see you tomorrow, sunshine.

I covered my mouth with a shaking hand because the things I was feeling, knowing he was Nick, knowing that he wasn't putting on some show to get me in bed, wasn't pretending to be something he wasn't, I could've burst into happy tears right there in his really awful family room.

I tried to type out a response, but it immediately came back as undeliverable.

Me: Tomorrow. I really, really wish you were here right now.

When the bright red notification that it was undeliverable popped up, I snatched up my dress with a frustrated huff. Tugging on my clothes with all this knowledge bubbling around in my body was so ... frustrating. No, it was worse than that. It was like hours of foreplay, but I was left without the climax, the thing that had been building and building and building.

There was no way I could just sit on this.

My message thread with Nick had my heart turning over again because all the things I knew about him, paired with what I'd learned about Dominic, I could hardly keep my fingers steady enough to type.

TurboGirl: Let me know when you get this. I need to talk to you.

The message sent, but I couldn't tell if it delivered or not, so I set my phone down with a groan. It got worse when I opened his kitchen cupboards and saw about ten boxes of cereal. My smile probably looked borderline psychotic. After a bowl of Captain Crunch, I finished dressing. And because I'd been raised to pick up my mess, I made his bed carefully, the edges of the sheets neatly folded.

As I walked out of the apartment, I tapped out another text.

Me: I don't know what your schedule is like, but this is a code red BFF situation, and if you have plans after work, I need you to cancel them pronto.

Tori: Code red? Yeesh. Okay. Did the bad boy turn out to be a waste of good underwear?

Me: Not even close to a waste. I'll tell you everything later.

Tori: I can be home by four.

Chapter TWENTY-FOUR

Faith

"**D**ID YOU KNOW THAT FEMALE KOALAS IN CAPTIVITY OFTEN mate with other females, and their sexual encounters can last up to five times as long as female-male encounters?"

Tori froze for only a moment but recovered quickly, setting down her drink and giving me an even look.

"First," she said calmly, "I have a degree in Zoo Science, you dingbat, so yes, I knew that." Then her lips curled up into a smile. "And second, are we actually surprised by the fact that men can't last long?"

Pushing the hardcover koala book away from me, I gave her a smug look. "Some men can."

"Oh geez, with the bragging and the smirking and the delicious sex memories." Tori took a sip of her drink. She was being remarkably calm, not pushing me for the dirty details. "So we like him? The tattooed bad boy who adores you?"

It made me laugh, but honestly, I couldn't argue. Three times, he'd worshipped me, and if we'd had time or the energy, he might have gone for round four, judging by the text I'd had waiting on my phone.

But instead of answering her question, I played with the edge of the koala book. Naturally, koalas reminded me of Ivy, which was why I'd pulled the book out in the first place. Reminded me of him. All day, I turned the situation over in my head until I thought I'd go crazy for not being able to process it with someone. Anyone.

And this wasn't something I wanted to tell him over the phone when he was working for one of his sponsors all day.

"I have to tell you something crazy," I started.

Tori's shoulders slumped in relief. "Holy shit, finally, I have been dying here pretending like I didn't want to shake it out of you."

"You know Nick, right?"

At my careful shift in the topic, Tori paused in confusion, then rolled her eyes. "Obvs. Drives me crazy when I can hear you tap-tap-tapping on your phone when you're sitting next to me on the couch."

I held my breath before I blurted it out on a rushed exhale. "Nick is Dominic Walker."

Her cup hit the table with a loud thunk. "I'm sorry, what now?"

"They're the same guy."

"Shut *up*."

With a shrug, I couldn't help but laugh at her dumbstruck expression. "I know! I couldn't believe it, but I saw a picture of his sister before I left his apartment."

"After your sex-fest. With the guy that is both people."

I covered my face with my hands. "Yes."

"How does this shit even happen to you? Honestly."

"I don't know," I wailed. My hands settled back into my lap, and I felt the whole roller coaster again. It was insane. And amazing. And insane. "He's like, one of my best friends, Tor."

"Umm, who's your best friend?"

I gave her a look.

"Sorry. Just wanted to verify that I haven't lost my place because that's like … the whole package he's got right there."

"You have not lost your place. But yes, it's him. He's Nick. Which is even crazier because he was such an asshole the day we met—" My voice trailed off. Everything clicked into place.

"What?"

"Holy shit," I whispered. "That's why he was acting so crazy the day we met. The attitude and why he reeked of alcohol. Oh my gosh, Tori, it was the anniversary of Ivy's death. That's why he got trashed on the field, and that's why he was in such a terrible mood."

Her face softened in understanding.

"He told me, on our chat that day, that he got in trouble at work." I speared a hand through my hair and shook my head. "This is so crazy."

"I'd be remiss not to point out, though," she said gently, "a lot of people have sad, awful days that remind them of bad things, and they don't get drunk at work." Whatever facial expression I made had her cackling. "Oh my gosh, you're ready to claw my eyes out for saying something bad about him. Look at little miss defensive girlfriend right now!"

"It's hard not to feel that way," I protested quietly. "He's … he's so different than I thought at first. And knowing that he's Nick, the guy I've talked to about so many things the last couple of years, it just makes it even better." I laughed. "I even talked to him about *him*. I told Nick that I wanted to sleep with Dominic after one date."

Tori's eyes sharpened. "He didn't know it was you, right?"

"How could he have? Millions of people live in Seattle, and we never talked about what we did for a living. I never told him about Allie or who my dad is or the Wolves."

"And he never told you he was a professional football player?" Her eyes widened dramatically. "Usually, they can't shut up about it."

"Usually, they can't," I agreed. I'd turned that part over in my head all day too. "I think … I think he didn't because of me."

"What do you mean?"

"I messaged Nick for the first time a little over three years ago." I raised my eyebrows meaningfully. "Right after Charlie."

"Ahh. And you told him about the douche?"

"I did indeed." Slowly, I spun my phone on the table. I'd read so many of our message exchanges when I should have been reviewing grants and following up on emails. Every single sentence from Nick was now a fascinating insight into the man I was falling in love with. That and some in-depth googling, something I didn't usually do on any player.

Dominic's entire life, he'd been underestimated. His potential was never recognized until he forced people to look at him. Once they did, it was impossible not to see how good he was at his job. And in a way, he'd done the exact same thing with me. The moment he had my full attention, there was no way I could unsee it. Whatever preconceived notion I'd had of Dominic Walker, he'd torn it down until I didn't have a choice but to see him fully.

"I didn't give him every detail about Charlie," I said. "But I was in my active *hate all the football players* mode."

Her eyes widened. "I remember. It wasn't pretty."

"I guess I'll add it to the list of things to talk about with him."

"And you're going to tell him at the ball? You sure you don't want to wait until you have a little more privacy?"

I nodded. "Not blowing up his phone right now is about all the restraint I can handle."

"But you messaged him at first, right?"

"I was so … shocked. I didn't think through the fact that he was flying. I tried calling, but his phone was off. And I don't think he's checking the messenger app where I talked to him as Nick."

"What'd you say in that one?"

I slid her my phone. But before she opened that app, she saw the text thread with Dominic.

When she scrolled up far enough that the pic appeared, she whistled quietly.

"Damn, girl. That's some softcore hot shit right there."

"It's always been my life goal," I said dryly.

"You've got a real-life *You've Got Mail* situation going on here, but he is no Tom Hanks waiting with a golden retriever and some daisies." She shook her head. "It's so much better than that."

The picture she painted made my heart positively gallop. The thought of Dominic in that type of scenario might make me spontaneously combust into a pile of love-sick, heart-shaped goo. He'd have a smirk on his dangerously handsome face, some wildflowers clutched in his big hands, and even as he'd sweep me into his arms like the end of an epically romantic movie, he'd probably whisper in my ear all the filthy things he wanted to do to me when we were alone.

I would walk into the Black and White Ball with my absolute dream man on my arm, and I wasn't sure there could be anything better than that.

"Uh-oh, I've lost her," Tori teased.

I blinked. "Sorry, you derailed me with the whole rom-com ending thing."

"What are you going to do?"

"Let him do his job. Tell him the first chance I get."

"It's a solid plan, kid."

"Thanks," I told her.

"So ... how good was it?" she asked with a sly smile.

I slumped in my chair with a sigh, and she laughed.

"If I didn't love you so much, I'd hate you."

I grinned. "Yeah?"

She leaned back. "You found a tattooed football player who is not only good in bed but he also has a tortured heart of gold that he hides from everyone except you. Yeah, you're a giant bitch, Faith Pierson, and I adore you until the end of time."

Listening to her discuss him, I got my first real flutters of reality. Dominic Walker was my boyfriend—before that, he'd been one of my best friends—and once he was back, there would be no hiding it. He wasn't someone I'd ever keep in the dark. I'd never pretend he wasn't important to me.

"I hope my parents have that same reaction when he comes with me on Saturday," I told her. "My dad is still wary after the whole Charlie thing. I can't blame him."

Tori whistled. "Yeah, Daddy Luke may have a coronary, but you know Allie will tell him what's up, and then Lydia will do something insane to distract him, and all will be normal again."

"Help me choose my dress?" I asked her. "If my dad is going to have a coronary, then I want Dominic to lose his *mind* when he sees me."

She was up and out of her chair before the words were out of my mouth.

In my room, she was already pulling out the two garment bags I'd had sent over from Allie's stylist. Tori unzipped the first bag and made some purring sound, like she was a satisfied cat licking cream off its whiskers. "Oh mah gawd, look at this one."

I peeked over her shoulder. "I'm fairly certain Lydia told the stylist to include it just to torment me."

"You have to wear it."

"What about the one with the high neck?" I touched the silky black material. "That's nice too."

Tori swatted my hand away with a tsking sound. "No, no, my child. Would I steer you wrong after the cardigan?"

"It really was magical," I conceded.

"Then you trust me." My friend turned and set her hands on my shoulders. "This will be your night, Faith. It's about time you're getting all the perks of being such a fucking amazing human being."

After giving her a tight squeeze, I studied the dress again. "I need that magic boob tape."

"Yes, that's a given because we cannot have the girls going anywhere." She eyed me with a wicked grin. "You going to tease him with what you're wearing? I would after that text he sent this morning. Wowza."

"No teasing," I told her. "This might be the craziest thing that's ever happened to me, but it's not a game. I just want to see him and know there are no secrets between us."

Chapter
TWENTY-FIVE

Faith

In the end, it was thunderstorms in Chicago that derailed my perfect rom-com plan.

Dominic was stuck there hours beyond what he'd planned because the pilots wouldn't risk takeoff in such moody weather, all reds and oranges and yellows on the doppler loop I'd watched all morning after he texted he would make it but might be a touch later than he thought.

He still hadn't seen my text to Nick, and for that, I was grateful.

The ballroom was bustling with athletes and celebrities, philanthropists, and the elite of the Pacific Northwest. They wandered the immaculately decorated tables, perused the silent auction, and wrote down bids as they sipped their expensive wine and ate the expensive food on china plates. And as the clock ticked forward, there was no sign of Dominic.

I'd been busy enough talking with people as they passed that I hadn't fully panicked that he was ditching me, that something I'd done had led to this. But when I left the ballroom, I was greeted with an empty corridor. It was just about the worst thing that could've happened to me, given the jittery energy I had coursing through my veins. Dinner would start in thirty minutes, and as it stood, the seat next to me would be empty while the keynote speaker stood to give their speech.

He was a graduate of one of the schools that Team Sutton supported when they branched out from Allie's initial mission. The addition of providing extracurricular programs for underserved schools and communities. His ability to take part in an arts program for the first time spawned a passion that he'd turned into a career, earning a spot at the prestigious ArtCenter College of Design in Pasadena. He'd bring in donations hand over fist, which was always the goal of evenings like that one, where Team Sutton had worked all year on a few hours in a fancy ballroom.

And there I was, the one at the helm of the organization, pacing an empty hallway because the boy I liked was late, and I was freaking out that I wouldn't have time to tell him this really big thing.

I laid a hand on my stomach, which growled ominously. My nerves were jacked so high from the night itself and now Dominic that I couldn't fathom touching any food. Against the white of my dress and the pale pink of my manicure, my hands looked tan even though it felt very much like the blood wasn't flowing properly through my body.

The asymmetrical neckline and sweeping cutout made it look like a river of skin showed through the dress. It started up by my collarbone in a gently flowing line, following the curve of my chest and giving the slightest peek at the top of the opposite hip. A slit cut up to the thigh exposed the leg in the opposite direction, like my body had been draped with a fluid column of white. The makeup artist kept my lips nude and my eye makeup in shimmering tones of gold, thick lashes the only real accessory needed to complement the dress.

It was, undoubtedly, the most glamorous I'd ever looked in my entire life. And inside, I was still a nervous wreck.

My phone was somewhere inside the ballroom, tucked away

The LIE

into a beaded clutch that held nothing except that and a tube of lip-gloss. When I last checked it, Dominic had told me he was on his way, and that was over an hour ago.

"You okay, sweetie?"

I looked up, not even realizing someone had joined me in the hallway. My mom's executive assistant was giving me a concerned look. She'd known me for so long, she could probably read my nerves all over my face.

I smiled, or as much of one as I could muster. "Yeah, just a little nervous. I've never had to give a speech at one of these things."

She touched my cheek. "You'll knock 'em dead, kid. You've got some tough genes, you know."

"I know." I gave her a brief squeeze. "Thank you, Connie."

"Need me to get Allie or your dad?"

"No," I told her immediately. "They can do more good in there schmoozing."

She laughed. "Okay. Good luck, Faith."

Feeling slightly calmer, I took a deep breath and turned to use the ladies' room before I went back in.

But I stopped short when I saw him at the end of the hallway. Dominic stood with his shoulder leaning against the wall, his hands tucked into the perfectly tailored tuxedo pants. The jacket was flawless, cut to fit his wide shoulders in a way that had my heart racing, and even with how immaculately it fit him, it held nothing on his face.

For a second, all I could do was drink him in, the dark shadow on his hard jaw, the sharp intensity in the way his eyes coasted down the curving lines that hugged my torso and hips.

I inhaled sharp and quick when his gaze locked on my face. Because what I saw there was like staring straight into the eye of a hurricane. He wanted me. It was there in the center of all the stormy chaos that he couldn't quite hold back.

Then he was moving, and so was I. We met in the middle, his

hands gripping the sides of my face as his mouth took mine in a fearsome kiss. His tongue swept into my mouth, a groan torn from his big chest as I clutched my hands to his back.

Dominic pivoted us to the side, and there was a wall at my back, so I could do nothing except hold on tight for the onslaught of whatever was happening between us.

This man, with his dangerous kisses and overwhelming heart, had somehow turned out to be exactly what I wanted. And not just wanted, but what I needed. Sometimes they were different, no matter how much we wanted them to be the same. When I writhed restlessly against his hardness, his hands slid down the curve of my waist, stopping to swipe his thumb over the peak of my breast. My hands wrapped around his neck, and I couldn't believe how quickly it was like this between us.

Right there, in the hallway with the Seattle elite just on the other side of the doors, I arched into his touch when he slid his hand up the slit in my dress, cupping my bottom with a firm grip.

His kisses were sharp and hot and wet, something desperate in the way he touched me, the way he breathed hard through his nose because neither one of us dared pull away. I wasn't sure if his reasons were the same as mine, but something inside told me that the minute we stopped, something would change.

That thought was enough to have me break away from his mouth with a gasp. Dominic kissed the edge of my mouth, slicking his tongue along my bottom lip.

"You look so beautiful," he whispered, stopping to suck my earlobe into his mouth.

I laughed shakily. "Thank you. I'll need to check my makeup before I go back in."

Dominic lifted his head, gaze tracing every inch of my face. "You're perfect."

"I missed you," I admitted. "You were gone for two days, and I missed you."

"Why do you say it like it's a bad thing?"

"It's not, I guess." I tucked a piece of hair behind my ear, and his eyes warmed when I did.

"Did I mention that you look beautiful?"

I laughed softly. "Thank you." Smoothing my hands along his chest, I stopped over his heart and took comfort in the hard, steady pounding underneath my palm. It was grounding to know that he was as affected by this as I was. I wasn't alone in this. "I'm glad we have a minute alone."

"Yeah?" he murmured, ducking his head to kiss the tip of my nose. "How much did you miss me?"

"You want a list?"

"Say it slow," he said, smoothing his hands up and down my arms. "In that voice I like."

I laughed. "We don't have long before I have to go in there, but I wanted to talk to you about something."

He was still staring at my mouth. "What about?"

In a halting voice, I told him about waking up at his place and going into his closet. Finding his jacket.

Dominic's face was an unreadable mask when I licked my lips and told him about the picture of Ivy.

"I-I saw her picture once," I told him carefully. "And I know how insane this will sound, but you're Nick ... aren't you?"

His jaw clenched, his gaze searching deeply into mine.

I gave him a tentative smile, gently touching my necklace, currently hidden under the white of my dress. "I'm Turbo. It was, it was my nickname growing up."

His chest expanded as his breathing picked up speed. Then it was his turn to lick his lips before speaking. "You knew when you messaged Nick about needing to talk?"

"Yes," I breathed. "I-I freaked out when I saw her picture, Dominic. I tried to call, but your phone was off because you were flying. I didn't even think. Then I knew I should wait until I could tell you in person." With a laughing exhalation, I pressed against him, sliding my hands up along his face. "I was such a wreck waiting for you to get here."

Dominic exhaled in a relieved rush. "I didn't open it. I... was worried you might have said something about our night being too much..." His voice trailed off.

It took me a second, in the heady exchange, the absolute relief of having the truth out there, for his words to penetrate.

"You knew before I messaged you?" I whispered.

There was a flare of panic in his dark eyes, gone in the next instant, but I saw it. If his desire for me was the eye of the hurricane, then this was bright bolts of lightning, a warning to stay back.

I didn't.

Chapter TWENTY-SIX

Dominic

I ALWAYS HATED THE SAYING ABOUT CURIOSITY KILLING THE CAT. Because in this scenario, I'd been really fucking curious. What would happen if Faith only had the one side of me to choose from? Would she want me?

I knew the answer now. Unequivocally.

And as for what would happen if she found out first ... this was it. Faith Pierson was pissed.

"When did you know?" she pressed. The color was high in her cheeks, her dark eyes flashing.

My jaw clenched tight because every defensive instinct roared not to concede this easily.

"Does it matter?" I asked.

Her mouth fell open. "Yes, it matters. When did you know?"

Only the smallest shred of self-preservation had me answering through a tight mouth because the truth of how betrayed she'd feel had me wanting to flay my skin off. "When I came back to the center. When your car wouldn't start."

"What?" She gasped. "You've known that long?"

"Faith," I started, "hear me out—"

She swept her arms out. "Oh, by all means, explain this to me, Dominic."

Panic crashed against my ribs at her sardonic tone, making my hands tingle and my heart race. What an idiot I'd been. And instead of saying that, something horrible hissed and snapped at the back of my head.

As I stood there silently, Faith stepped away from me, her face draining of color.

"I talked to you, *about* you," she whispered. "About wanting to *sleep* with you."

My eyes burned. "Faith." My voice cracked on her name.

"How did that feel?" she asked. "Hearing me tell you how badly I wanted to screw you."

The air around us went cold, and if she'd taken a knife to my gut, it probably would've hurt less. And I deserved all of it.

"Don't make it ugly," I begged. "It wasn't easy for me."

Her eyebrows rose on her forehead. "I bet it wasn't. To lie to me. To ... what? See how far you could take it?" She exhaled a shaky laugh. "God, everything you knew about me. Asking me about my dating rule. No wonder you knew exactly what to say. I practically handed you a script of how to get me into bed."

"It wasn't like that," I hissed.

"Wasn't it?" she asked quietly. If she'd yelled, it would've tripped the wire on my temper, and because it was her, she knew that. From the beginning, she'd known exactly what I needed, exactly how to dig out the most vulnerable parts of me. Then her eyes filled, and for the first time in my life, I knew true and real self-loathing.

I paced the small hallway. "I'm sorry, Faith. It was ... it was stupid." I came to a halt in front of her, clasping her hands in mine. "I was wrong, and I'm sorry."

A tear slid down her cheek, and she pulled her hands from mine so she could wipe it away. "I *trusted* you."

"You still can," I told her fervently. "You still can."

Faith stepped back. "Dominic, you used my past as a way to benefit that part of you that still doesn't ... I don't know ... doesn't believe that I'd actually want you. You used this awful thing I went through as a way to manipulate me."

Her voice grew in strength, and as it did, I felt her slipping through my fingers. It didn't matter if she was right in front of me. Didn't matter what I said at this moment, if I tried to kiss her anger away, if I touched her in just the right way.

"I wasn't trying to manipulate you." I jammed a hand through my hair and tugged, a useless outlet for my frustration. What I really wanted to do was break something, just to see it shatter into a million un-fixable pieces. Something that would be more work than fixing whatever drove me to do such stupid, stupid shit. "I knew I needed to tell you, Faith. Every fucking time we were together, I thought about it."

"Then why didn't you?" she cried. "Why didn't you tell me?"

"Because I don't always do the right thing!" I yelled. "I'm fucking human, and I mess up. It's not always so simple as knowing the right thing and just doing it."

Her cheeks were high with color. "I don't always do the right thing, Dominic, but I would never lie to someone I was fall—" Her voice broke off.

My attention sharpened on her face. "Someone you were what?"

Her mouth flattened into a line.

"Someone you were falling in love with?" I finished, voice growing louder. "Why do you think I didn't say anything? It was almost too good to be true. You were exactly the kind of thing I never thought I'd have. Even before I knew who you were, I wanted you. And not for a million dollars did I think you'd ever want me back in the same way."

"So you had to what, prove a point? That I could fall in love with you even if you weren't the man I've respected for so long? That is bullshit, Dominic." Maybe Faith was feeling that hot rush of anger like I always did when I gave in to the snapping, snarling impulse to make someone feel just as shitty as I was inside. And I couldn't blame her. Not for a single second. "I have *never* made you feel like you were below me."

"I *was* below you," I yelled. "Look at what I did."

She glanced down the hallway. "Calm down, please," she begged. "Please don't make a scene. Not here."

A door opened just around the corner, and when I caught a glimpse of Allie leaving the ballroom, I swiped a hand over my forehead, then looked down at my hands. "Look at what I did," I said more quietly.

Faith sniffled, tears streaming down her face unchecked.

"Faith?" Allie called. Her eyes darted uncomfortably between us. "What happened?"

"Go," she whispered to me. Her stepmom hurried to her side, but I couldn't tear my gaze from Faith. My insides were ice cold, and I wanted to take a crowbar to my ribs, pry it out, and get rid of this feeling coating my veins.

If we'd been alone, I might have fallen to my knees in front of her. Tried to make this right.

I wanted to let Faith warm me, take all that goodness in her and absorb it. But until I could fix what I'd done, until I could repair all the broken shards laying around us, I'd lost the right to do that.

"I'm sorry," I said again, staggering back.

How had I let it get this far? Why did I think it wouldn't leave her feeling betrayed and manipulated?

With a final look, memorizing that absolute fucking heartbreak on her beautiful face, I turned and did as she asked.

I walked away.

Faith

My knees gave out, and I sank back against the wall. Allie was in front of me in the next heartbeat. "Oh honey, come here."

I held my hand out. "No. If you hug me right now, I will lose it," I whispered.

My dad joined, concern stamped all over his face. "What happened?"

We both ignored him. I couldn't say it. And Allie, I think she knew if she said anything of what she'd just seen, my dad would go after Dominic without a second thought.

Allie looked me straight in the eye with her hands on either side of my face. "Tell me what you need, Faith. Do you need to get out of here? We can do whatever you want."

"What happened?" he repeated. "Are you okay?"

Somehow, I nodded. "I just ... I think I just had my heart broken again," I choked out.

Allie's eyes filled.

"I could go slash his tires," my dad muttered. "Or rip his balls off."

A watery laugh escaped my mouth on a sob. "No, I don't want that."

I tilted my head up and took a few deep breaths.

"Turbo," my dad said quietly.

"I'm so sorry this happened, Faith." Allie shook her head. "I really thought underneath all of that, he would turn out to be something special."

"He is," I said quietly. When my dad opened his mouth to argue, I held up my hand. "He is. But I think, I think he doesn't know how to let people see it. Not that it makes it okay," I added.

From the hallway, Connie joined us with a gentle clearing of her throat. "Dinner is starting if you want to join us. Allie, they're ready for you in five."

"Go," I told her. I dabbed my face with a handkerchief that my dad produced from … somewhere. It came away with a smudge of makeup, but that was it. I blew out a slow breath.

She shook her head. "No, not if you need me. They can wait."

It was said so simply, with such certainty, that I almost collapsed into her arms and let the tears flow again.

I held her face like she'd held mine. "Go, Mom. I'll be right in after you. This is important."

"So are you," she said. Her eyes, so bright in her beautiful face, sparkled with unshed tears. "I love you."

"Love you too." Gently, I pressed my forehead to hers. "And when it's my turn up there tonight, I'm going to kick ass because I learned how from you."

Disobeying my no-hug rule, Allie gave me a tight squeeze and then pecked my dad's lips.

She gave me one last look. "Are you sure you can do your speech?"

I nodded.

Connie handed me a small bag. "There are eye drops and some blush in there, sweetheart."

"Thank you, Connie." My dad smoothed a hand along my back, and I gave him a tremulous smile. "I ruined your handkerchief."

"I don't give a shit," he said, studying me with concern.

I laughed quietly. Setting a hand over my chest, I took a quick inventory of whether I could actually do this.

Could I set aside that huge part of me that wanted to run after him? My entire body hurt from what had just happened. All the skin covering my bones ached from sheer heart-hurt.

Allie was still standing with us. "Faith, I'm serious. I can step in if you need to go."

I shook my head. "No. I can do this. But can I maybe sleep at home tonight?"

My dad smiled. "Of course."

Allie blew me a kiss. "You can do this."

"I can." Because that was part of life. Things hurt. They were difficult, and we didn't use them as an excuse to knock over the things that mattered. To hurt people the way we were hurting. Maybe it wasn't that simple for everyone, but I knew it was true for me. "I'll see you in there."

She left with Connie, and my dad cleared his throat, blinking a little more rapidly than was normal.

"You okay?" I asked gently.

His eyes were a little red. "Never better, Turbo." He held out his elbow. "You ready?"

My eyes watered again, but I did the same rapid blinking that seemed to work for my big, burly, tattooed dad, who was only brought to his knees by the women he adored.

"I think so," I whispered. "But my heart hurts a little."

I curled my hand around his elbow, and he patted it with his hand. "We'll walk with you until it doesn't hurt so much."

Which was what he did.

Somehow, I made it through the event with a smile on my face, even if everything else was curling up in agony inside. By the time I got back to my apartment to pack up some clothes, slipped off my heels, and sank onto the couch with an exhausted sigh, I finally pulled my phone out of my clutch.

My heart stopped when I saw a call and message from Dominic about an hour earlier.

With shaking hands, in the quiet of my place, I hit the button to play the message. I should've braced for impact at the sound of his voice, but I didn't, and it was stupid.

"Sunshine, I…" He stopped, voice uneven and slow and rough. "I'm such a fucking asshole."

The tears started immediately, and I did nothing to stop the trails they left down my face.

"I don't know why I let it go that long. I knew it was wrong. I just…" He paused, letting out an unsteady breath. "I was scared that because I didn't tell you immediately, I had to tiptoe around it until things were exactly right. It was so fucking stupid. I fell in love with you so fast, sunshine."

A sob escaped my mouth before I could stop it, and I pinched my eyes shut because I was so glad he wasn't in front of me.

If he'd been in front of me saying those things, admitting how scared he was, I might have forgiven him, might have overlooked how screwed up his reaction was. Still, my body fairly shook from the desire to wrap my arms around him, and I had to pause the voicemail and let the feeling pass before I could continue.

I hit play and let the message continue.

"You are the first girl I have ever wanted to be with, Faith Pierson. The first girl I have ever fallen in love with. And I don't know how to do that," he admitted quietly. "I should be saying this to your face, and I know this is all wrong, but I want you to hear it in a way that you can… I don't know, process it or whatever. That's probably selfish too." Dominic breathed out a harsh laugh. "But you know me, you know me so well, and I hope you can forgive me. I wish I could say that I'd never hurt you, but I already have. And I don't…" His voice broke off. "I don't know how to forgive myself for that."

Silence stretched out in the message, and I held my breath.

"That's it, I guess. If you want to call me, talk to me, anything, just let me know. And if you don't, I-I get it. Good night, sunshine."

WASHINGTON WOLVES

Chapter
TWENTY-SEVEN

Faith

"Can I watch it again?"

I threw a pillow at Lydia. "Please don't. I've heard the sound of my voice quite enough."

"You were so good, though, Faith." My sister, propped on her stomach with her pillow scrunched underneath her chin, swiped her finger across the screen of her tablet again. "Look how many views already. You're going to go viral!"

"Just what I always wanted."

She laughed at my muttered answer. My old bedroom was empty because instead of using the room down the hall with the soft white walls and big windows overlooking Lake Washington, I snuggled under Lydia's blanket instead, which was where we'd slept.

My little sister was the perfect person to host a post-breakup sleepover.

Which was why Tori was here too. She popped her head up from the mattress we'd dragged into the room and set up on the floor. In a house with six bedrooms, we'd turned my sister's old room into a chaotic mess.

"I'd watch it again," my best friend chimed in. "At least the end. Gawd, you were so freaking amazing, Faith. I hope he sees it."

My chest hurt when she said it because the timing of my speech sure did look like I was making a jab at him.

"It wasn't about him, Tor," I told her. "I've had that speech written for over a week."

Lydia gave me a look.

"It was! I can show you the note on my phone when I last edited it."

"I'm sharing it to my page," my sister said, speaking out loud as she typed.

"You are not," I chided.

Lydia hit a button with relish. And Tori snatched her phone off the floor, cackling when she saw it. "Oh, she did. You think he'll see it?"

"It's not about him," Lydia mimicked me in a sweet voice.

I threw a pillow at her blond head.

My voice filled the room as Tori listened to the clip, again. I shoved my face in the blanket with a groan.

"Stories like our amazing keynote tonight are just one of thousands that we hear at Team Sutton every single year. With each application, each funding request, stacked high on the desks of our incredibly talented staff, it would be so easy to numb ourselves to the truth of what those papers mean. It would be easy to ignore the reality that schools and community centers all across the country simply lack the funds to be able to give these kids what they need to nurture their passions. We shouldn't numb ourselves to that, not ever. Looking it in the face every single day is the ability to respect their incredible resilience." I paused, smiling at Allie and my dad at the table in the front. "One of the lessons my sister and I were taught growing up is that raw talent is only one piece of a much bigger puzzle. Without it, you can only get so far. But without grit, without the ability to persevere, you can't get anywhere. It's tenacity in the face of never-ending challenges. It's adaptability in the constantly shifting tides of life. We might be able to write checks tonight, we might be able to look these amazing young people in the face and recognize what they're able to achieve with the right support, but something we cannot hone, something we cannot purchase for them is the grit they have running through their veins. They don't hide from their challenges," I said softly. "And as the director of the Team Sutton Foundation, I will not hide from mine either."

Tori flopped back on her mattress. "Ugh, it was so good, Faith. You were such a fucking rock star."

I gave her a look. "Yeah, who went backstage and burst into tears as soon as the spotlight was off me. Poor Connie was not expecting my snot on her chiffon."

Lydia rolled over and rubbed my back, something Allie used to do for us whenever we were sick. My eyes filled up for the hundredth time in the past twenty-four hours, and it pissed me off. I wanted to stop crying over him.

"You okay?" my little sister whispered.

Tori set her chin on her hands at the edge of the bed and watched us with a small, sad smile.

"I don't know," I answered quietly. "I'm still so hurt. He lied to me to my face, over and over. I don't know how to be okay with that."

They knew he'd called, but I couldn't bring myself to share what he'd told me. Even now, I felt the need to protect him, allow that window of vulnerability to remain private.

"You should be mad at him," Tori added. Then she held up a hand. "I know, we're probably not ready for the vilifying of the boyfriend yet."

I sat up and ran my hands through my mess of hair, courtesy of the tossing and turning I'd done all night. "Maybe not just yet."

Lydia sat up too, tucking her legs up against her chest. "What part are we at then? I'm not used to seeing you like this, so I feel a little ... lost."

Swiping at the tears on my cheek, I gave her a watery laugh. "I feel a little lost too. But I know that I can be mad at him and still just"—I pressed a fist to my chest—"*hurt* for how hell-bent he seems to be to undermine anything good that might hurt him. I wish I could make him stop." I let out a deep breath. "But the only person who can make Dominic stop is him."

"Why do you think he does that?" Lydia asked.

I shrugged. "Why does anyone self-sabotage? It's scary to think about giving your heart to someone if you've never done it before." My fingers plucked at the edge of the pillow I'd hugged to my chest all night. "Even for me, it was terrifying to feel all those things for him, especially so quickly. He was the first man I truly trusted."

Tori settled her hand on mine. "But you didn't take a baseball bat to it, even if you were scared."

"No, I didn't." There was something hard about acknowledging it out loud. But it was the truth. Falling in love with Dominic was like a jump off the edge of a cliff, no net, no parachute, no notion of what was waiting for me once my feet were off the ground. Maybe it was just as scary for him to leap into the unknown with me.

"Are you going to reach out to him?" Lydia asked. "Tell him you got his voicemail."

Tori got a look on her face—the protective friend look, and I held up a hand to stop whatever she was about to say.

"If Dominic wants to work through his issues, I will be his number one supporter. But I'm not going to be the proverbial punching bag while he figures out how to be in a healthy, functional relationship. This isn't high school. It's not cute or sexy to manipulate people because you're scared. He's a grown-ass man, and even if it breaks my heart to stay away from him"—my voice wavered, and I caught Lydia wiping under her eye—"I'm not going to put myself in the position to be treated like that by someone I care about."

Tori blew out a relieved breath. "Okay, good."

"I think he'll call you again," Lydia said. "Or email you. Or show up with some romantic gesture to show you how much he loves you."

"The only gesture that boy better show up with is receipts from a therapist," Tori added.

I smiled at the two women reacting so differently to this first heartbreak of mine. "Lydia, I didn't know you were such a romantic."

"I'm not," she protested weakly. Then she rolled her eyes. "Don't tell anyone."

"Your secret is safe with us."

My little sister sighed. "Should we go see if Dad will make us some pancakes?"

"Yes." Tori stood from the floor. "I like this plan. Maybe after we eat, we could go to the zoo and feed some babies?"

Lydia clapped. "I'm in! Am I allowed to film it?"

Tori shrugged. "Don't think the kangaroos will care. Go for it."

It took me a second to drag my exhausted ass from the bed, and when I did, my sister gave me a quick hug. "I still think he's going to call soon," she whispered.

I smiled at my sister. "I'll be right up."

Once I was alone, I sat back down on her bed and pulled up Dominic's name.

Me: Please don't answer when I call. Just wanted you to hear my voice when I say this.

Dominic: I won't. I'm sorry. I'm so, so sorry.

Me: I know, Dominic.

When the call connected, I said a quick prayer that he'd respect this little boundary I'd erected. His first hurdle, at least in my head. His voicemail picked up almost immediately, and I breathed a quick sigh of relief.

My nerves were lit like firecrackers, popping all along the

surface of my skin because I hadn't even thought about what I wanted to say. When his automated message was done, and the beep to record sounded in my ear, I took a deep inhale.

"Thank you for your message last night," I said quietly. "I told my sister this morning that I feel a little lost, Dominic. I don't know what I'm supposed to say. Or what's helpful for you—helpful for me—in navigating all this. You hurt me so badly," I whispered, tears crowding my throat. "And I do accept your apology. I'm relieved that you can see how ... how fucked up it is that you lied to me like that. You're the first man I've ever wanted to be with, Dominic. The first man I've fallen in love with. And I wish I was saying this to your face too, but it's too hard. Because as much as I want to save you from your own worst tendencies, I *can't*. I can't take on that responsibility. Only you can do that. And I hope you do because I miss my friend. And I miss the man who convinced me to take a chance on him."

I sniffed noisily.

"I forgive you for lying to me, hotshot, I do. But if you want to be with me, I need you to figure out how to live in that ... that tension of the in-between. Where something scares you, something worries you, but you don't take it out on everyone else, just so you can stay in control of what happens next. Because that's what you did. Even if you didn't intend to manipulate me, that's how I feel. I *trusted* you, and because you were scared of what might happen if you trusted me in return, you set off a ticking time bomb under this really great thing we were building. I won't be that person in your life. I respect myself too much." I stopped, wiping my endless tears. "But I miss you. And I hope you can hear how much I care about you in this message. I would never say these things if I didn't. And I hope that makes sense."

After that, my words just dried up. There was nothing else I could say to him, at least for now. And even as I disconnected the call and left my phone on Lydia's bed, a huge chunk of my heart hoped Lydia was right. That he'd call. He'd show up and sweep me off my feet with some huge gesture showing that he could change this one side of him.

That I'd get that chick flick ending I'd imagined when I found out who he was.

But for the next week, my phone stayed silent. And I promised myself I'd be okay with him respecting what I'd said. But my heart, it still didn't get the memo because each night, I lay awake and thought of him.

Chapter
TWENTY-EIGHT

Dominic

"**Y**OU'VE BEEN QUIET TODAY.**"**

James appeared next to me on the deck as I stared out at the crashing ocean waves. We'd been at his place all week, a trip I wasn't sure I could handle making until I realized I couldn't stand the sight of my shiny fucking apartment. I saw her in every inch of it. I'd wandered around my family room, studying each piece simply because she'd done the same, wanting glimpses of who I was.

Before I knew it, I'd shoved clothes and some deodorant in a bag, and I was climbing onto a private plane with James and the other guys he'd invited.

Maybe I'd gone because it would keep me from going crazy, beating myself up for what I'd done, and maybe I'd gone because Faith had encouraged me to. But either way, once those plane doors shut, there was no going back.

And with each day that passed, yet again, she was proven right.

I didn't approach them with a chip on my shoulder. Didn't expect the worst, bracing for impact on each interaction I had.

But they could all sense that something was wrong. James was just the first who was willing to ask.

"Yeah, had a rough couple of days before I got here," I told him. "Been thinking about it more since we're leaving tomorrow."

James folded his big body into a teak chaise lounge next to where I was sitting, and he sighed. "This is my favorite place in the world."

"I can see why."

For a few minutes, we sat in silence, the roar of the powerful water churning along the coast the only sound between us.

"You wanna talk about it?"

At first, I shook my head.

"No problem," he said easily. "But you can, if you want."

Turning slightly on the deck, I gave him a curious look. "You play counselor to every guy on the team?"

James laughed. "No. But there's something about you, Walker."

"Yeah, I've heard that a time or two," I muttered. "Usually, it's not meant as a compliment."

Down in the grassy yard area underneath the second-story deck, three of the other guys were sitting in the hot tub. Christiansen—a fifth-year running back—tried to dunk the rookie, and the other guy—Washington, the all-pro receiver, with more catches than almost anyone in the league—laughed so loudly at the wrestling that ensued that it echoed up to where we sat.

Maybe I'd been quiet, but now I knew more than their names.

I knew that John Cartwright, the rookie from Florida, had a mom sick at home with terminal cancer. Hence the tequila on the day he signed because she might never get to see him play a single game.

Christiansen was a third-generation professional football player, had three kids under the age of three, and a wife he met in high school.

Washington had a similar background to mine. A walk-on in

college, he ended up destroying every school record at Michigan State. Like Christiansen, he was married. No kids yet, but they were trying. We heard all about the shots and the hormones and the ovulation sticks, whatever the hell those were.

Everyone there was nice. They were friendly. And the thing I'd noticed was that they relaxed immediately around me when they saw that I was approaching without clenched fists and a scowl. We hadn't cried together in a trust circle or anything, but it was a really good start.

I kept thinking about what Faith had said in her voicemail to me. She'd trusted me fully from the moment we had our first date. But I hadn't trusted her at all.

I *wanted* her. That wasn't the problem. Fell in love with her. Could've spent all my free time with her. The way I felt about Faith, as a person, was never the issue. But trusting how she'd react to me was in an entirely separate category. But I still couldn't figure out what to do about it. How to fix it.

With another glance back at James, I left my spot on the deck and joined him on one of the chairs.

"How'd you know I wouldn't come this week and make a mess of everything?"

He smiled. "I didn't."

My brows lowered at the ease in his answer.

"You think you're the first guy I've played with who's mad at the world?"

"I'm not mad at the world," I corrected. "Well ... sometimes I am. I played for someone who wanted us all that way, and it, I don't know, brought out all the worst sides of me."

"I've met those kinds of coaches." He set his hands on his stomach and stared out at the water again. "That kind of leadership is the quickest way to ruin really good players. They piss me off, Walker."

I smiled. "You're the calmest pissed-off guy I've ever met."

"Tell me a situation where you got really angry, and it actually solved anything." His gaze came to rest on me, and I saw the challenge there. "If you can."

Resting my head back on the chair, I thought about it. I'd been angry about a lot. Ivy getting sick. Her treatments not doing what we'd hoped. My parents not wanting to discuss her after she was gone. People's expectations about what kind of player I was, my ability to do something great in Washington because of it. And now ... I was really fucking angry with myself for how I'd handled things with Faith.

Separately, each situation fell flat when I tried to hold it up under what James had asked. Nothing had changed because of whatever was happening inside me. Didn't matter if the burn of my reaction was quick or slow or if I had time to second-guess it or not. Didn't matter that I knew I had two options of how to react, opposing forces whispering into my ear trying to sway me one way or the other.

It didn't even really matter if my reaction to that thing had been valid. The validity of my anger, the ability to rationalize why I felt it, didn't really change my ability to answer his question.

"It's okay if you can't."

"You gonna tell me how to fix that, master of the Zen?"

James cracked a wry smile. As he did, I couldn't help but marvel at this side of him, when I had seen firsthand his intensity on the field, his ability to manage the offense with efficiency and ruthless intelligence. But never with anger. Never with heavy-handed dominance.

"We get angry, defensive, self-destructive for the same reason we worry ourselves to death, Walker." He closed his eyes. His entire body relaxed as he spoke. "It tricks our brain into thinking we're in control of whatever that situation is. You're doing something if your reaction is big enough. But that reaction? Probably makes no difference on the outcome, other than to make you feel a false sense of control."

Self-destructive, he'd said. That phrase made my skin feel two sizes too small, shrunk tight to my body until it was uncomfortable. I wanted to shuck it off me with brisk movements of my hand, so it didn't settle for too long.

"Uh-oh," he said. "Something I said hits wrong, judging by the look on your face."

Before I could speak, I thought of my parents and how they'd dealt with Ivy. My completely opposite reaction. All of it was a way of managing this giant thing that we couldn't actually control. I thought of the press conference on my first day in Washington. The choices I made that tipped over an endless line of dominoes. Even now, they were still falling in a winding line that I couldn't slow. The result of where they'd fall wasn't in sight, and I hated that too.

And at the end of the day, none of the things I'd done to keep a tight grip on those situations had actually helped at all. My teammates had only started warming up to me when I approached them, hands raised and defenses down. No matter where it was, what jersey I wore, my ability to play the game I loved wasn't enhanced because I let my anger take the wheel. And worst of all, I'd still broken the heart of the woman I fell in love with because everything I'd done to protect my own fragile fucking ego only served to break something precious—her trust in me.

"Settle in, James," I told him on a sigh. "I've got a story for you."

With infinite patience and no interruptions, he listened as I told him.

After a few minutes, we were joined by the rookie and Christiansen, and they listened, eyes wide, as I told them about my sister. About Faith. How everything came to a head at the ball.

By the time I finished talking, my throat was dry and my chest ached from the reliving of all the separate pieces. They weren't separate, though. Not really. That was the thing that was hard to see when you were in the middle of shit, no matter what it was.

It was almost impossible to see how it all weaved together, how it formed the net that we fell back into day to day. It was in our reactions, our thoughts, the stories we told in our head of what other people were thinking. I wasn't even aware how tangled up in that net I was until Faith started showing me what it was like to be free of it.

The rookie shook his head slowly. "You need some serious therapy, dude."

Christiansen knocked him upside the back of his head.

"Ouch," Cartwright muttered, rubbing his scalp. "I didn't mean it in a bad way."

James smiled.

I did too. "You're probably not wrong."

Washington, who'd joined us about halfway through, along with the other two receivers, gave me a sympathetic look. "What are you gonna do?"

"I don't fucking know," I admitted. Frustration bled into every syllable. But I did everything in my power not to let that frustration turn to anger. "She's right. She can't fix all that shit for me. And I don't expect her to. But how am I supposed to even know what that means?" I dropped my head back on the chair and swiped a rough hand over my face. "Live in the fucking tension," I muttered.

"It means you let it be uncomfortable," the rookie said. "Your parents don't talk about Ivy because it makes them sad. So they do everything in their power to avoid that feeling, when really, if they admitted it and stayed there for a while, they'd probably find some sort of healing. You avoided helping those little girls because they reminded you of your sister, so you're really not much different than your parents in how you avoid it. And you can be afraid to admit something to Faith, but don't make some rash decision to make that fear go away because you're not actually solving it. You face her like a man and say, I love you and I'm afraid to lose you by telling you this. Then you wait and trust she'll believe you."

My eyes popped open. Every head swiveled in his direction.

Cartwright glanced around at us. "What?"

"The hell, man," Washington said. "Where'd *that* come from?"

He shrugged. "Therapy. That was my agreement with Allie when we met in her office. I told her about my mom and why I got so trashed after signing my contract that I puked on the field."

Now every eye swung in *my* direction.

I glared at the rookie.

"It's fine, Walker," he said. "You didn't need to take that rap then, and you sure don't need to take it now. I'm okay if they know that I did something stupid because I've already had to work through the shit that made me do it in the first place, and I'll never do it again." He held his arms out wide. "Living in the tension, motherfuckers."

After a beat of silence, I was the first to start laughing. By the time they joined, my whole frame shook with it. I still didn't know exactly what it all meant, but it was the first time since I'd walked away from Faith that there was a new small burning feeling buried deep in my gut.

Hope.

WASHINGTON WOLVES

Chapter
TWENTY-NINE

Dominic

Trying to mold yourself into a person who wasn't constantly waiting for someone to take a wrecking ball to their life was hard fucking work.

Not that things were always that dramatic, but in the couple of weeks that followed the retreat with James and the guys, it was hard to swallow all the warning signs I'd had along the way. Some of the things that had been said to me at the beginning.

Coach Ward, in the weight room, had told me if I failed here, there was only one person to blame, and I looked him in the mirror every single day. I remembered those words as I showed up to practice every day and worked harder than I'd ever worked in my entire life. As I slowly got to know my teammates, my coaches.

I remembered things Faith had told me as I sold that ugly-ass apartment and found something that was at a less impressive address and a significant reduction in reflective surfaces. As I started laying the foundation for the kind of life I really wanted to have, instead of shoving myself into a role that never really fit me in the first place.

And because I owed it to her, I forced myself to remember

all the things my sister had told me. At nine, she'd been so much smarter, more intuitive than I ever was. Even though I'd lived more than half of my life without her in it, before she was born, and now after her death, I knew that Ivy's purpose was so much bigger than just to leave a silent hole in our family.

Once a year, I could still do something to honor her, but as I drove to my parents' house for dinner, I wasn't willing to let it only be that.

After parking my truck in the driveway behind my dad's, I tucked my laptop underneath my arm and grabbed the bag on the floor of the passenger seat.

"Young man, you got a set of spare hands for me?" Miss Rose called from across the street.

I straightened, grinning in her direction. "For you, always." I set the computer and bag down on the ground and waited for a car to pass before crossing the street to her driveway.

She was trying to set up a ladder by the side of her house, where some gutters were hanging at an angle.

I gave her a chiding look. "I know you weren't going to get up there on your own, Miss Rose."

Miss Rose waved that away. "I'm no fool. I would've asked your daddy."

As I climbed up the ladder, I held my hand out so she could pass me the screwdriver. Tucking the extra screws into my mouth, I pressed the drillbit into the notches and hit the button, the whine of the screwdriver giving me flashbacks of college. I used to work under the hot sun as many hours as they'd take me, between shuffling to classes and practice.

It was what I had to do in order to play the sport that I loved.

I had to blink a few times when I realized that I could finally see all of it connecting. The line of dominoes finally curled around in a way where the purpose in all of this, the buildup stretching back years of my life, was becoming clear. Without Ivy, without my parents reacting the way they had, and—with a rough swallow, I forced myself to bring her face to mind—without Faith, I might not have arrived in this place.

As I finished hanging the corner of Miss Rose's gutters, I let myself think about how much I missed her. I didn't dismiss it, and I didn't let those feelings redirect to something less productive.

Every day, I thought of her. It never hurt less. Still, a month later, I struggled with knowing when I was ready. I trusted Faith's ability to forgive me. She never would have said it if she didn't mean it. But where I still felt unsteady was in my ability to trust myself with her heart.

Descending from the ladder, I handed Miss Rose her screwdriver. Her gently wrinkled face studied mine. "You all right, Dominic?"

I patted her back. "Getting there, Miss Rose. I messed up with a girl, and I'm trying to fix things."

She clucked her tongue. "Lord. Hope she's a patient one then."

I laughed. "She is."

"She pretty?"

"The prettiest," I told her. "But what's on the outside doesn't come close to what's on the inside."

She whistled. "I think you'll get there just fine, young man, with words like that."

"I think I need more than words for this one."

From across the street, I heard the squeak of my parents' front door, and my mom waved at us.

"I gotta go, Miss Rose. Let me know if you need anything else before I leave, okay?"

She patted my cheek. "You're a good one, Dominic. I always thought so."

I was still smiling as I walked into my parents' living room. My dad looked over the edge of his paper. "Son," he said.

"Pops." I glanced at the paper. "Mariners win yesterday?"

He grunted. "Barely."

I kissed my mom on the cheek. "You look pretty today."

She blushed, swiping a hand down the front of her purple blouse. "Had a hair appointment."

As I set up my computer on the small dining room table, I could feel both of my parents study me, but neither said anything. I took a deep breath as I sat and clicked open the folder I needed. There were two videos that I'd dug up from my old cell phone, emailing them to myself so I could save them on my computer. If everything panned out the way I wanted, I'd need them saved in a place they could never be lost.

"What's that for?" my mom asked. She set her oven mitts down and leaned up against the kitchen counter.

"Dad, can you join us in here?"

My parents shared a look, and he slowly got out of his chair. Like he did every day, and like he had for years, he was wearing the same white T-shirt he always changed into after he was home from work. In fact, if the video on my computer panned to him, he was probably wearing it there too.

With wary expressions on their faces, my parents joined me at the table. It took me a moment to get the courage to click on the first video. My mom's brows lowered, recognition dawning.

"Dominic, what is this?"

I laid my hand on hers. "Please, just trust me. I need you to watch this before I explain something to you."

My dad's chest expanded on a deep breath. "I don't think I can watch this, son."

Already, my mom was shaking her head because she didn't want to either.

"Yes, you can," I said quietly. "And there's a reason, I promise."

After giving them both another look, I hit the play button. The sounds of Ivy's last little soccer game filled the screen. She'd already started losing her hair, so her head was shaved at her request. But she'd had enough energy to play, and her coach put her in for the last quarter of the last game at striker—her favorite position.

My mom wept openly at the way she ran across the field, dribbling the ball past two defenders with a huge grin on her face. But the tears overtook her because she covered her face when Ivy pulled her leg back and kicked a beautiful shot into the top corner of the goal, just past the goalie's hand. With the sound of Dad and me yelling triumphantly in the background, Ivy's teammates surrounded her, with hugs and shrieks and screams and applause filling the video with happy noise.

Because I was that obnoxious brother, I'd run onto the field and hoisted her up on my shoulders like she'd just won the fucking World Cup, instead of scoring a goal in the rec league soccer at the park two blocks away from our house.

I refused to look away when she raised her arms, waving to all the people cheering. She was wearing a tie-dye scarf over her head, and when I pulled her off my shoulders, she gripped my neck in a tight hug.

Even though my face was wet, and my throat felt choked and full, I still didn't look away.

My mom pushed her chair back. "It's too much, Dominic."

"Mom, please."

She paused. "Why are you making us watch this? She's gone."

Dad's eyes were bright red, his jaw tight. But he didn't say anything.

"I miss her too," I said. "I miss her so fucking much. She'd be almost sixteen, you know? And I know it's hard to look at kids who were her age, or would be the same age as her now, but it doesn't feel right to just ... ignore it anymore."

Slowly, my mom sat back down at the table. "What are we supposed to do then? It won't bring her back."

"I know that. But I think we should be able to talk about her, how tall we think she'd be, or what a fucking rock star she'd be if she was still playing because she would be. Or how ugly that tie-dye scarf was," I managed.

My mom's smile trembled, but it was there.

"It was." My dad's voice was gruff. "It was so ugly."

We all laughed.

"We're always going to miss her, but I think we can do something great with that. In order to do that though, I'll need your help."

My parents, holding hands under the table, shared another look. My dad gave her a short nod. After a deep breath, she finally met my eyes. "Okay. Why don't you tell us what you're thinking."

The next day

Across the wide desk, they faced me as a single entity, an unbreakable unit. Luke stood behind his wife's massive executive chair, his arms crossed over his chest and his eyes hard. With her hair pulled severely off her face, Allie had slightly more open body language, but her eyes warned me without a single word:

Fuck this up, and you are finished.

She didn't resemble the woman I'd met with on my first trip to her office. Back then, she'd been a bit warmer and a bit more willing to give me the benefit of the doubt.

Back then, I hadn't broken her daughter's heart.

The tension in the office was thick and heavy, and instead of running my mouth to make it disappear, I folded my hands in my lap and took a deep breath.

"Thank you for being willing to meet with me."

"I didn't want to," Luke said.

I nodded. "If I had a daughter like Faith, I'd feel the same way."

My voice didn't stumble over her name, and I was pretty proud of myself for that because no matter that it had been almost eight hundred hours since I'd seen her, I still missed her like someone had cut my arm off. It was the reason I was sitting in front of the two people who had every reason in the world to hate me.

"What did you want to talk about today, Dominic?" Allie said. She was wearing a sharply tailored red suit, the exact color of the Wolves logo, and I couldn't help but marvel that she'd been commanding the Wolves organization for twenty years and hardly looked old enough to have two grown daughters.

"How did you start Team Sutton?"

Slowly, Allie sat back in her chair, surprised by the question.

Luke's eyebrows lowered, and his gaze narrowed skeptically.

She tilted her head to the side for a moment, studying me. But then she blinked. "I had an idea one day to help girls find opportunities to find their passion and nurture them. A lot of those opportunities happen to come in the form of extracurricular programs at schools. We've expanded our mission, obviously, as it's no longer run out of our basement by me and a friend, but it all started with an idea, a big check to get us rolling, and"—she shrugged—"a meeting with the team lawyer to make sure I was setting up the structure of the foundation properly."

I nodded. "I'd appreciate it if you could pass along the number of a lawyer that you would trust."

Luke's arms unfolded from his chest, set now on his hips. "This is why you wanted to meet with us? Not to convince us why you should be with Faith?"

For once in my entire life, I chose my words carefully. "With all due respect, Mr. Pierson, and while I apologize for what happened at the ball, you're not the person I need to convince. I know I should be with Faith, and so does she. I'm just ... I'm trying to prove worthy of the fact that she does believe it."

A muscle in his jaw ticked. "And that's why you've ignored her for a month?"

Even with their stone-faced demeanor, it was the first real jab that had me feeling a brief flickering of anger. Allie sat thoughtfully, not in any rush to calm her overly protective husband.

"I'm respecting what Faith asked of me," I said after a minute. "I have a terrible temper. Impulse control problems. And I fuck things up when I'm scared. That's not something she can fix."

It was Allie's turn to interrogate. "And starting a foundation is what you think she wants you to do?"

I met her gaze head-on. "No. I'm doing that for my sister. But before what happened with Faith, I always…" I paused to take a deep breath. "I always skipped anything with kids because they reminded me of Ivy. And I'd do anything to avoid that feeling. But I can help. More than that, I want to."

Allie glanced up at Luke, then back at me. "Tell us about her, what you want to do."

I stood from the chair to hand her a manila folder with everything I had so far.

Wordlessly, she flipped through the first couple of pages of bullet points, the mission as I'd outlined it. Allie paused when she got to Ivy's picture, held to the page with a paper clip. Luke settled a big hand on her shoulder and squeezed.

"I like the name," Luke said quietly.

"Thank you," I managed.

"Do you want this to be a private foundation or a charitable foundation?" Allie asked, eyes still glued to the paper.

"Charitable," I answered. "If I break my leg off tomorrow and can never play football again, I want to know that others can donate to what I'm trying to do."

She eyed me briefly. "Please don't break your leg. Preseason starts tomorrow."

Allie handed one of the papers to Luke, and he studied it with an even expression on his face. If I saw the man smile, I might think the apocalypse was upon us. Because of the lights in her office, I could tell which paper he was reading. It was the page where

I described the mission and why it was so important to me. Where I described what my parents went through, working jobs that didn't pay very much, and trying to afford treatments for their eight-year-old daughter with a rare leukemia. My sister's dream of being a professional athlete, that even if she'd recovered, how impossible it would have been for my parents to afford that dream.

"You'll need a strong team to help you," Allie said. "Female athletes on your board, no shirking the tough conversations they'll force you to have."

"Yes, ma'am. I'm working on that."

She grabbed a small notepad off her desk and scrawled something on it with a very expensive-looking pen. When she carefully ripped the paper off and handed it to me, she didn't let go immediately.

"Do this the right way, Walker. Or don't do it. The worst thing an athlete can do is promise to help and then screw up the delivery to the point they disappear from those people's lives. I'm giving you this name because she knows everything there is to know about successfully starting a foundation, finding volunteers, and building a strong board of directors."

"Thank you," I told her.

"You'll need a lot of help with the season starting tomorrow. I'd call her as soon as you leave, if I were you."

"I will."

Luke set down the paper. "Your parents okay now?"

I swallowed. "How would you be if you lost one of your daughters?"

His answer came without hesitation. "Empty. Heartbroken."

I nodded. "Pretty much. Grief doesn't fade, no matter what bullshit people feed you after someone dies. It's always fucking there, crowding the base of your throat and weighing down the bottom of your gut. You just ... get used to it to the point it doesn't ruin your every waking thought." I took the folder back when Allie carefully closed it and handed it to me. "Even if I've been quiet with Faith, make no mistake about it, every moment, I'm thinking about what I can do to make things right. I am going to try to win her back. You don't have a woman like her in your life and then let her walk away without a fight."

"And this is you ... fighting?" Allie asked quietly.

I gave her a wry grin. "I figured I'd try it without throwing any punches for once. See how it works for me."

Luke bent over and pulled open the top drawer of Allie's desk. She watched him with a slight smile on her face. They had this whole silent communication thing going, and it was weird. Maybe that was what twenty years of marriage did to people.

He tossed a checkbook out on the desk and held out his hand. She set the pen on his palm.

I fidgeted in my seat, not sure what I was supposed to say next.

"How much of your own money are you using to start this thing, Walker?" Luke asked as he began to write.

My eyebrows lifted in surprise. "Ah, I spoke to my financial planner yesterday, and she's setting aside five hundred k as an initial fund for families to apply for. I've got one family going through the paperwork process right now. Someone who works with my dad. Their daughter wanted to play for a traveling soccer team, but they couldn't afford the registration. I'm meeting with Keisha later today about others she might know."

The pen scratching across the paper was the only sound in the office. He ripped it off the checkbook and straightened. But instead of handing it over the desk, he took measured steps around it until I was forced to stand just so he wasn't towering over me.

In his gaze was a challenge, clear and direct.

I didn't reach for the check, simply lifted my chin and tried my best not to fidget under the weight of his stare. It was no wonder that when he played, defenses absolutely fucking hated lining up against him.

Luke held the check out.

"Don't lose it on your way to the bank," he said.

When I glanced down, I almost couldn't believe it. They'd matched my initial investment, dollar for dollar.

"Thank you," I replied, voice a little gruff from emotion.

It wasn't just a generous donation. It was an olive branch.

"My daughters are my world, Walker," he said quietly. "Prove that I made the right choice in trusting you."

Behind him, Allie smiled.

"I will," I told them both. "I'm getting there."

Chapter THIRTY

Faith

Day thirty-three was the worst. Probably because it was the first time I saw him in person.

For the thirty-three days prior, I'd caught glimpses on Wolves social media channels. A few clips from training camp on *SportsCenter*. I might or might not have watched one particular clip about seventeen times.

They showed a series where James lined up, did a play action—faking a handoff to the running back—then tossed the ball laterally to the wide receiver to his left. Because the defense pulled to the running back, and James blocked the linemen who hadn't been fooled, the receiver was able to step back and heft a beautiful thirty-yard pass over the head of the safety. Dominic stretched to his full height and caught it one-handed before he took off, spinning around a defender to run it in for a touchdown.

It wasn't even the play that was incredible. It was the smile on his face when his teammates rushed him in the end zone.

Oh, the things that happened in my heart when I saw him smile like that. It was a little strange, truth be told. The happiness at seeing him celebrate with the team was almost enough to make me all weepy and ridiculous.

And there was a dull, throbbing ache because I still missed him as if I'd been with him for years. And in a way, we had been.

I missed talking to Nick about my day. About his. Even though the details of when and where had stayed offstage, we shared so many of the small building blocks that made up our days, the things we liked and didn't.

And I missed the overwhelming fire of my short span of time with Dominic.

Sometimes I thought about reaching out, but I didn't know if it was fair. I was certainly busy enough to stay distracted with work. Which was how I found myself face-to-face with Dominic Walker for the first time in thirty-three days.

The second I pulled into the parking lot, my heart was off to the freaking races at the sight of his truck. I shot off a text to Keisha immediately.

Me: He's here????

Keisha: Did I not tell you about that?

Keisha: Oops.

Me: KEISHA. Warn a girl next time.

With a quick glance in the mirror, it didn't take long to realize it was not how I would've chosen to look upon seeing this man who still held a massive piece of my heart.

My hair was back in a simple braid, there wasn't a stitch of makeup on my face, and I'd grabbed a vintage Tootsie Pop T-shirt out of my closet. Digging around in my purse, I breathed a sigh of relief when I found a tube of mascara because honestly ... what woman would judge me for that?

I had a healthy enough sense of vanity. Mascara was the least I could manage.

But it didn't take long, walking with my chin high and my heart hammering in my chest, to realize that mascara was about as effective as a paper plate protecting me from a hurricane. Because he was the first thing I saw when I walked through the door.

At the sight of his broad back, covered in a black T-shirt, it felt an awful lot like someone hit the flat of my back with a steel pipe. Keisha was facing me, a clipboard in her hand, and she caught sight of me first. The hallway was blessedly empty of kids because when Dominic noticed the shift in Keisha's attention and did a double-take at the sight of me, I almost passed the frick out.

Whatever hit me in the back must've hit Dominic straight in the gut because I could see the shocked gust of air as it left his body.

His eyes, dark and intense, swept me from the top of my head to the bottom of my Converse. And when he stopped at my T-shirt, his lips curled up in a crooked smile.

I tucked my hair behind my ears, and his smile went a little pained at the edges.

His gaze only left mine so he could say something to Keisha. She nodded, giving me a tiny wink as she went back into her office.

Dominic tucked his hands into his jeans and approached me slowly.

"Hey, sunshine," he said.

My throat went dry at the sound of his voice. It took everything in me not to throw myself into his arms.

"What are you doing here?" I asked. "I know you're not scheduled for any official volunteer time."

His eyes searched mine. "You checking up on me?"

I breathed out a laugh and stared down at my feet for a second. "Once or twice," I admitted when I could look at him again. "How have you been?"

The LIE

"Fucking miserable," he said immediately. "But … I'm working on it."

My nose tingled, a warning siren for incoming tears, and I willed them back. "I'm … Dominic…" My voice trailed off because I wasn't even sure what to say now that I was faced with him. In my last message, I'd charged him with this massive thing, and now as I saw him, smelled him, desperately wanted to curl myself into his arms, I wasn't even sure that what I'd said was fair.

Or that it wasn't fair to disappear once I'd said it.

I didn't even know anymore.

I miss you.

I'm still in love with you.

Please … tell me we can do this.

All of those thoughts stayed locked tight because I wanted some sign from him that he felt ready to try again. Maybe what he was working on was a way to live without me.

"I know, Faith," he said quietly. "You were right, you know. For what you said to me. How you held me accountable to fix my own shit."

"It doesn't feel right," I whispered. "Not right now."

His jaw clenched, his eyes moving over my shoulder while he nodded. "It doesn't." When he locked gazes with me again, it was so powerful, what one look from him did inside me. Before, I remembered thinking that his eyes were the center of the hurricane, the quiet around all that chaos. But they were different now.

Everything about him looked different, even if it was still him.

I opened my mouth to comment when Keisha cleared her throat. "I'm sorry to interrupt, but here are those names I told you about, Dominic."

He smiled. "I can't thank you enough, Keisha."

"You're doing a great thing, Walker." Then she looked at me with a twinkle in her eyes. "You better ask him what he's been up to, Faith."

When she disappeared, he gave me a rueful smile. "She's subtle."

"What does she mean?"

Dominic blew out a breath and handed me the file tucked under his arm. When I flipped it open and saw the letterhead, I covered my mouth with one hand.

"Ivy's League?" I said. My finger traced the logo, and once I could get past that, I saw what was on the paper. The mission statement—a scholarship program for girls from low-income families who wanted to pursue their athletic dreams. The names from Keisha were well-known supporters of the philanthropic community, and lined up with who he'd listed from the sports community, he'd have a home run. It was exactly who I would've suggested he reached out to. "Dominic." I paused, shaking my head. "This is amazing."

He blushed, just a little, at my praise, and I wanted to heap about a hundred times more of it on him. "Thanks."

"Do-do you need any help?" I heard myself ask. "I mean, if you want. I don't have to."

At first, Dominic didn't answer. He just stared at me in that way of his, where I very much felt like he was digging a foothold into my heart or my soul or whatever intangible thing still hummed between us.

"It might be too hard," he said finally. "Even seeing you like this"—he shook his head—"when I don't think I'm where I need to be."

I miss you.

I'm still in love with you.

Please ... tell me we can do this.

It was the kind of answer that spoke to how much he was trying, and again, my heart was split straight down the middle. Happiness and the gut-wrenching ache of missing him.

But if he could respect me, what I'd said to him, then I could do the same.

"I understand," I told him. "I'm so proud of what you're doing."

The LIE

Carefully, he took a step closer, and with a sharp inhale, he lifted his hand and tucked a piece of hair behind my ear. His finger lightly trailed the curve, and I shivered, my eyes falling shut.

"I miss you." He whispered so quietly, I almost didn't hear him.

With my eyes still closed, a tear slid out, and I expected Dominic to wipe it away with his thumb.

But when I opened my eyes, he'd backed away a step, his forehead wrinkled like he was in pain.

The breath that left my lips was shaky, as unsteady as my wobbly, Jell-O legs that could hardly hold me up.

Dominic smiled. "I should go."

My heart was breaking all over again, just from being near him. I'd never get over this man, and I didn't want to.

As that thought entered my head, my selfish heart pushed words straight out of my mouth. "Do you think you'll be ready soon?" I asked. "Because I miss you too."

He swiped a hand over his mouth as he studied me. His jaw clenched before he answered. "I'm close."

My hand brushed away another tear, and I barely managed a shaky nod. This was what I'd asked for.

"Good luck in the game tomorrow," I told him.

"Will you be there?" he asked.

I smiled. "Yeah. We always watch the first preseason game from the sidelines. I'll ... you won't even notice me."

Dominic grinned, a small dimple appearing in his cheek. "Impossible."

Then he turned and walked away.

Day thirty-three. What a dick.

And at that point, I had no clue what was waiting for us on day thirty-four.

Chapter
THIRTY-ONE

Dominic

I T MIGHT NOT HAVE BEEN THE REGULAR SEASON KICKOFF, BUT the energy heading into our first preseason game had me amped. Music pumped loudly through the speakers in the stadium, a deep throbbing bass that rattled my bones as we lined up in the tunnel. Around me was a sea of black and red and white, the growling rumble of the stands reminded me very much of the howling wolf on our jerseys, that decorated the middle of the field.

My headspace now, about to enter the field for a very different reason, couldn't be further from the first night I'd signed my contract.

The buzz of the crowd, the jumping and jostling of my teammates as we waited to take the field to fireworks and screaming and waving flags, it all rolled through my body in a wave that I never wanted to end.

It was the high that every football player experienced and craved when the season—or our career—was over.

For a moment, I let my mind wander from the game, the stadium, the fans, and I thought about seeing her the day before.

There was hope.

I knew it. It was no longer a slight glow or a slow build.

I saw it in her eyes, in how she held her body so carefully in that hallway.

And tonight, I'd get a glimpse of her again. It was enough to sustain me, those little snippets. Until I could walk straight up to her and trust myself to love her the way she deserved. No secrets between us, no minefield to navigate.

James approached with a slap to the back of my helmet. "You ready, Walker?"

"I'm ready, cap." I punched a fist to the C on his chest proclaiming him one of our leaders.

He grinned. "Proud of you. Want you to know that, before a single snap happens."

"Thanks." For just a moment, I allowed myself to absorb the full impact of his compliment, handed to me so casually.

Until I was at Washington, I didn't think I ever would've recognized what true leadership looked like. And without the years at Texas, clawing my way to a starting position when my coaches never thought I could hack it, and then at Vegas, where the bad behavior became a badge of honor, I never would've fully appreciated that leadership either.

The announcer started, stirring the fans into a crazed roar as he teased our entrance.

"But you know, you can still get a *little* angry out there," James yelled over the noise.

I laughed. "Good. Not sure I could ever fully turn that off anyway."

He smacked my back. "Let's do this, Walker."

At the sound of his name and the answering roar of the Wolves fans, he took the field first with his fist raised.

In front of us, ready to usher us through the tunnel with shouts of encouragement were Torres and Ward, walking past each player to tap their helmets. Torres grinned when he hit mine, and before Ward did the same thing, he paused, then held his fist out for me.

I tapped it. "Ready, Coach?"

He smacked my helmet. "Always."

After that, the music cranked louder, and so did the fans. We all hopped once, twice, and took off sprinting down the line of waving flags.

Preseason games were almost always the same. A chance for the starting players to take a few snaps, run a couple of plays to get the initial kinks out and give the fans a small preview, but the majority of it would be left to the rest of the team.

We won the coin toss, and it took everything in me not to scan the people gathered on the Wolves sidelines for Faith.

This entrance to a new season with a new team, and an energy that was electric, I wanted her to witness it along with me.

It was just another way we would be so right for each other. Not just loving something, but experiencing something together that very few people could understand. Even in the midst of all these things I was trying to balance in my life, I worried that I wouldn't be patient enough to wait for my head to straighten out before going to her.

If seeing her yesterday proved anything, it was just how real this thing with Faith was. A month of nothing, and all it took was five minutes with her, and I had this jittery, frantic need to finish what I'd started.

I could do it, right? I could manage to keep my focus on this job I had to do and not wonder all the time if she was watching. Wonder what she was thinking.

James and the captain of the other team chatted amiably as the camera crews filmed their exchange, and just as we turned to let the kickoff return team line up, I caught a glimpse of blond hair, and a wide set of shoulders right behind, take off running down the tunnel.

It was Allie and Luke.

Running out before kickoff of the first preseason game.

My eyes narrowed as I watched them disappear from view. My eyes scanned the rest of the sidelines, unable not to look for her anymore, and there was no sight of Faith or her sister.

Coach Ward had a cell phone up to his ear, which was odd enough by itself during a game, but it was the concerned look stamped on his face that caught Cartwright's attention, just as it caught mine.

"What happened?" I heard the rookie ask James, who was listening to something in the mic piped through his helmet.

James glanced at me. "Come on, let's review this first offensive series, okay?"

"What happened, James?" I asked.

He gave me a steady look. "I'm not sure, and I don't think it'll help anyone to speculate when we've got a game to start."

"James," I snapped. "What the hell happened?"

Players around us shifted uncomfortably at my tone. Torres approached the huddle, his eyes serious and his jaw set. "What's the problem, boys?"

James looked at Torres, then back at me. "Just trying to keep everyone focused."

The three of us weren't even watching the field while the return team brought it up to the forty-yard line, a more than respectable starting line.

Something was wrong.

"Why did Allie and Luke just leave?" I asked Torres.

James dropped his chin to his chest.

Torres' jaw twitched. "There was a family emergency."

"What kind?" I managed between gritted teeth. My stomach was a giant block of ice.

"We will figure that out, and they have our thoughts and prayers in the meantime, but we have a game to play, Walker. Time to get your head on straight."

I pointed at the tunnel where they'd escaped. "Where did they go? Why doesn't James want me to know what happened?"

"Hey," he said firmly, "I'm trying to be the quarterback you need right now, which is someone to keep you grounded when we don't know anything."

"You know something." I looked between them. The kick-off team left the field. I should've been going out there. James too. The ref yelled for us to line up.

Torres gave us a firm command, even if his eyes were kind. "Go line up, Walker. Run the play, and I'll try to get more information."

"Fucking tell me what happened," I yelled. "Is it Faith?"

Coach Ward strode over. Torres dropped his gaze to the ground.

"The girls got in a car accident on their way here," Coach Ward said. Even as my heart dropped out of my stomach, down to my feet, and I tried to pull in a shallow breath, he held my gaze, and I could see how badly he was willing me not to freak out by saying it. Almost like you'd speak to a spooked horse, in gentle, hushed tones. *Steady now*, I could practically hear him say.

Torres said something under his breath, and Ward snapped his attention to the offensive coordinator.

"What happened?" I asked around the rock in my throat. "Are they okay?"

"We lining up, guys?" the official came over. "Come on. Game clock won't wait for you."

"Give us a second," Ward asked. The official nodded reluctantly.

My eyes stayed locked on Ward. "What happened?"

He held up his hands. "I don't know. My wife got a call from

Allie. The girls got in a car accident. All they knew was that one of them was being transported by ambulance."

The ice wasn't just in my stomach. It was my entire body. I'd never known fear like that, not even when Ivy was sick. That was an impossibly slow process that sapped away one small piece of your sanity as each day passed. But this, it was immediate and all-consuming. And I had to get out of there.

"Fuck!" I yelled. A camera guy eyed me from the side of his camera, but thankfully, he kept it trained on the field. I started toward the tunnel, heart racing, and Torres grabbed my arm.

"You can't leave, Walker. We'll find out what happened, and you can go to the hospital as soon as the game is done."

"Fine me," I told him. Before, I might have shoved my way out, might have whipped my helmet off and threw it, just for an outlet for my helpless energy. But instead, I just let the fear roll through me. "Take half my fucking paycheck, Torres, and see if I lose a second of sleep over it. You don't need me out there right now, and I swear on everything I hold dear, if it's Faith, and something h-happens…" My voice stumbled, just once, as my brain entertained the image of Faith strapped to a gurney. "If something happens to her before I can get there, you won't want to be within a city block of me, Torres."

There was chaos and noise and yelling, the palpable energy of the stadium all around us, blissfully unaware that I could feel the foundation crumbling underneath me at the thought that something had happened to her.

It would've been so easy, to let all that fear turn to anger, to slowly color my insides until I became something—someone—different. But I curled my hands into fists, took a deep breath, and locked eyes with Coach Ward.

"Help me out here. *Please.*"

Ward set his hand on Torres' shoulder, gave him a quick

glance, before turning to me. "Go," he said, his tone brooking no arguments. "I'll deal with the fallout."

Torres glanced between us, then nodded slowly.

"Where?" I asked urgently.

"Swedish on First Hill."

Without a backward glance at the other players, the cameras who panned to film my sprinting exit down the tunnel, or the coaching staff with raised eyebrows, I left.

A custodian in Wolves gear was in the empty locker room when I shoved the door open, his hand clutched over his heart at my abrupt entrance.

"You all right, Walker?" he asked.

As I tore off my jersey, then my pads, my gaze narrowed on his face. He was the same guy I saw during my very first meeting with Allie, when I'd met Faith.

My chest heaving, I ran my hands through my hair as I tried to steady my racing heart. "You're Max, right?"

"You okay? You don't look so good."

I shook my head, snatching my wallet and keys from the top of my locker. The pants were staying, as was the sleeveless T-shirt I wore under my pads and jersey. "I don't know, Max."

Sounds from the field filtered into the locker room, and he watched me curiously as I ripped off my cleats and shoved my feet into my Nikes.

"Aren't you supposed to be out there?" He hooked a thumb out to the field.

Knowing it probably wouldn't do anything, I pulled up Faith's phone number and hit the button to call her. It rang and rang and rang. With a frustrated groan, I threw the phone into my backpack, along with my wallet.

Because I knew I should, I took a second to steady myself before I ran to the parking lot and got behind the wheel. The last thing I needed was to get into a car accident on the way.

The LIE

"Walker?" he said.

I hadn't answered his question.

"No," I said slowly. "Not right now."

He nodded. "Then you better go wherever it is you're needed, don't you think?"

My heart was still lodged in my throat as I rushed toward the door, but I paused to set a hand on Max's shoulder. "Yeah, I think I should."

Chapter THIRTY-TWO

Faith

"AND YOU DON'T REMEMBER ANYTHING ELSE?" THE OFFICER asked.

Allie smoothed her hand up and down my back. My hands were shaking so hard, and no matter what I did, I couldn't stop them. I shook my head. We were sitting in a small waiting room at the hospital. My dad was in with Lydia while the doctors X-rayed her arm, which was most likely broken in a couple of places. My eyes welled up again because driving behind her car and having to witness the accident unfold was one of the most terrifying moments of my entire life.

The sound of metal on metal, the shriek of her brakes, the sound of glass breaking, and my voice screaming her name before I'd even made the decision to ... I wanted to park myself in Allie's embrace and never, ever move.

I shook my head. "No, I'm sorry. I hardly noticed the car itself because I was so concerned about my sister."

The officer, sitting on a chair in front of us, gave me a

The LIE

sympathetic smile. "You're very fortunate you weren't in the passenger seat of that vehicle, miss."

It was the side that bore the brunt of the impact.

"I know," I whispered.

Allie sniffed loudly, curling her arm around me. "You don't have to talk about it anymore if you don't want to."

The officer nodded, her eyes softening when she noticed me gripping my hands together so tightly that the skin went translucent. "She's right. Here's my card. I want you to call me any time if you think of something else. Anything else."

"I will."

"Fucking paparazzi," Allie whispered fiercely. "A girl can't drive herself down the road without them risking life and limb just to get a picture."

The police officer set her hand on my back before she walked away. "It's hard to witness something like that. Might not be a bad idea to talk to someone if you find it hard to sleep, okay?"

Dumbly, I nodded.

Allie's arm around me was a solid anchor, but in my trembling, adrenaline overload, I just wanted Dominic. Thinking about him was enough to start the tears for the first time since I watched my baby sister swerve off the road and into a massive tree because a psycho with a camera swerved at her.

"Oh, Faith," Allie whispered. "Lydia will be okay. She'll be in a cast for a while, but you know that won't stop her."

"I know." I swiped at my face. "It's not even that…" My voice trailed off. "I just want …"

Allie sighed, pressing a kiss to the top of my head. "I know, sweetheart. Big moments like this do a really good job of erasing all the bullshit reasons, don't they?"

I glanced up at her. "You think us being separated is bullshit?"

She shook her head. "Not exactly. I think you were right in

asking for some space, and he listened to you, which shows how much you mean to him."

"I miss him," I said. "I wish he was here. I wish … I wish that none of this had happened. And I just met him like a normal girl meets a normal boy."

Her smile was soft. "We all have wishes like that. But Faith, the way you met him was exactly right. And I think you'll find your way back to each other."

"Was it wrong to ask him when he thinks he's going to be ready?"

Allie smoothed my hair down. "Dominic has impressed me." She spoke carefully. "I don't think it would hurt to let him know that you're still in this."

After I nodded, she kissed the top of my head. "If you're okay, I'm going to go see if they brought your sister back to her room."

"Go ahead," I told her. "I might try to leave him a message while he's at the game."

She smiled. "Good idea."

Alone in the alcove, I let my head rest against the wall for a second. Even though I hadn't physically been in the car when it slammed into the trunk of a hundreds-year-old tree, every muscle ached as if I had. All day, I'd counted down the minutes until the game—seeing him again—and the reality was exactly the kind of discomfort I'd told Dominic he needed to be okay with.

Before I dug through my purse to find my phone, I made sure that my reasons for reaching out weren't just to make things easier, make things simpler. I was ready for whatever version of Dominic waited on the other end of the phone call. This wasn't an action caused by desperation or fear. It was knowing that even if things were uncomfortable for a while, it was still right in the end.

He was it for me.

The truth was so, so sweet to admit, to swallow down and let it fill my tired body. Like a lungful of fresh air or a sip of cold water after stumbling through smoke.

I sat up and tugged my purse onto my lap, but when I sifted my hands through it, my phone wasn't there. I glanced under the seat and frowned. Rubbing my head, I stood, trying to remember if I'd been on it since arriving at the hospital with Lydia in the ambulance.

No, because I'd used her phone to call nine-one-one, as I tried to keep her calm and still in the driver's seat. There was a bag of Lydia's things in her room, and I turned the corner to see if my cell had been tossed in along with her clothes.

At the end of the long hallway, the sun glared painfully off the doors when they swung open. I could hardly see from the flare of bright light, but it was his height that had me stopping.

Then the glimpse of bright white football pants, the black shirt hanging off his muscular shoulders. He sprinted to the nurses' desk, and even from down the hallway, I heard him bark my name.

The nurse gave him a stern look but started speaking.

He tilted his head back, and the look of pure frustration was so clear.

Dominic had left his first game because he thought I was hurt.

"Dominic," I called out.

He went still for a beat before pivoting in my direction.

And that big man, with his wonderfully big heart, positively deflated with visible relief. His hand rubbed at his chest, and when he lifted his head, his dark eyes locking on mine, I wasn't sure I'd ever be able to breathe properly again.

Then he strode toward me. I was moving before I could take another breath.

A moment later, an eternity since the last time, I was swept into his arms, his face buried into my hair, his arms shaking from how tightly he held me.

"Oh thank God," he breathed into the side of my hair. "I thought it was you."

I pulled back and cupped his face with my hands. His face was blurry from the tears. "You left the game?"

"Fuck yes, I did. Are you serious?" Dominic stamped a hard, hot kiss over my mouth, and I sighed happily. He broke away almost as quickly as it began, his forehead pressed against mine. "You're okay?"

I nodded, smoothing my hands over his face. "I'm okay. I wasn't in the car with Lydia. She … she broke her arm, but she'll be okay too."

His eyes traced over every inch of my face. We stood like that, my feet dangling in the air while he held me to him as nurses and doctors breezed past us.

"Faith," he said, "I am still so fucking impatient. And I don't always do the right thing. I'll probably drive you insane sometimes."

I breathed out a laugh.

"But I love you," he proclaimed with such fervency, I felt it in my bones. "And I will never hurt you like that again. I know you may not be ready yet—"

I set my hand over his lips. "Hotshot?"

"Wha?" He spoke against my fingers.

"You're exactly who I need you to be," I whispered. "I don't need you to be perfect, or be something you're not. Whatever this version of you is, I want to be right next to you for all of it. Because I'm not perfect either."

"The fuck you're not," he argued.

With a laugh, I kissed him again. Dominic moved us back into the quiet alcove and settled himself on a small loveseat. My legs split over his thighs and with my arms wrapped tight around his neck, we sat like that for a few minutes.

Not kissing.

Not talking.

Just breathing each other in.

After another moment, I pulled back and smiled at him. "I love you too," I said.

His eyes warmed. "Took you long enough to admit it."

"Someone has to keep you on your toes, you know."

Dominic slid his hand along the side of my face until his fingers wove through my hair. "I always want it to be you, sunshine."

Slowly, so slowly, he leaned in, sipping sweetly from my bottom lip, until I curled my hands tight around the back of his neck. His tongue was cool and slick against mine when I deepened the kiss. Soon, he was directing my head to the side, the angle of our mouths hot and wet and exactly what I needed after so many days and weeks without him.

It was enough, the feel of him against me, after the afternoon I'd had, that tears pricked my eyes again. I broke away and took a deep breath, my forehead against his.

He tucked my hair behind my ear. "Talk to me," he said, brushing his lips against my cheek as he spoke.

"Just glad you're here." I turned my face to catch his lips again. "I was trying to find my phone to call you, you know?"

His face softened into a devastating smile. "Were you now?"

I nodded. "Thirty-four days was my limit, I guess."

"Mine too," he murmured. "It was what I needed, but ... still too fucking long."

I couldn't help but smile. "So impatient."

"You have no idea." He stamped a kiss over my mouth. "Do you want to check on your sister before we go?"

Leaning back, I settled my hands over his broad chest. "Where are we going?"

"My new apartment."

My eyebrows popped up. "Really?"

Dominic hummed. The way he was staring at me made me squirm on his lap. "It's got brick. And wood."

"Does it?" I giggled.

"Very, very hard over at my apartment," he said against my lips. "Can I show you?"

He stood with me in his arms, and we went down the hallway like that, garnering stares and whispers and giggles as we did.

"I'll go anywhere with you, Dominic Walker," I told him.

Faith
Eighteen months later

I was so nervous I could've puked. I'd never been like this for a single game I'd watched in my entire life. Regular season, postseason, not any of the Super Bowls I'd watched Washington play in. And judging by the way Dominic was gripping my hand as I sat next to him in the massive theater, packed with every single elite player in the league, the greats that came before him, he might have been feeling the same way.

His leg bounced up and down as the next set of announcers strode onto the brightly lit stage. Next to me, Dominic's mom smoothed a hand down her pretty pink dress, which I'd helped her pick out.

"You okay?" I whispered.

She nodded, patting my arm. "Just fine, sweetie. Do you think anyone will notice if I pass out?"

I laughed quietly. "Nope. Not at all."

Dominic's eyes warmed, watching me talk to his mom. I loved his parents. Like, *loved* them. And they had been so firmly adopted by the Sutton-Pierson clan that they could never ever leave, no matter what happened with Dominic and me.

Not that I was letting him go anywhere either. My fingers squeezed his back as the two veteran players bantered on stage, using the teleprompter to introduce the next award.

Dominic's chest expanded on a huge inhale. I leaned closer. "I'm so proud of you," I whispered.

He turned, catching my mouth in a light kiss. While they moved to the small intro for Dominic's nomination, he could hardly look at the screen. His mom and I both sniffled quietly, and he wrapped his arm around my shoulders while I did.

"There's no crying in football, sunshine."

I emitted a watery laugh. "Wrong sport, hotshot."

At the mention of Ivy's favorite movie, he closed his eyes while the presenters opened a huge envelope.

"And this year's Walter Payton Man of the Year award goes to…" He paused, eyes scanning the audience. "Dominic Walker."

He turned into me while I cried, his arms tight around me. His whole frame shook. Behind me, I heard his mom weeping audibly.

"I love you so much," I said into his ear. "And she would be so proud of you."

When the man I loved pulled out of my embrace, he wasn't even trying to hide how overwhelmed he was. He wiped his face and stood while the entire theater got to their feet in a standing ovation. He made his way to the stage, and I clasped his mom's hand so tightly. From where they sat in the row in front of us, my parents were just as overcome.

When Dominic accepted handshakes and hugs from the two presenters, I could see how huge his eyes were. He couldn't believe it.

While they handed him the award, film played across the massive screen. Pictures of Ivy, footage from her last soccer game, then pictures from the Ivy's League recipients who'd benefited from the tremendous amount of work he'd done for the past year and a half. The crowd finally quieted as he stepped up to the microphone, the iconic statue in his other hand.

He blew out a hard breath, eyes finding me in the crowd.

"*I love you*," I mouthed.

Briefly, Dominic looked down at the floor and then looked back up. "Thank you," he said in a choked voice. "I, uh, I'm just as shocked as anyone else that they're actually letting me have a microphone."

Laughter rippled through the auditorium. My dad looked back, then slid a handkerchief in my direction with a wink. I wiped under my eyes.

Dominic cleared his throat, and I knew he was getting his emotions under control. "When I started Ivy's League, I knew a few things to be true. First, it's really hard for kids with a rough start to get a leg up. Maybe I'm not the best guy to start something like this, to help young girls with a dream to play, but I've met so many incredible female athletes who helped me find the right places to look for kids just like them. Who had a passion and a fire inside them. Some of them have come on board with Ivy's League, and to them, I'll be forever grateful for letting me step into the space that they've worked in for so long. Together, we've been able to put scholarship and mentorship programs in place in middle and high schools across six states, and next year, we're going to triple that. And second, I know how hard it is to see someone's dream not come true." He stopped, his eyes going red. "My sister didn't live long enough to achieve her dream of becoming a professional soccer player, but if she'd beaten cancer, I can guarantee that she would've kicked so much ass doing it."

I laughed through my tears.

"I started Ivy's League because of her. Because she couldn't do the thing she wanted, and if she were here, she'd have bugged me like only a little sister could until I helped as many kids as possible reach their full potential, no matter what financial barriers they face. But I also started it because of one other woman." His eyes locked onto mine. "Faith, I never would've taken this step without you. It scared the hell out of me to try something like this when I was probably the last person anyone expected to take on a project of this magnitude. Your belief in me has never wavered, and because of you, I might come close to being the best man that I can be."

There was nothing I could do to stem the flow of tears going down my face. My hand was lying flat against my chest because my heart was so impossibly full I had to make sure it was still beating properly.

He stuck a hand in his pocket and took a deep breath. "In fact, I was going to do this later, but what the hell." He turned to the presenters and held out the statue. "Can you hold this for me? I'll be right back."

With my mouth hanging open, I registered the ripple of excited murmurs sweeping through the auditorium as Dominic jogged down the steps off stage and strode back in my direction.

Then he was in front of me, eyes bright, hands gripping mine. Cameras ran after him because of *course* they were.

"What are you doing?" I whispered, just before he gave me a sweet, lingering kiss.

"Something a little crazy," he whispered back. Then he got down on one knee and pulled a small black box out of his pants. "You are the only woman I will ever love, Faith Pierson. I don't know how I got so lucky to find you in this life, but you are it for me." He opened the box, and under the lights, a simple cushion-cut diamond sparkled beautifully against the black velvet. When he slid it on my finger, it was a perfect fit. His eyes glowed. "Marry me, sunshine?"

I tugged him up because I needed him against me, needed his arms around me. "Yes," I breathed against his mouth as he folded me into his strong embrace. "*Yes*."

The place went crazy. As the room filled with raucous applause, yells and cheers and celebration, I curled myself into his arms.

Dominic kissed me again, and when we finally broke apart, he was grinning widely. "I meant to do that later when we were alone."

"Sure you did, hotshot."

His laughter was big and happy, and I loved him so much that it hurt. He was my home. And I was his. And this entirely perfect, crazy night was entirely us. I wouldn't change a thing.

Second Epilogue
Lydia

"You cannot live there forever."

Watch me, I thought, as I attempted a one-handed fold of one of my sweaters. A broken arm was absolutely murder on organizational attempts, but after ten weeks of the cast, I was getting pretty good at it. My friend Jill couldn't see me, because I was not in a FaceTiming sort of mood, but my determined silence didn't deter her.

"We all get it. The accident was super-duper scary and everything, but you're like, twenty-one and living in your parents' basement. It's not a cute look."

I pinched my eyes shut, because she had no idea how little I cared. I still couldn't get behind a wheel of a car without having an anxiety attack. The second I was out in public and a paparazzi aimed a long lens camera in my direction, my entire body went cold and prickly. But my friend—whose concern was motivated by her lack of social scene without me—didn't want to hear any of that.

All Jill wanted was my access to really cool people and really cool places back. My shiny new hermit lifestyle didn't appeal to her at all.

"Besides, the accident was *months* ago. Like ... let's find a good shrink who'll give you some good pills and move the hell on, you know?" Jill pushed on, completely unaware that her blasé tone had me wanting to punt-kick my phone into Lake Washington, just beyond the stretch of my parents' backyard.

Carefully, I set the sweater onto a shelf in my closet and ignored the fact that my hand was shaking a little bit. It did that a lot. Anytime someone backed me into this particular corner, where I was forced to think about moving back into my apartment.

The unfortunate truth was she wasn't the first to have a mini-intervention.

My sister was concerned.

The LIE

My parents were concerned. And not because they gained a blonde squatter in their basement with excellent taste in clothing. The last ten weeks, I knew exactly how much I'd changed, and what that must look like to them. Unlike Jill though, their worry—coming from a place of love—actually made me feel safe. Cared-for. Protected. It made me never, ever want to live by myself again. I loved the chaos of their home. The people filtering in and out who worked with and for my parents. I loved falling asleep in my bedroom knowing that I wasn't alone in the house.

Like I'd conjured him with the thought, my dad knocked gently on the doorframe. I held up a finger and then pointed to the phone laying on the dresser next to me.

"Jill, I gotta go," I told her. "Something just came up."

"Ugh. Fine. Call me later, bitch."

My dad smiled when I disconnected the call with a vicious punch of my thumb.

"I hate when she calls me that," I said. "It's not a flattering nickname."

"It's really not," he agreed. "Do you have a couple minutes?"

I eyed him. "What's with that tone?"

Dad adopted an innocent expression. "Can't a father ask his daughter to come upstairs?"

"For what?"

"Your mom and I want to talk to you about something."

I shoved my feet into my fuzzy black slippers, tugging up the hem of my favorite gray sweats so they didn't drag on the floor. Lately, they'd been slipping off my hips, as some unintended weight loss had been another unfortunate side effect. Pre-accident Lydia *loved* her curves. "Lead the way."

He set his hands on his hips and studied me for a second. "Do you maybe want to," he gestured vaguely at my hair, "brush that?"

With a self-conscious pat to the birds' nest sprouting out of the top of my head, I glanced in the mirror hanging on the wall next to my dresser. Yikes.

Maybe I did look a little ... homeless. With a yank and a twist, I attempted to smooth my hair into something a bit neater, but honestly, with the amount of dry shampoo we had going on in that situation, it was kind of a lost cause.

As I tugged the last few loose strands into place, I narrowed my eyes at the look on my dad's face. He looked nervous. He never looked nervous. "Is there someone up there or something?"

Dad pinched the bridge of his nose, then let out a sharp exhale. "Okay, your mom thought we should do this a different way and if you don't act completely surprised, she'll know I warned you."

"Oh Lord, what?" I groaned.

"Just remember, we love you and we're worried and that's the only reason why."

"What did you do?" I set my hands on my hips.

He did some hand-hip-setting of his own, which was how I knew this was really serious. "He's ... he comes highly recommended."

"Who does?"

Dad held up a hand. "And he's a former player, I got his name from Logan."

"Who is?"

"He only played for a few years before he got injured, but he ended up working security."

"*Who?*" I stomped my foot. Like a toddler.

It wasn't my finest moment.

"He's a ... professional driver. Sort of," my dad hedged. "And he's going to escort you wherever you need to go."

"*What?*" I yelled. There was no cold tingling in my body now, no shaking hands, as I brushed past my dad and started up the stairs.

"You're supposed to act surprised," he whispered frantically.

"Too late," I tossed over my shoulder.

The LIE

As I cleared the landing, I only caught the briefest of glimpses of my mom's face, obviously my yelling had reached her ears.

She said something to my dad, or me, but I couldn't hear a thing, only garbled words that didn't penetrate the buzzing in my ears as *he* unfolded his great big body from the couch in the living room.

Tall and scary. It was the only way I could describe him, with the arms and the beard and the chest and the eyes. If I crossed him in an alley, I'd run the hell in the opposite direction.

Those eyes of his, even darker than the hair on his head, never moved from my face, but I felt like he'd taken my measure in a single heartbeat.

"No way," I said. "Not happening."

His expression never changed.

If my parents thought they were saddling me with this terrifying driver slash bodyguard slash guard dog, they were sadly mistaken.

What happens when the grumpy bodyguard and the football princess are stuck together?

I cannot wait for you to find out.

Lydia's story will hit your Kindle early 2022!

The Bet, a standalone sports romance, is coming soon.

Curious how Luke Pierson and Allie Sutton fell in love? If you like hate to love/single dad romance, then their story is for YOU. Here's a small snippet from **The Bombshell Effect** *(Washington Wolves book 1)*

"I, umm, I came to bring you these." I held out the plate of cupcakes and he stared at them for a weighty second. If it were possible, his eyes got even flintier. His chest was heaving, and the white t-shirt he wore was soaked in sweat like he'd been working out. His hands were wrapped in boxing tape, and it made my stomach curl, but not in the good way that you want your stomach to curl when standing in front of a gorgeous, sweaty man. "I just wanted to introduce myself."

"Why?"

My smile dropped a fraction. "Why did I bring cupcakes?"

His eyes met mine and one dark brow lifted slowly. The cold, icy flush of embarrassment slipped down my spine, which I straightened stubbornly.

"Why did you want to introduce yourself?"

"Because I thought it would be a nice thing to do," I told him, pushing brightness into my voice and refusing to drop my smile further. Jerk. That was the unspoken addition to the end of my sentence.

"I don't eat sugar." He folded his arms over his chest.

"Okay, fine." I pulled the plate closer to me like it was my very sugary, cupcakey shield. Rational, I know. "Sorry I was trying to be neighborly."

"Neighborly," he repeated, and his mouth twisted like he just sucked on a lemon.

I lifted my chin and smiled again, determined to salvage this. "Yes. Neighborly. Your … daughter waved at me and I thought I'd be nice and come say hi."

If I thought he looked cold before, it was nothing compared to the way his face transformed at the mention of the little girl.

His eyes narrowed and pinned me with enough ice that I actually stepped back. "So you're as smart as you are original, that's good to know."

My mouth dropped open. "Excuse me?"

"I've got a list of reasons that have been used by women prettier than you, blondie, and that's on the flimsy side when it comes to reasons you show up on my doorstep."

The absolute friggin nerve of him made my jaw pop open. "Who do you think you are?"

One side of his lips curved up, but it was cold. "Uh-huh. Can we be done now?"

"Are you kidding me right now?" I gasped. It was amazing how the body could switch from cold to hot without changing the shape of your skin and bones, because now I was on fire.

"Do I look like I'm kidding?" He flicked his eyes up and down my body, and my sugary shield was no match from the derision I saw on his face. "You can go back next door now. We're set on baked goods for the foreseeable future."

You know, there were moments where I prided myself on my even temper. My ability to stuff my immediate reaction and keep a pleasant expression on my face, honed by years of practice of being marginally well-known and judged for every single piece of my life, from my face to my body to my upbringing, my parents' money.

This wasn't one of them.

Everything I'd been shoving down for the last week since I got the call about my dad's heart attack, all the silence that I'd ignored because it was hiding too much, the empty house, my empty family tree, the crappy cupcakes and the fact that it was difficult enough for me to lift my hand to knock on the door in the first place, oh, it all came roaring through my body in an ugly, cacophonous rush of anger.

That's the only reason I can explain why I shoved the plate of cupcakes at his chest.

KEEP READING with your KindleUnlimited subscription

OTHER BOOKS BY
KARLA SORENSEN
(available to read with your KU subscription)

The Ward Sisters
Focused
Faked
Floored
Forbidden

The Washington Wolves
The Bombshell Effect
The Ex Effect
The Marriage Effect

The Bachelors of the Ridge
Dylan
Garrett
Cole
Michael
Tristan

Three Little Words
By Your Side
Light Me Up
Tell Them Lies

Love at First Sight
(Published by Smartypants Romance)
Baking Me Crazy
Batter of Wits
Steal my Magnolia

Acknowledgements

Oh my, this book was a glorious test of my patience. I thought it would go one way, and as I was writing, it just … didn't. Faith and Dominic were a big leap from my last book, and that's always a little scary as a writer. The vibe of their story was always going to be very different from Forbidden (which is what I wrote before this), because I knew Faith needed someone to shake her world up a bit.

Instead, Faith and Dominic shook up mine.

Through it all, I had a couple sounding boards who probably wanted to duct tape my mouth shut when I kept questioning whether I was on the right path for their story. To Fiona Cole and Kathryn Andrews, I just cannot thank you enough. You walked me through the hardest rewrites I've ever done, and I owe you both tremendously.

To my husband and kids, for just … all the things.

To Julia Heudorf for taking the time and energy to beta.

To Najla Qamber/Qamber Designs Media and Regina Wamba for such a fun, sexy cover.

To Jenny Sims and Julia Griffis for the edits and proofreading.

To Ginelle Blanch for giving it a last read.

To Tina and Michelle for being invaluable to me the last few months.

To my readers—I adore you.

"Those who hope in the Lord will renew their strength. They will soar on wings like eagles; they will run and not grow weary, they will walk and not grow faint."
Isaiah 40:31

About the
AUTHOR

Karla Sorensen is an Amazon top 20 bestselling author who refuses to read or write anything without a happily ever after. When she's not devouring historical romance or avoiding the laundry, you can find her watching football (British AND American), HGTV or listening to Enneagram podcasts so she can psychoanalyze everyone in her life, in no particular order of importance. With a degree in Advertising and Public Relations from Grand Valley State University, she made her living in senior healthcare prior to writing full-time. Karla lives in Michigan with her husband, two boys and a big, shaggy rescue dog named Bear.

Printed in Great Britain
by Amazon